I0527808

Legend of the Oracle Runes
3

ENTHRALLING IMMINENCE

A fantasy novel

by Debbie Stansfield

Books by Debbie Stansfield

Legend of the Oracle Runes 1: Nornien Odyssey
Legend of the Oracle Runes 2: Allegory of the Milieu Stone
Legend of the Oracle Runes 3: Enthralling Imminence

CONTENTS

To my mom, gone from my sight but never from my soul, whose love continues to guide me through every step of life; to my angel babies, loved beyond words, missed beyond measure, and forever carried in my heart; and to my husband, who stands beside me with unwavering love and laughter, supporting every wild, crazy idea and sharing in the joy of every dream. You are my anchors, my angels, and my inspiration, and this is for you.

Chapter 1

Echoes of the Past

From the moment she stepped through the dense veil of trees and into the enigmatic forest, an undeniable sense of urgency gripped her heart, compelling her to run and escape the unseen eyes that seemed to follow her every move. Despite the cautionary tales she had been warned about, she felt an unyielding determination to witness the truth for herself. The world yearned for a hero, especially after the mysterious disappearance of others who had once safeguarded it. And she, with every ounce of her being, was striving to become that beacon of hope. The haunting rumors of women being subjected to unspeakable acts had reached her ears, leaving her hesitant to believe their validity.

However, when she heard whispers that it was not just the Centaurs responsible, but their vile minions as well, she knew she could no longer remain idle. Initially, she had hesitated, praying that these were merely rumors, but as more harrowing stories reached her, she knew the time for action had come. The past year and a half had been a period of quiet solitude, yet an unsettling restlessness had settled within her. She yearned to find purpose, to be of use, and perhaps, just to escape the ceaseless melancholy that seemed to have taken root in the Castle and village. A relentless cycle of despair seemed to grip them, with tragic events unfolding one after the other. Then, fate delivered an unexpected turn of events when Sachiel appeared alongside Adriata, demanding to see Amethyst.

The guards feigned surprise, but beneath their façade, a collective sigh of relief seemed to echo through the halls, as if Sachiel's arrival offered an unusual respite. Yet, she could no longer be content with merely finding solace in the shadows of the Castle's walls. The call to action beckoned her, and she resolved to face the dark forces head-on. She knew that within her heart, the seed of a true hero lay, and she would nurture it with courage, determination, and an unwavering spirit. As she ventured deeper into the mystical forest, she could feel the weight of responsibility settling on her shoulders, but the knowledge that she could make a difference spurred her forward. In the face of darkness, she would become the light the world desperately needed.

With every step she took, she embraced her destiny, knowing that her journey would be arduous, but in her heart, she carried the hope of a brighter future for all. As the days passed, the situation seemed to spiral further out of control, leaving Amethyst overwhelmed with grief and confusion. It all began on that fateful day on the battlefield when her dear friend, Alexandria, disappeared without a trace. Despite numerous attempts to find her, their efforts proved futile, leaving an empty void that nothing could fill. A few months after the battle, another heart-wrenching blow struck when Shadick vanished in the dead of night, leaving behind only an eerie silence and no clue to his whereabouts. Astarte's messages offered some solace, stating that Shadick had been staying with them, but his sudden disappearances persisted, leaving everyone mystified.

Chadromida attempted to reassure them that Shadick was well and focused on unfinished tasks, but Amethyst remained in a state of perpetual shock. The absence of Alexandria, combined with Shadick's enigmatic vanishing, had taken a heavy toll on Amethyst's well-being. The doctors, too, believed that these events had a profound impact on her mental state. Despite their best efforts, no remedy seemed to alleviate her pain.

One evening, Adriata, Amethyst's daughter, sat beside her mother, tears streaming down her cheeks. For a fleeting moment, it appeared as though Amethyst might respond to the emotional display, but alas, it was a false hope. The situation was disheartening, and their desperate attempts to comfort her seemed to lead nowhere. Amidst her turmoil, Amethyst toyed with the idea of returning to Atlantican, seeking solace in her grandparents' embrace. However, the thought of explaining Alexandria's absence and not knowing her sister's whereabouts made the prospect daunting and impractical.

At times, Amethyst couldn't help but wonder if Alexandria had somehow encountered the Centaurs and, for unknown reasons, joined their ranks. Yet, this theory seemed improbable, as she would have been involved in the subsequent battle. The puzzling question of why her sister felt compelled to play the hero haunted her thoughts, even as the harsh reality of grunts and the somber surroundings engulfed her.

When Sachiel suggested she take guards for protection, Starlansha stubbornly insisted on venturing alone, yearning for solitude. As she walked, a sudden and immense shadow cast itself before her, causing her to scream and whirl around to her right, fear gripping her heart.

"Why do you keep on insisting on running, little girl? You know as well as we do that we will eventually surround you, and there will be no way out," one of the Orcs bellowed menacingly from behind her.

Starlansha's heart pounded in her chest, but she summoned her courage and retorted, "And why is it that the Orcs decided to join the Centaurs during this battle?" She hoped to divert their attention and gain some insight into their motivations. "I know that you were offered a place in our army but denied it."

"That is an easy question to answer," another Orc called out. "The Orcs only follow the strongest when they engage in battle."

"And you believe Balditha when he tells you that his army is the strongest?!" she challenged, hoping to sow doubt in their minds.

"He has given us proof of not only his strength but that of his army," the Orc replied confidently.

Starlansha's mind raced as she sought to unravel the truth. "Ah, I see! He waited until the end of the last battle to make sure that his army is strong before recruiting you. And making sure that Alexandria wasn't around so she can't talk to anyone about it." She paused for effect. "This way, he would be assured of your loyalty, and there would be no competition. So tell me, which other creatures was he able to recruit? Are there more betrayals we should be aware of?"

The Orcs hesitated, uncertainty flickering in their eyes. Starlansha's gamble to exploit their doubt appeared to be working. Yet, she knew she needed to tread carefully. With each word, she was peeling back layers of deception, trying to expose Balditha's schemes and unite the creatures against the real threat they faced. In this moment of truth, she hoped that her determination and quick thinking would be enough to sway the Orcs from their misguided allegiance and reveal the larger web of deceit they had unknowingly become entangled in.

"That be none of your business!" the Orc retorted, frustration evident in his tone.

"Oh, very well then... I was hoping that my distraction would be a little more successful, to be honest," Starlansha replied, trying to maintain a semblance of calm despite her racing thoughts.

She turned and took off running, pushing herself harder. Her legs moved swiftly, but exhaustion bit at her determination. The Orcs seemed to multiply in number as the minutes ticked by, a disconcerting sight that fueled her urgency to escape. The dark forest disoriented her, and she found herself questioning every sound she heard, her senses playing tricks on her. The relentless pursuit left her unable to distinguish the distant footsteps of the Orcs from the pounding of her own heart.

With sheer determination, she pressed on, her eyes widening with hope as she caught sight of a glimmer of light from the edge of the forest. Freedom beckoned, and she knew she had to reach it to find a place to hide. Attempting to outmaneuver the Orcs within the dense forest seemed futile; they knew its secrets all too well, and evading them would be nearly impossible.

Finally, as she reached the forest's edge, a ray of optimism filled her. If she could only break free from the trees, she believed she could find refuge. But just as she neared escape, something fell upon her from above, catching her off guard, and she let out a startled and fearful shout. The unexpected obstacle sent her tumbling to the ground, momentarily stunned and vulnerable.

As she struggled to regain her composure, she couldn't help but wonder if her desperate flight had led her into yet another perilous situation. The light that had offered hope was now shrouded in uncertainty, leaving her to face the unknown. But Starlansha was determined to rise once more and confront whatever awaited her, for she knew that surrendering to fear would only hasten her peril. With a deep breath, she steadied herself, ready to face the next challenge that fate had laid before her.

"If you were to just keep quiet, little girl, it would go a lot faster. And perhaps we will even take mercy on you," the first Orc taunted, his sinister grin belying his words.

"In the same way that you showed the other 'little girls,' your mercy?" Starlansha shot back, her voice laced with defiance. "I am really sorry to disappoint, but there is no way I am falling for your lies. There is also no way that I will stay quiet."

She squirmed slightly, maneuvering until she was on her back and able to watch her attacker with unwavering determination.

"It's just you and me now... so there is no need for you to worry about your comrades attacking me. They know very well that when I choose someone, they will die a quick death if they try to take it from me," the Orc boasted with a twisted sense of self-importance. "And, to be completely honest with you, you are one of the most succulent ones that we have come across so far."

Starlansha's heart raced, but she refused to let fear overpower her. Instead, she met his gaze with unyielding resolve. "So I take it that you are the so-called 'leader' of this band of misfits?" she inquired, trying to keep him engaged in conversation, hoping to find a way out.

"Aye, that would indeed make me the leader," the Orc affirmed, though he seemed dismissive of the fact. "Not that it should matter to you, one way or another."

With every word exchanged, Starlansha was learning more about her captor, trying to discern any weakness she could exploit. She knew that her life hung in the balance, and any wrong move could prove fatal. Despite the odds stacked against her, she remained resilient, determined to find an opening or an opportunity to escape. As they faced each other in the tangled shadows of the forest, a battle of wills raged on—one fighting for control, the other for freedom. The next moments would test Starlansha's mettle like never before, and she steeled herself for the inevitable clash that would determine her fate.

As Starlansha bravely faced her tormentor, she retorted with a determination that caught him off guard. "I only ask because I would like to know who will be raping me, just so that I can remember for when I send the guards to come and avenge me."

The Orc, though initially taken aback, seemed to derive pleasure from her defiance. "You definitely talk a lot more than any of the others," he remarked with a sinister grin. "It makes it a lot more exciting, to be honest."

Yet, as he proceeded to violate her personal space, a voice rang out, stern and resolute, breaking through the dense atmosphere. "There will be no chance for you to go through with this heinous act!"

Starlansha, frantically looking around, couldn't locate the source of the voice. The Orc, too, seemed momentarily puzzled but quickly disregarded it, continuing his menacing advance. Her fear and desperation intensified, but before her tormentor could proceed further, something remarkable happened. Two blades materialized out of nowhere, inches away from her face.

The Orc's eyes widened in disbelief as the blades found their mark, extinguishing the light from his eyes. His lifeless body fell on her, causing her to gasp in horror. Pushing the lifeless Orc aside, Starlansha scrambled to her feet, her eyes searching desperately for her savior. It didn't take long for her gaze to find the figure—a dark silhouette standing a few feet away.

"Than... thank you," she stammered, still trying to see the person clearly. "I will forever be indebted to you."

The mysterious figure replied with a hint of familiarity in their voice, "Do you really think that I would have allowed that beast to hurt you?"

Her mind raced, trying to place the voice. "I'm sure that I recognize that voice... do I know you?"

"You do; or rather, you did a couple of years ago."

Drawing closer, Starlansha finally got a clear view as a wing shielded the person from the sun. The revelation left her stunned, but an overwhelming joy surged within her. Without a moment's hesitation, she ran straight into the person's embrace, hugging them tightly.

It was Alexandria, her long-lost friend, standing there with her Coral Daggers still stained with the Orc's blood. In that unexpected moment, the friends were reunited, their bond stronger than ever. Starlansha felt a mixture of relief, love, and gratitude as she clung to her friend, cherishing the miraculous twist of fate that had brought them back together in the darkest of times. With their strength combined, they were ready to face whatever challenges lay ahead, united once more against the forces that sought to tear them apart.

"I'm sorry that I just threw my arms around you earlier," Starlansha said, chewing her bottom lip

"It's okay; I understand," Alexandria replied gently, her voice tinged with sadness. "I'm sorry for causing you so much worry. The truth is, after that day with the Elementals, everything became a blur. I don't have a clear recollection of what happened afterward."

Starlansha nodded, her concern for her friend evident in her eyes. "What exactly do you remember?"

Alexandria furrowed her brows, trying to piece together fragments of her memory. "I do remember that I was able to kill Diliante, the leader of the Elementals. After that, it gets hazy. I recall a fierce battle against Balditha, but the details are fuzzy."

Her friend's admission only deepened Starlansha's worry.

"What happened after you fought Balditha? Why did you leave without saying anything?"

Alexandria's gaze drifted away, and a weight seemed to settle on her shoulders. "I wish I could provide you with clear answers. All I know is that I needed to disappear for a while. I needed time to heal, both physically and emotionally. The battle took a toll on me, and I felt lost, unsure of who I had become."

Starlansha reached out and gently touched her friend's hand. "You don't need to explain everything right now. Just know that we are here for you, and we will face whatever comes together."

A tear glistened in Alexandria's eye, and she gave her friend a grateful smile. "Thank you. I've missed you more than words can express."

The friends embraced once again, finding comfort in each other's presence. There were still many questions unanswered, but for now, they chose to focus on their reunion and the strength they drew from being together again. As the hours passed, they shared stories of their separate journeys and the challenges they faced. Their bond only grew stronger, reaffirming their love and the unbreakable connection they shared. With Alexandria's return, a renewed sense of hope stirred within them, and they knew they were ready to face whatever the future held, side by side.

Alexandria listened to Starlansha's account of that fateful day, her own memories slowly resurfacing, piece by piece. Her expression shifted between surprise and recognition as she absorbed the details of her extraordinary transformation.

"I remember some of it now," Alexandria said, her voice tinged with wonder. "The power of the Elementals coursing through me, the fiery wings, the changed daggers, and the forcefield of Spirit. It was like I was one with the elements themselves."

Starlansha nodded eagerly, recounting the events with enthusiasm. "Yes, you were magnificent! The way you commanded the elements and defended us all was beyond anything we had ever seen. You were fierce and powerful, like a force of nature."

"And convincing Balditha to retreat, even for a moment, was no small feat," Alexandria added, her gaze distant as she relived the memory. "He was so intent on destruction, and it took everything in me to appeal to whatever shred of reason he had left."

"The Elementals' intervention was both awe-inspiring and mysterious," Starlansha continued. "When they surrounded you, it was like they were protecting you, guiding you. And in the blink of an eye, you were gone, vanished with them."

"I don't know how they did it or where they took me," Alexandria said, her curiosity piqued by her own experiences. "But their presence and power were undeniable. They saved me that day, and for that, I'll forever be grateful."

"It's incredible to have you back, Alexandria," Starlansha said, her eyes shining with love and admiration. "You may not have all the answers yet, but we'll face whatever comes together. We're stronger when we're united."

"I agree," Alexandria replied, a smile gracing her lips. "I may not remember everything, but what I do know is that I have you, and I have the Elementals. Together, we will face whatever challenges lie ahead."

In that moment, the friends shared a profound understanding, knowing that their reunion had brought them strength and hope for the future. With their bond rekindled and their shared memories, they were ready to face the mysteries of their past and the adventures yet to come. As Starlansha listened to Alexandria's harrowing account of her time in the strange world, she couldn't help but feel a mix of emotions—relief that her friend was safe, anger at the treatment she had endured, and admiration for her strength and resilience.

"I'm so sorry you had to go through all of that," Starlansha said softly, reaching out to hold Alexandria's hand. "It must have been incredibly difficult and painful for you."

Alexandria nodded, appreciating her friend's understanding. "It was, but I had to find a way to survive and protect myself. Necrontyr and Claudia were there to support me, and together, we managed to come up with a plan to escape."

Starlansha's concern deepened when she heard that their friends, Necrontyr and Claudia, had helped Alexandria. "I hope they are safe too, and that their leader didn't harm them."

Alexandria's eyes reflected the worry she felt. "I hope so too. We managed to get away, but I haven't heard from them since. I can only pray that they are okay."

Starlansha squeezed her friend's hand reassuringly. "We'll find them, Alexandria. We'll do whatever it takes to bring them back safely."

As the conversation turned to the mysterious transformation of Alexandria's wings, Starlansha was both fascinated and concerned. "Dragon scales with extra abilities... that's incredible. But it also sounds like it comes with its own set of challenges."

"It does," Alexandria confirmed. "Controlling and concealing the wings require a great deal of energy and pain. But they can be a formidable weapon when I need them in battle."

Starlansha admired her friend's adaptability and determination. "You've become so powerful, Alexandria. I've always known you were special, but now it's like you're something more, something extraordinary."

Alexandria smiled warmly, grateful for her friend's support. "I don't know about extraordinary, but I do know that I'll use my powers to protect our world and everyone I care about."

As the two friends continued to talk, their bond grew stronger, and the promise of facing the unknown together became a source of strength and hope. They knew that the path ahead would be challenging, but with their friendship and resilience, they were ready to overcome any obstacle that lay in their way.

"It's a testament to how much you mean to them," Starlansha replied, her voice filled with warmth. "You may not have realized it, but you've touched the lives of so many in our village. Your strength, kindness, and leadership have left a lasting impact on everyone."

Alexandria looked touched but still uncertain. "I never thought of myself as someone worthy of such devotion. I was just doing what I thought was right."

"That's exactly why they admire you," Starlansha said with a smile. "You never sought recognition or praise; you simply acted with compassion and courage. People look up to you because of who you are."

As the conversation turned back to Amethyst and Sachiel, Alexandria's concern deepened. "I'm glad Sachiel has been there for Amethyst and Valencia, but I worry about the burden it must have placed on him. He shouldn't have to shoulder all that responsibility alone."

Starlansha nodded in agreement. "I understand your concern, but he's been doing his best. Adriata has been a source of strength for him, too. She's growing up to be a bright and spirited young girl."

Alexandria's expression softened as she thought of her niece. "I wish I could have been there to see her grow up. And I hope Shadick is okay wherever he is. I never wanted to bring any pain to anyone, yet it seems my absence has caused so much."

"You can't blame yourself for what happened," Starlansha reassured her. "None of this was your fault. And now that you're back, we can face whatever challenges come our way together. You're not alone, Alex."

Alexandria smiled gratefully, feeling the weight of her friend's support. "Thank you, Starlansha. I'm grateful to have you by my side."

"You've always been there for me, and I'll always be there for you," Starlansha said firmly. "Let's focus on the present and the future. We'll find our missing friends, rebuild our lives, and protect our world together."

As the two friends continued to talk, their bond grew stronger, and the reassurance of their friendship gave them both renewed hope and determination. No matter what challenges lay ahead, they knew they could face them together, standing as a united front against any darkness that might threaten their world.

As Starlansha settled into the comfortable bedroll provided by Alexandria, she couldn't help but feel overwhelmed by her friend's kindness and the depth of their connection. Her heart was filled with gratitude and admiration for the woman who had faced so much and yet still managed to be a source of strength for others. As she lay there, trying to relax and drift off to sleep, she couldn't shake the feeling of awe at Alexandria's abilities.

The way she conjured the bedroll and other things with such ease was truly remarkable. Starlansha had always known her friend was special, but now it seemed like she possessed powers beyond their imagination. Closing her eyes, Starlansha felt a mix of emotions swirling within her—the joy of Alexandria's return, the sorrow for the hardships she had endured, and the uncertainty of what the future held. She knew that the road ahead would be challenging, but she also had faith in Alexandria's resilience and determination.

As Starlansha's breathing gradually slowed, Alexandria kept watch from her perch on the tree, her gaze fixed on her friend. The night was peaceful, and the sounds of nature surrounded them, creating a soothing atmosphere.

It had been a long and eventful day, but Alexandria was determined to stay vigilant and keep her promise of protecting Starlansha while she rested. As the hours passed, Alexandria couldn't help but reflect on everything that had transpired—her return, the reunion with her friend, and the prospect of facing her past and finding their missing friends. The weight of responsibility rested on her shoulders, but she drew strength from the knowledge that she wasn't alone in this journey. As the first light of dawn began to illuminate the sky, Starlansha's breathing became steadier, and she slept peacefully.

Alexandria, feeling a sense of relief, knew that her friend was finally finding rest after a long and tiring day. With a soft smile, Alexandria continued her watch, ready to face whatever challenges the new day brought. The bond between her and Starlansha had never been stronger, and she knew that together, they would face the future with courage and resilience. The world awaited their presence, and with their unwavering friendship and the support of their loved ones, they were prepared to shape their destinies and protect all they held dear.

Chapter 2

A New Dawn

As Alexandria prepared breakfast in the early morning light, her mind was filled with a mix of nostalgia and uncertainty. It had been quite some time since she had been in this world, and while she remembered what was considered 'normal,' she couldn't help but feel like a different person now. As the aroma of cooking filled the tent, Alexandria's thoughts drifted to the experiences she had with the Elementals. The time she spent with them had been transformative, exposing her to a world of magic and power she never knew existed. It had changed her in profound ways, and now she found herself questioning where she truly belonged.

Looking over at her friend Starlansha, still sleeping peacefully, Alexandria felt a pang of sadness for the loss of her sister. She knew that Starlansha must be going through a difficult time, and she wished she could do more to ease her friend's pain. Lost in her thoughts, Alexandria considered the responsibilities that awaited her back in Valencia. The villagers relied on her to ensure their well-being, and Amethyst needed her support and guidance. But after everything she had experienced with the Elementals, returning to her old life felt strange and unfamiliar.

"Alex...? Is everything okay? You seem to be lost in some rather deep thoughts." Starlansha whispered from behind her.

Alexandria turned to see Starlansha looking at her with concern. She appreciated her friend's intuition, knowing that Starlansha had always been perceptive.

"I'm just... trying to process everything," Alexandria admitted with a sigh. "The time with the Elementals has changed me, and I'm not sure how to navigate this world now."

Starlansha nodded, understanding evident in her eyes. "Change can be overwhelming, especially after what we've been through. But remember, I'm here for you, and we'll figure it out together."

Alexandria managed a small smile, grateful for Starlansha's support. "Thank you. It's just that nothing feels the same anymore, and I'm not sure where I fit in."

Starlansha reached out and took her friend's hand in hers. "You don't have to have all the answers right away. We'll take it one step at a time, and I believe we'll find our way."

As Alexandria glanced back at the breakfast she had prepared, she realized how much she appreciated the simple act of caring for her friend.

"I didn't want to disturb your sleep," Alexandria said, feeling guilty for not waking Starlansha earlier. "But I thought we could have breakfast together before heading back to Valencia."

You are always more than welcome to wake me up! Even if it is just to talk about what you have on your mind."

Alexandria smiled gratefully at Starlansha's offer, appreciating her friend's willingness to listen and support her. "Thank you, Starlansha. It means a lot to me knowing I can talk to you."

As they sat down to eat, Starlansha's compliment on the food made Alexandria feel a sense of warmth. She had always enjoyed cooking, and it was comforting to know that some things hadn't changed despite everything that had happened.

Watching Starlansha as she ate, Alexandria couldn't help but feel a twinge of frustration. She wanted to understand the social cues and dynamics of this world better, but it felt like an uphill battle. She had spent so much time with the Elementals, who were different from humans in many ways. Inwardly, she sighed, feeling torn between her two worlds. The Elementals were humanoid in some sense, but their ways were vastly different. Yet, she knew she couldn't let her confusion and frustration distance her from her friend.

"I hope the food is to your liking," Alexandria said, trying to focus on the present moment. "I'm glad you're here with me. It feels... normal."

Starlansha smiled, reaching over to place a hand on Alexandria's. "We'll figure things out together, just like we always do."

"Are you okay with walking back to Valencia today? It never

crossed my mind that I would be here for as long as I have, so I walked. And it isn't as though it is that from here, though." Starlansha asked smiling

"I'm fine with walking back," Alexandria replied with a smile. "It's been a while since I've been back in this world, and I don't mind the journey. Plus, it'll give us some time to talk and catch up. Unless, of course, you're not against me teleporting us there? Or if it would make you feel safer, I could fly?"

Starlansha looked at Alexandria with curiosity, "So I take it that you were able to learn how to control the teleporting? From what I remember, you had some trouble with it before you disappeared. I wouldn't mind traveling that way at all, it would save us so much time!"

Alexandria chuckled softly. "You're right, it would be much quicker. And I've actually become quite comfortable with teleportation now. The Elementals helped me overcome my initial struggles."

Starlansha nodded approvingly. "That's great to hear. I trust you completely, Alex."

Alexandria's expression softened, touched by her friend's words. "Thank you, Starlansha. I guess I'm just adjusting to being back in this world after my time away."

"You don't have to worry so much," Starlansha reassured her. "Even though we haven't seen each other in a while, our friendship is still strong. I know I can count on you, and you can count on me."

Alexandria smiled gratefully. "I'm glad to hear that. It's good to be back with you, Starlansha."

Starlansha smiled reassuringly at Alexandria, understanding the internal struggle she was going through. "Do not worry about it, you will get back to the way you were soon enough. I assure you that once you are surrounded by the people who love you, it will be as though you never left. Except, of course, for the not-so-subtle changes."

"I doubt that anything will ever go back to the way it had been before," Alexandria replied with a hint of sadness. "Not only have I changed, but so have the other people around here. It feels as though I've changed so much this past year and a half that I'm not even sure if I know myself anymore."

"You are Alexandria... the Witch that not only has Faerie powers but Elemental powers as well," Starlansha said firmly. "Also, the person who has been a true, as well as a kick-ass friend from the very first day that we met!"

A genuine smile crossed Alexandria's face, touched by her friend's words. "Thank you... you have no idea how much it means to hear that. Especially seeing as I feel as though I have become a stranger in my own body."

"Then let us get back to what you used to call your home... Valencia," Starlansha suggested. "Not McLeod's, that is, just in case it was confusing."

"From what I can recall, McLeod's was completely destroyed and would never be inhabitable ever again, so I do understand what you meant," Alexandria replied, grateful for her friend's understanding.

As Alexandria held out her hand, Starlansha took it with a smile, feeling a rush of excitement and anticipation for their teleportation. As the makeshift camp disappeared back into the ground and the fire was swallowed by the earth, Starlansha watched in awe, impressed by her friend's abilities.

She knew that Alexandria had become more skilled during her time with the Elementals, but seeing it in action still amazed her. With a nod from Alexandria, they closed their eyes, and the world around them seemed to blur as they teleported. The sensation was like a brief moment of weightlessness, and then they found themselves standing in a familiar room in Valencia.

"Huh... that was even less painful than I thought it would have been," Starlansha remarked, opening her eyes slowly.

"I realized too late that I wasn't sure where I should be teleporting to and whether it would have changed at all," Alexandria admitted. "The only place I thought might have remained unchanged would be the room I had been living in."

"You made a very good choice," Starlansha said with a grin. "If you had teleported us into the middle of the village, I do believe that it may have caused a bit of a panic. As much as you have been missed, people don't normally just appear from out of nowhere."

"You have a point there. I wouldn't want to cause a commotion. Why didn't you freak out when I appeared from out of nowhere?"

"I've already told you the answer to that. You're my friend; you don't scare me. And the truth is that I have missed you so much that I had been hoping you would just appear. Even if that meant that I had lost my mind."

Without any warning, a group of soldiers burst into the room with their swords and spears raised, their faces tense with urgency. Warnings were shouted at them, demanding that they stay put. In that moment of tension, Princess Starlansha acted swiftly, stepping in front of her companions just as she tensed, prepared to defend herself against the unexpected intrusion.

"There is no need for violence! Or for any of you to even have your weapons out!" Starlansha's voice rang out, firm but composed, trying to defuse the situation.

"Princess Starlansha! When we heard noise from inside the room, we were worried that we were being invaded by the Centaurs, somehow," one of the guards explained, his eyes narrowing with confusion. But then he froze as if struck by a revelation. "How were you able to get in here? There was no sign of you passing us to enter the room. And the last report we have is that you left for the forest the day before last but had not returned yet."

"You are correct that I was in the forest; although I have Alex over here to thank for making the long journey so much shorter."

The guards stared at her for a few seconds before falling onto their knees as they realized who she was. A blush ran across her cheeks, and she fidgeted slightly, trying to appear as though this was what was expected of her.

"We welcome you back, your majesty! King Sachiel will be happy to know of your return," another guard said, trying not to stare at her wings. "I do apologize in advance if this is too bold a question to ask or even disrespectful in some way. The last time I saw you, there were no wings on your back, and now you have the most beautiful pair."

"It has been a rather new acquisition..." Alexandria replied, feeling uncomfortable with the attention drawn to her wings.

"Perhaps you should give her at least some time to settle back into the Castle; perhaps she will tell you then. But for now, I believe that she would just like to go and see her sister," Starlansha interjected, trying to protect Alexandria from further inquiry.

"Of course! Please allow us to escort the two of you to her room," the guard replied, bowing deeply.

"I can assure you that no one within the castle or the village wants to hurt you, so there is no reason for you to be so on guard the entire time. All it is, is that everyone is surprised that you're finally back with us," another guard added.

"I was not expecting them to rush into my room..." Alexandria said, her hand subconsciously touching one of her wings, a reminder of the magical encounter that had changed her life.

"Shadick declared that your room needs to be guarded shortly after your disappearance. You know, just in case some fool thought it a good idea to steal something. It kind of felt as though he wanted to make sure that everything stayed the same as how you left it," Starlansha explained to Alexandria.

"Ah, that explains a lot," Alexandria replied, realizing the reason behind the heightened security around her room during her absence.

"Captain Darvies, would you please send one of the soldiers to go and give Sachiel a heads up? And also request that he join us in Queen Amethyst's room?"

"Very well, Princess," Captain Davies said, saluting her before disappearing down the hallway to fulfill the request.

"There isn't really a need for Sachiel to be around..." Alexandria said, furrowing her brow.

"After all of this time, he will want to know as well as be given a chance to greet you."

As they continued walking, they reached Queen Amethyst's room. Starlansha informed Alexandria that Amethyst had been moved to her rooms once things had settled down, and she seemed to be in better spirits. Two of the guards opened the doors and slowly stepped back so that Alexandria and Starlansha could pass them.

The minute they stepped over the threshold, it felt as though the temperature had dropped a couple of degrees, causing Alexandria to frown, but she did not say anything. Her eyes rested on the bed where her sister and best friend lay, staring into nothingness and looking as lost as a little lamb.

"Amethyst? I hope you don't mind, but I have a little surprise for you... someone special has come to visit you," Starlansha said, beckoning Alexandria closer to the bed. "Someone that none of us have seen for about a year and a half."

"Hi, Am..." Alexandria said uncertainly, her voice filled with emotion. "I have been really missing you the last year and a bit, and it was my biggest wish to be able to talk to you again."

"I will give you a couple of minutes alone," Starlansha said, stepping back towards the doors as Sachiel appeared, staring wide-eyed at Alexandria in shock. "Why don't we give her a few minutes alone with Amethyst before bombarding her with a gazillion questions?"

"I really am sorry that I had just disappeared when you needed me the most. You should know that it wasn't by choice, and I made sure that everyone knew that I was not happy about any of it. Not that anyone listened to me... wouldn't even allow me to send you a letter to let you know I'm still alive. In some way, it was good, I guess, because I learned so much! However, if it had been up to me, I would much rather have been here than have gone through all of that."

She paused, feeling the weight of her experiences and the changes she had undergone during her time away. The memories of the enchanted realm and the Elementals are still fresh in her mind.

"I have changed quite a bit since the last time you saw me, and I'm not sure whether it's a good thing or not. All that I do know is that people can't stop staring at my wings. Wings I wish I could just take off and give it to you, perhaps it would allow me to have my sister back then. The Elementals took me to their world so that I could train and gain proper control over my powers without the fear of me hurting someone, if you were wondering where I had been. Although I have to admit their leader wasn't very happy about my presence when he found out. Even though I kept shouting at him that he should just send me back, he kept refusing. Whether he was just too interested in my abilities or if he just wanted to keep me there because he was afraid I would cause trouble, I don't know. But I do have to say that I made sure that they knew I wasn't happy and didn't make it very easy for him or any of them, for that matter."

Alexandria's voice trembled with a mix of frustration and

determination as she shared her experiences with her sister, hoping that somewhere within Amethyst's consciousness, her words would reach her. She knew that the road to her sister's full recovery would be challenging, but she was willing to do whatever it took to break the enchantment that held Amethyst captive.

As she sat there, pouring her heart out to her sister, Alexandria could feel a glimmer of hope, a sense that Amethyst was somehow aware of her presence. The magical bond between them, strengthened by the love they shared, gave her the strength to believe that they would overcome the trials ahead, together.

"Could you please just inform me what happened from the time you left here to getting back here, with Alexandria?! Because, as far as I know, you went to the forest to investigate the claims of Creatures attacking and raping women?" Sachiel whispered, his concern evident.

"I really was! Unfortunately, I underestimated that there would be more than just one of these creatures. It was as I was running away from the Orcs that I was tackled by their leader. He was about to harm me when Alexandria appeared without warning and killed him!" Starlansha replied, smiling. "If it hadn't been for her and her excellent timing, I would have been in serious danger. Of course, I was putting up quite a fight and not making it easy for him."

"Was this not why I told you to take guards with you? In case something like this were to happen?! And wait a second... did you say Orcs?"

"I did, yes. It would seem that the Centaurs were able to recruit some new monsters and haven't really been giving a damn about what they get up to."

"Papa! I have been looking all over for you, but just couldn't find you!" a little voice said from the door, making Alexandria freeze in surprise.

"I apologize, my sweetheart, but Daddy had to come and greet an old friend of his," Sachiel replied, bending down next to Adriata.

"Good morning, Adriata," Starlansha greeted the girl.

"Adriata?!" Alexandria whispered, getting up and walking towards them. "Is it really you?"

"Aunty Lexa?" Adriata whispered, her eyes widening and quickly being replaced with a happy smile. "I haven't seen you in such a long time, Aunty Lexa!"

Adriata ran towards Alexandria, and she bent down to allow the girl to give her a tight hug. In that moment, as she held the little girl close, Alexandria felt a sense of belonging and comfort. The worries and insecurities she had carried since her return seemed to melt away in the warmth of Adriata's embrace. She realized that this little girl made everything better, and her presence reassured Alexandria that she was not an inconvenience or burden to others.

In Adriata's innocent joy and love, she found a renewed sense of purpose and acceptance. As Alexandria stood up, she smiled at

Adriata, feeling a newfound sense of determination to protect her family and friends from any threat that may come their way.

With Starlansha, Sachiel, and Adriata by her side, she knew that together they would face whatever challenges the enchanted realm had in store for them. And for the first time since her return, Alexandria truly felt at home.

Chapter 3

A Warm Reception

She lightly kissed Adriata on the top of her head after she had fallen asleep in her bed for an afternoon nap and stood up. She quickly but quietly walked out of the room, pausing briefly to look back at the little Princess. There was finally peace in her heart, and she knew that it was all because of that little girl.

The fact that her sister was still in a coma after she had lost her wings had not been easy to hear, and she still felt bad about it. The fact that no one had really heard from Shadick in more than a year made it feel as though her heart was being ripped out of her chest.

What made her feel a little more at peace was the fact that Sachiel had relocated his entire village to Valencia to help rule while Amethyst was out of it. The fact that she had been recognized and was able to see her Goddaughter made everything worth it. As though everything that had happened the last while had not just been for nothing.

"It seems as though Adriata showing you around the Castle was a good thing; you are a lot more relaxed. Can you perhaps now take some time to tell me what has been happening to you?" Sachiel asked her the second she had closed the door, "You know very well that I respect you and I understand some things might be too hard to talk about, but I need to know at least something about what happened."

"She hasn't even told me everything yet, Sachiel." Starlansha said, standing up. "We do not want the villagers to hear of a ghost haunting the castle and cause a panic, so it might be for the best for her to not only clear her mind but to allow people to see her. And you know for a fact that is what will happen."

"Sachiel... I agree that you deserve to know at least some of what happened, but before I can do that, I need to clear my mind of everything before reliving hell. There have been a lot of things that have happened over the last couple of years that I have not been able to process properly. I give you my promise that I will come and talk to you before nightfall, to the both of you. Although I figure that you would like to join me, Starlansha?" she said, smiling.

"If you don't mind me tagging along, then I really would love to join you."

"Then I shall expect you to be back here for dinner so that we can have a conversation about what has been going on."

"Patience, Sachiel... if we push too hard, Alexandria might just get spooked and run away again."

He muttered something under his breath before quickly turning on his heel and walking back to his study to finish what he had been busy with. Starlansha laughed softly, shaking her head and putting her arm through hers, lightly steering her to the front doors and out into the village.

"Now… I expect that people will be both shocked and surprised to see you; some might even truly think that they are seeing a ghost or something equally similar and scary. Do not let it get to you, though. Once they get over the shock of seeing you, they will be happy to have you back. When they stare at you, don't let it get to you, as there will most definitely be stares of shock and surprise."

"What would you think of some of the guards following you, Princess?" Captain Davies asked her as they walked past.

"Hmm… I do believe that two guards wouldn't go amiss. Just in case."

"You're making it sound as though the villagers will be storming me with pitchforks and swords in hand, ready to get rid of me," she replied, looking at the guards following them.

"That's how I wanted to put it, as I know they wouldn't actually do that. Rather safe than sorry though, you know? Everyone will see not just you but your wings and start questioning themselves, and whether they have finally lost it. Having myself and some of the guards around you will help reassure them that all is well."

"Perhaps it would be better then if I were to retract the wings?"

"There is definitely no need for you to do that, as they will see you with the wings at some point in the future, and perhaps showing it now, it will stop a lot of questions. More important than that, I don't particularly want you to be in any kind of pain."

"If you will forgive me, your Majesty. If you were to retract your wings, you might have to do it every time you go into the village to ensure no one gets uncomfortable. We do not want the villagers to start spreading rumors that you had been visited by death, which is why you have these wings. The very last thing we need at this point in time is to cause mass panic to break out, not with the Centaurs still running around." Captain Davie said, smiling.

"If you put it that way, I have to agree. Causing slight panic now is better than having a full-on rebellion in the future. In all honesty, I would rather not retract the wings after what has happened over the last year and a half. Perhaps once things calm down a little more, I might consider retracting them."

"Once you feel up to it, you really should tell me a little bit more about those busy days of yours," Starlansha said smiling.

It was as though a chill descended all around, not just them but the entire village, the second they stepped out of the front doors. The further they walked into the village, a hush seemed to spread throughout everyone. She was not sure whether that was a good thing or not. Were they staring at her because they believed that she was some kind of ghost? Or were they looking at her in that way because they thought she had been taken over by something evil and had been sent to invade the village and kill them all?

"If you do not relax right this second, then I might just be forced to smack you over the head, Alex. The nervous energy is vibrating off of you," Starlansha said softly. "I give you a promise that they aren't looking at you as though you are a monster or something like that. It has been almost two years since they have seen you, and they are just wondering if you aren't perhaps something of their imagination. As they have done time and time again. There have been several occasions when I was walking through the village, and I heard the whispers of how one of them had seen you.

"They have been waiting for you to come back here for the longest of time, and I am sure that most of them dreamed of this day happening," Captain Davie said seriously. "There are even stories of how some of them have been trying to summon you."

"How can you be so sure that my being back would be a good thing? They may just be fooling themselves when they said that they wanted me back," she said, sighing. "I have a feeling that all they see when they lay eyes on me is regret and the knowledge that battle will soon follow. That every time I have returned from wherever it was that I had been training, fighting seems to follow closely in my wake."

"You should stop thinking so negatively about yourself, Alex. Be the girl who saved me from the Orcs yesterday, the confident and a little too serious girl," Starlansha said as they reached the middle of the village, pausing as they noticed the villagers surrounding them. "Show them you are actually here and show them that you aren't just a figment of their imagination. Although I have to admit that the Captain and I being here has helped show them that you are already here."

"We have been hoping for your return ever since the very second that you had disappeared, your Majesty. Happiness surrounds us now that you have finally returned, as we are sure that you will once again bring peace to our world and let there be no more suffering. Hopefully, it will also be your return that will bring our beloved Queen back to us. Then we will be able to celebrate two miracles," a villager said, stepping towards them, bowing. A couple of seconds later, all of the villagers sank to their knees in unison.

"Alex!" a voice shouted from her right, and she glanced quickly towards the voice to see Terri rushing towards her, enveloping her in a tight hug. "It has been the very best of days so far! When I awoke this morning, I had a feeling that something good was about to happen, but I could not say what it would be exactly. So I have been wandering around the village in the hopes of figuring out what it is that made me have this feeling, in the hopes that I would see why I had woken so early. But I cannot tell you enough how much I have missed you the last couple of years."

"It really is good to see you as well, Terri! I can assure you that I have missed you as much as you have missed me. To be honest, it has been a long couple of years, a lot of them I wish that I would be able to take back or redo, truth be told," she whispered glancing back at the still kneeling villagers, blushing. "You are free to rise."

It was with great applause that they did so, making her blush even more. She still could not see how it was possible for people to be so happy to see her when she did not consider herself anything special. No matter how hard she tried, she was not the same person as she had been. While she had still been around, she had not shown Terri much friendship, and it made her feel bad.

"You have welcomed back a long-time friend of ours! I know that we have all missed her quite terribly, and I am sure you all will have a lot of questions for her that you would like to have answered. However, I thought that perhaps we should give her some time to settle back into her home before we bombard her with a thousand and one questions." Starlansha said, quickly stepping forward, lifting her hand for silence. "I do see some of the local children in the crowd, and perhaps if we ask her nicely, Alexandria will answer a few questions. From the little ones in our midst. Would you mind?"

"All I hope is that I will be able to answer the little ones' questions," she replied, smiling and nodding.

"Where did you get your wings?! Could I also perhaps have a pair?" one of the girls asked her wide-eyed.

"A nice lady named Claudia gave them to me, hoping that I would be able to use them well. It is really heavy and gets in the way most of the time, so I can honestly say that you wouldn't want a pair."

"It looks amazing how they seem to glitter between black and red the entire time."

"I do agree with you that they look amazing. Who wants to ask the next question?" Starlansha asked, shooting her a grin.

"I really like the outfit you are wearing. Would I be able to get one as well?" one of the other girls asked, hiding behind her father's leg.

"Maybe one day, when you are older, I could organize a similar one for you, but I do believe that you might just give your mom a heart attack if you were to wear it right now," she replied, winking at the girl's mother, who blushed.

"My daddy told me that you have blades made of water and air! But I think that he has been lying to me because I can't see anything like that?" a boy asked with narrowed eyes.

"I promise you that he did not make it up; I won't be able to show you, though, because at the moment they are just normal blades."

"I think that is pretty amazing!"

"It is indeed amazing, especially when I hold the blades in my hands."

"Is it true that you are able to turn your wings into fire?!" another boy asked.

"Yes, I have the ability to turn my wings to fire."

"But doesn't it burn your back and arms?"

"It is a special kind of flame that doesn't burn me, which is a good thing. Although I have been told that they have burned some of their hands or arms, so I really have to be careful when they are on fire."

"Those are enough questions for now, I believe. Perhaps we could ask Alexandria..." Starlansha started freezing mid-sentence as the kids gasped.

"You... you called her majesty by name!" they all whispered in unison.

"Oh deary me... you are indeed correct. I accidentally called her by her name, and I have to apologize profusely for my little slip-up, your majesty."

"I am not sure whether you should be forgiven for your little mistake... but perhaps it would be a good idea to ask the children what they think I should do."

"Forgive her!" they all shouted, making everyone laugh.

"Then it has been decided that you will be forgiven for your little error," she giggled.

"If you were to please excuse us... her majesty was in the process of touring our fantastic village, and I am sure she would like to finish it," Captain Davie said, stepping forward. "You are now free to continue in the tasks you had been busy with."

"Thank you, I believe that helped quite a bit with all of the nervousness of my returning so suddenly," she whispered to Starlansha as everyone went back to their day.

"That is what I am here for, if you remember… your majesty," she replied grinning.

Chapter 4

The Quiet Anticipation

"Starlansha told me a little about not just Shadick but some of the others, and I am thankful for that. You and Shadick were quite close while I was still here and had more conversations together. Is there perhaps anything you are able to tell me? Something that you may know that no one else would be able to?" she asked Terri, walking again.

"I am sorry to say that I have not heard much from him. What I can tell you is that he has been on the hunt for the Glacier Sword. Unfortunately, he had refused to tell me where his search was taking him, so I would not even be able to tell you that. I'm not sure whether he knew that I would follow him or if he was afraid that I would insist on him taking guards with him. In case you say that I should have at least followed him. I did, but he almost immediately lost me when he transformed into a wolf and disappeared into the forest," Terri replied. "I really had been trying my best, but he knew what I was up to and made it impossible for me to follow him."

"It would not have been fair of me to ask you to babysit a grown man, Terri. There really is no need for you to feel guilty about anything. Shadick did what he did to make sure he gets his mission done, whether that is alone or with someone. I believe if I hadn't disappeared, he may have asked me to join him."

"You have matured a lot since the last time I spent time with you. I have not made up my mind as of yet whether that is a good thing or not. What I can say is that you have become a lot more serious and stoic."

"Honestly, from what I have gone through with not just the elementals but their leader, I'm shocked that I still know how to deal with humans. The lessons I learned while there were life-changing, dangerous, and honestly scarred me for life. But it has made me stronger than I have ever been, even if those things hadn't happened to me. A couple of years ago, I was too immature and too stupid to realize how much I had been taking life and everything that happened for granted. I lost my youth due to a lot of unforeseen circumstances, and I wouldn't wish it on anyone, except maybe the Centaurs. I kind of lived my life once I moved back to the village as though there was absolutely nothing for me to worry about, the life of a girl full of innocent dreams."

"At times, it is for the best to grow as well as learn instead of just accepting that things are the way they are. It is one of the things that make us stronger as well as more assured of not just ourselves but what we are capable of doing. Not to mention, there is nothing wrong with being innocent; just make sure it doesn't make you blind to what is around you."

"Since my return, I have heard a lot of words, but nothing has been as simple and straight to the point as the words you just spoke. So I thank you, Terri."

"It is one of the things I am here for, amongst others."

"And do you have any news of Chadromida?"

"He has been trying to send me weekly reports, but as we all know, the Dragons sometimes keep him busy, and then I hear nothing for a month or more. He has been spending most of his time ensuring that when the next fight breaks out, the Dragons will be ready and give us proper assistance. Astarte... has made sure that some of the humans who aren't exactly ready to live with Magical creatures have a place where they do not have to worry about their safety too much. She has requested some of the Magical creatures to pop in every now and then, so that the Humans can get used to them and that they aren't all bad."

"There is absolutely no reason why all the humans should just automatically accept that they have to live with the Magical creatures. It makes me feel better that they at least have a place to call home. Since the moment I started the journey, it has been tough on everyone to accept the change, but it shouldn't mean people start stagnating back to an old school idea of who is good and bad. There is no need for us to go around and try to convince the people of how bad the Centaurs are, as they did that on their own. Unfortunately, there are some creatures that have always thrived on the bad and negative, so they were attracted to the Centaurs."

"That is very true... it is a sad reality to know that most of them will be slaughtered as though they are nothing. And they mean nothing to the Centaurs, and they are set in their ways and believe they are right."

"Has there been any news on how Balditha and Justren have been handling the death of Diliante?"

"As you saw on the day you killed her, he was not happy with what you did..." Terri replied before glancing at Starlansha.

"There is no reason for you to stop there. There is something that you wanted to add, but Starlansha just gave you some kind of hint to rather not tell me. I would rather find out what is going on now than at some point in the future, hearing about it from someone else."

"Balditha made the decision to put a bounty on your head, and it is not a small one. Once more, people find out that you are alive, they might start coming after you so they can claim the bounty he put on your head."

"From recent reports, he has promised any creature or human who brings him your head not just gold but a place with them in their troops. To give the person a rank that has not been heard of before, and it will assure them that nothing at all will happen to them or any of their family."

"And what if I were to give myself up to him?" she joked.

"That would leave Balditha with an interesting conundrum. I ask that you please not do anything stupid." Starlansha said, sighing. "You have been gone for far too long, and there is no way that I can survive without you ever again."

"You can rest assured, Star, that I was not actually planning on doing it. There is no need for you to worry about it. I was just trying to lighten things up a little."

"I have a question to ask of you," Terri said.

"You wouldn't be the first person wanting to ask me questions since I got back here. Please go ahead, though."

"Your wings seem to now be a part of your body. How is that possible? I remember that they were fire, and very obviously they aren't right now, but there are still wings on your back that weren't there before."

"Then I think it would be the best for us to return to the Castle, as I know that is one of the questions Sachiel would like answered as well. And as fantastic or whatever it looks like, it hurt a lot to get them, and I had to go through things no one should ever have to endure."

"That is a very fair request..." he said, nodding and walking towards the Castle once again. "We have all missed you terribly since your disappearance and have been hoping beyond hope that you would return soon. So it is with a happy heart that I inform you of how pleased I am to have you back. And if you do not believe me, then just look back at how the villagers reacted when they saw you."

"It still feels strange to see people being so happy for me to be back when I have been the cause of all of the fighting since the very start."

"Why is it you believe that you are to blame for all of the fighting? You did not go to the Centaurs' home and personally insulted them and then forced them into an unstoppable rage or anything along those lines."

"You were the one to kill Diliante; you did, however, do it for a good reason," Starlansha said before stopping. "They were the ones that started attacking us years before you even considered killing her."

"You can relax, Star... I know that my actions during the last fight were my fault because I made the decision to attack and kill Diliante. I was just talking about the war from when it started," she replied, smiling slightly.

"You have just been the one trying to find out who is responsible for these attacks and doing your best to stop them before they get even worse than what they already are. The fact that they were happening before has not been your fault."

"Then could you please explain why it is that every time I return, the Centaurs decide to start the war again?"

"There is really nothing for you to worry about, Alex. As Starlansha just told you, it isn't your fault that the Centaurs decided to do what they are doing. It is not your fault that they decided to attack not just you but all of us. They have been unable to get rid of this grudge that they have been holding against us for a very long time, and there is no way that we can stop them from changing. I can assure you that if you were to approach the Centaurs and ask them why they were fighting, you would only receive nonsensical responses without ever truly receiving a proper reply," Sachiel said, walking towards them.

"Is there something wrong with Adriata? Or is it Amethyst?" she asked wide-eyed.

"Both of them are absolutely fine, don't worry about it, Alex! It has been a couple of hours, and I was just starting to wonder where you had gotten yourselves to. Also, the chefs have informed me that dinner will be ready in about half an hour."

"I have to agree with Sachiel on this. You really do need to try and relax a bit more. Amethyst has been fine for the last two years or so, and she will be alive and well for a long time still," Terri agreed, inclining his head to Sachiel.

"From your time away from home, you have become so serious. But if you think that your family and friends are in danger, you are ready to take on whatever is in front of you."

"It makes me a little happier knowing that I am not the only one who noticed how serious you have become since your return."

"That is all I have been hearing ever since my return," she whispered

"Then please tell us what is on your mind so that we can perhaps make it better. Or at least tell us so that we can ease your mind of some of the difficulties that have been weighing on you," Sachiel said, turning towards the Castle.

"I was thinking of not telling anyone about what happened when I was in that other world, but perhaps it would ease my mind if I were to tell you," she said with a sigh. "I do not want Adriata to be anywhere around us when I do tell my story, as I do not want to scar her."

"I will go and have a quick chat with Iva, so that she makes sure she does not come close to the meeting room. That way, we can be sure that she will not bother us. You do need to spend some serious time with her once you have settled down because she has been missing you."

"Once I feel a little bit more relaxed and feel that we will not be attacked within the next couple of days, I will spend all of my time with her. I have missed her just as much, if not more than she has missed me."

"Perhaps it would be best for you to take a couple of minutes just to breathe and clear your mind as much as possible before you tell us your story. As we will be in the meeting room and missing dinner with Adriata, I will organize some of the food to be brought to us."

"That sounds like a really good plan, and I thank you for the thoughtfulness," she replied, nodding and walking towards her room, still lost in her own thoughts, but ready to take on whatever would happen next.

Chapter 5

In the Realm of Elements

With a heavy heart, she made her way towards the meeting room, knowing that the time had come to face the truth. The burden of withholding information was becoming unbearable, and she realized that honesty was the only path forward. These people, her colleagues, were not just mere acquaintances; they were like a family, and they deserved to know the truth about her past year and a half. As she stood in the middle of the hallway, grappling with her emotions, a breathtaking sight unfolded before her.

A magnificent wolf sat gracefully, its eyes fixed on her. Her heart skipped a beat as she whispered in disbelief, "Freya...? Is that really you, girl?" The possibility that it could be her beloved wolf, long lost, filled her with both hope and trepidation. She approached cautiously, hoping for a reunion that seemed too good to be true.

As she stood there, the air thick with anticipation, she watched the wolf's every move with trepidation. The growls reverberated in her ears, causing her heart to race. Could this truly be her long-lost companion, Freya? The doubt lingered, but as the wolf drew nearer and sat down before her, gazing up with familiar eyes, her skepticism melted away, replaced by a surge of joy.

Tears welled in her eyes as she knelt to meet Freya's gaze, their souls connecting once again. It was a bittersweet reunion; the pain of their separation and the longing for her loyal friend all washed over her in that moment. With a soft smile, she spoke to Freya in a hushed tone, pouring her heart out to her wolf companion.

"Freya, my dear friend, I've missed you so much. The days and nights have been filled with loneliness and the weight of our adventures together. I wished you were by my side, to share the trials and train alongside me. Your presence would have brought me comfort, and I know Shadick would have kept me sane amidst the chaos."

She gently touched Freya's fur, feeling the connection between them grow stronger with each passing moment. Recounting her time away, she shared the longing she felt for her loyal companions and how she pleaded with the Elementals to reunite them. Yet, it seemed fate had other plans, and Freya's presence remained a distant hope.

"During my journey, Claudia and Necrontyr did their best to ease my loneliness, but they had their own challenges to face. The leader's selfishness only amplified my longing for you and Shadick."

As she spoke, she sensed an understanding in Freya's eyes, as if the wolf had been with her in spirit all along. Freya's warm tongue gently licked her face, a gesture of reassurance that brought tears of joy to her eyes.

As Starlansha approached, Alex offered a small smile, appreciating her concern. "I'm alright, Starlansha. It's just been a lot to process, but I'm glad to be back."

She crouched down to meet Freya's gaze, feeling a rush of emotions welling up inside her. Freya's presence was like a warm embrace, reassuring her that she was truly home.

"I missed you too, girl," Alex said softly, running her fingers through Freya's fur, feeling the softness of her ears between her fingertips. "You've been taking care of the village, huh? I knew I could count on you."

As Starlansha indicated they should head to the meeting room, Alex took a deep breath, gathering her thoughts for the upcoming conversation. With Freya at her side, she felt a newfound sense of strength, knowing that she didn't have to face everything alone.

Walking beside Starlansha, Freya by her side, Alex felt the weight of the past year and a half slowly lifting off her shoulders. She knew that this meeting would be difficult, but the truth needed to be known. Inside the meeting room, familiar faces looked up, their expressions a mix of curiosity and relief.

"I was just telling his Majesty to relax as you hadn't disappeared again," Captain Davies said, flinching as Sachiel playfully hit him on the head from behind. "I apologize for the insensitivity, Your Majesty! It was not my intention to come across as unfeeling or mean."

"Well, as far as I was able to tell, you were only trying to break the tension," she said with a hint of amusement. "Though I must admit, it was a rather miserable attempt."

She settled into her seat, glancing around at the guards. "At times, I really believe that the guards have no idea how to act in front of royalty or show proper manners without being rude and crude. Tomorrow, I shall call a meeting with all the guards so that I can have a conversation with them on how to react when talking to royalty."

"Yes, Your Majesty, I understand. I will make sure to convey your message to the others." Captain Davies nodded solemnly

"Good. Now, go and guard the door. Make sure that nothing interrupts us, unless it is of the utmost importance."

Captain Davies saluted and positioned himself by the door, ready to protect the privacy of their meeting. As the room fell silent, Sachiel leaned forward, her mind focused on the matters that needed addressing. Despite the occasional challenges of royal life, she felt a deep sense of responsibility and dedication to her kingdom, and she was determined to ensure that everything ran smoothly.

"I have to apologize, it seems that I have lost some of my humor in the last couple of years," Alexandria began, her voice tinged with sincerity. "I am hoping, however, that it will return once I have settled down a little bit more."

"There is no need for you to rush, Alex," she said gently. "You don't need to force yourself to be someone you're not just because you believe it's what we want."

"That was your way of trying to break the ice, wasn't it?" Terri chimed in, recalling Alexandria's attempt at humor.

"As fun as idle chit-chat might be," Alexandria interjected thoughtfully, "this is not why we're here. I know you all have been wondering what happened to me ever since the day I was taken, or as I've been hearing since my return... disappeared."

If it would make you feel better, we can make sure that the villagers know that you hadn't just disappeared." Sachiel offered a suggestion

"It doesn't really matter much to me. They are free to call it whatever they wish."

"So, where do you wish to start with your story, Alexandria?" Terri then asked the crucial question

Alexandria took a deep breath, steeling herself to recount the events that changed her life forever. She knew it was crucial to share the story from the beginning, leaving no details behind. The weight of her experiences bore down on her, but she knew she had to be honest and open with her friends.

"On the battlefield, when I summoned the Elementals, they merged with me, and we became one," she began, her voice steady yet tinged with emotion. "It was an overwhelming and exhilarating feeling to have such power coursing through my veins. I could sense the immense strength at my disposal, and for a moment, I believed I could easily defeat Balditha."

She continued, her words carrying the weight of the consequences that followed. "As I looked into Balditha's eyes, I saw hate and fear. I knew he would stop at nothing to kill me, just as I had inadvertently caused the death of his wife. It was in that moment that I felt something shift within me, but I brushed it off, thinking it was just nerves."

Alexandria knew she had lost control over her newfound powers. In her determination to wield them for the greater good, she had yet to learn how to harness them properly. Her intentions were noble, but her lack of training and understanding led to unforeseen consequences.

"When the volley of arrows was unleashed, time seemed to slow down," she continued, her voice carrying a mix of pain and determination. "I knew the arrows were aimed not at me, but at everyone surrounding me, my friends included. I couldn't allow more lives to be lost, so I instinctively conjured a wall of vines to protect them. It was a split-second decision, and I believed it was the right thing to do."

"But that moment marked the breaking point. I lost control of the powers I thought I could wield. The Elementals sensed the instability and intervened, surrounding me and taking me to their world." As Alexandria continued her tale, the weight of her past experiences hung heavily in the air. She recounted the fateful encounter with the leader, a being shrouded in darkness, and the confrontation that followed.

"Claudia tried to explain what was going on, but he silenced her with a glare. I couldn't stay silent, not when faced with such arrogance and cruelty. I asked him why he hid his face from his 'minions,' and in response, he muttered derogatory words under his breath. His anger towards me grew, and without warning, he touched my Fire wings. The pain was excruciating, and I couldn't help but scream.

"Smoke surrounded me, and when it cleared, I saw that my wings had been transformed, now permanently attached to me. He told me that he would ensure I got my wish of flying and using my wings as weapons since I craved it so much. His coldness and disregard for my well-being were chilling. The Elementals intervened, explaining to the leader that they saw potential in her, believing she could endure his training. But the leader laughed, his disdain evident before he vanished from their sight.

"After that, he was gone, and I was left with my changed wings and the knowledge that I was trapped in his realm, facing an uncertain future. They tried relentlessly on a daily basis to convince him to take me under his wing, or at least attempt to do so. At that point, I was determined to free myself from their grasp and refused to comply with anything they asked of me. My defiance only fueled their frustration, as they were eager to prove to their leader that underestimating me would be a grave mistake.

"It must have been about a month later, after enduring countless scratches and broken bones, that I finally relented and agreed to let them train me. Perhaps, if they showcased my progress, their leader would allow my return home. To my surprise, my willingness to work hard and the strength I exhibited did impress their leader, but it also seemed to reinforce his conviction that sending me back was not an option.

"Whenever I managed to get close to him and questioned why he wanted to keep me away from home, he would either ignore me entirely or respond with an enigmatic grin. The Elementals, those who had been training me, started suspecting that their leader allowed it merely to consider replacing one of them. His ever-changing stance bewildered them, as one day, he would angrily reprimand them, claiming they shouldn't be teaching me anything and that I was merely exploiting their secrets for myself."

"So he really thought that you were there to steal secrets, yet he was impressed with what you were able to do?" Starlansha asked, unable to contain her curiosity, but then quickly apologized for the interruption.

"Yes, you're absolutely right. Despite his suspicions, he couldn't deny the progress I was making and the potential I showed. It was a strange dynamic, but his uncertainty played in my favor."

"How is it that you were able to escape?" Terri asked, still frowning

With a thoughtful look, she recounted the pivotal moment. "One day, when I had nothing to do, Necrontyr came to my room and offered me a way out. I expressed how it would be the best day of my life if such an opportunity arose. Necrontyr, Claudia, and Jace devised a meticulous plan to secure my escape, but they knew it couldn't be rushed. We had to wait for the right moment.

"After about two months of careful planning and observation, we finally knew the time was right to put the plan into action. Necrontyr took on the crucial role of distracting their leader by engaging him in a conversation about how they could improve not just me but their entire world. While he kept their leader busy at his 'Castle,' Claudia, Jace, and I executed our daring escape. It was common knowledge that he loved talking about himself and his world, so we knew that he would be preoccupied for quite a few hours.

"Claudia played a vital role in this plan. She was tasked with opening a portal for me, allowing my escape, but it was a dangerous endeavor. Jace stood at the 'halfway point' to serve as a distraction in case their leader grew suspicious. Everything became a blur, and the next thing I heard was Starlansha's panicked screams, and I knew I was home."

She looked down, her emotions still raw from the memories. Freya, understanding her pain, moved closer in silent support. "To be honest, I never thought I would get out of there. I was a prisoner, and no matter what I said or did, nothing seemed to help."

"But you did make it out, and we are all incredibly proud of you," Claudia emerged from the shadows, reassuringly addressing the woman. "When our leader realized you had escaped, he was furious, but he couldn't figure out how you did it. He had no proof to accuse us, nor did he suspect us."

"Claudia?!" Starlansha couldn't believe her eyes, yelping in surprise.

"There's no need to panic, Starlansha. I'm not here to harm anyone. I just wanted Alexandria to know that we are safe and doing well. Our leader might eventually come after you all, but I don't think it will be anytime soon," Claudia smiled, calming her fears.

"I am really happy that no harm has come to you, Claudia. It had been one of my biggest worries from the start," Alexandria expressed with a hint of relief, though she still tensed at the thought of the dangers Claudia faced.

"If you were to think back, we had to convince you on numerous occasions that no harm would come to us," Claudia nodded, understandingly.

"That is true enough. Would you be able to stay here for much longer?"

"Unfortunately, no. Our leader has been growing more suspicious of everyone and everything, and if one of us is gone for too long, he becomes even more wary. However, I knew that you would be worried, and I just thought that I would come to tell you that we are all okay." With that, Claudia disappeared.

"It sounds as though you have had an amazing journey, albeit distressing. But I can now understand why you haven't been able to sleep for the last couple of years," Terri said seriously.

"If it had not come from you, Alexandria, I would have had a hard time believing that it was real," Sachiel said, shaking his head in disbelief. "What are you planning on doing next? I have known you long enough to know that you won't be able to sit still for much longer. I also know that the Centaurs will eventually catch wind of your return."

"You're right, Sachiel. I was thinking of going to Dargona village to see how things have been going over there and if they perhaps have any news on Shadick. Astarte might have been in contact with him recently and could tell me something more. Even if he doesn't want anything to do with me anymore, he has the right to know that I am still alive." Alexandria smiled, acknowledging his insight into her restless nature.

"I will not argue over that, as I know you can be stubborn. I do, however, believe that you are wrong."

"I have a request of both of you, Alexandria, as well as Sachiel. Would it be okay if I joined the journey to Dargona village? I have failed slightly as a friend by not doing my best to check if Shadick is still alive and well. I would like to see if there is perhaps a way I can help find him," Terri queried, standing up straight.

"You will have to ask Sachiel that, as he is the leader of Valencia. I, however, have no problem with you coming with me."

"I would have tasked you with going with her if you had not mentioned anything, Terri," Sachiel said, nodding in agreement. "While you are there, perhaps you could talk to those still living in Dargona village and convince them to join us here in Valencia. I think it would be a good thing if the villages were to join forces. Living so far apart is not the most secure, and it would be for the best if they were to move here."

"You are right, Sachiel. Chadromida's connection with the Dragons is deep and strong. Convincing him to leave their worlds for an extended period might indeed be challenging, and I wouldn't want to put him or the Dragons in a difficult position. When I first heard about a child being taken and raised by Dragons, it felt like a fantastical tale. I never imagined that they would allow a human into their worlds. Bringing up the idea with him and the villagers might be a good starting point. We can discuss the possibility of occasional visits or temporary stays, rather than a permanent move."

"I will do my best to talk to them and share the idea with them, but you're right. It's ultimately their decision whether they choose to leave their homes or not. I won't force them into anything they're not comfortable with. We must approach it with respect and sensitivity." Terri chimed in

Sachiel nodded approvingly, "Exactly, Terri. We can present the idea as an option, emphasizing the potential benefits of cooperation and unity between the villages. But we must be mindful of their feelings and priorities."

"Please do not get me wrong! I will not be forcing anyone to leave their homes, and it is truly up to them to join us here or not. It might just be a good idea to have more people around for when the fighting starts. And it might be for the best for all of us to unite the villagers," Alexandria reassured, understanding the sensitivity of the situation.

"I will approach them with the idea if I see an opportunity to talk to them," Terri affirmed.

"I hope that you don't mind me going with you?" Starlansha whispered hesitantly.

"There is absolutely no reason for you to even ask. You are more than welcome to join us!"

"I really do appreciate it, Alex. Our travels together have been missed quite a lot! It would also give me an opportunity for us to catch up a little more."

"It would be an honor for you to join me once again, as we have been through a lot."

"Very well then, I shall make sure that all is in order," Sachiel acknowledged, understanding the need for rest before their departure. "I also know that Adriata will want to spend some time with you, so if you wouldn't mind?"

Alexandria smiled warmly, "There is no reason for you to even ask me to do that. It has been a really long time since I've been able to spend time with her. Hopefully, things won't be too crazy, and I will be able to spend more time with her. Thank you for everything, Sachiel. I truly appreciate it."

"You're like family to me, Alexandria. It's only natural that I would support you and be here for you."

As Alexandria walked out of the room, she felt a mix of emotions—excitement for the journey ahead, nostalgia for reuniting with friends, and a sense of determination to face the challenges that lay in their path. She knew that together, with her companions and newfound allies, they could make a difference in their world.

The preparations continued as the group readied for the journey to Dargona village. Each step they took would bring them closer to their goal of uniting the villages and finding Shadick. As they settled in for the night, they could only hope that the morning would bring a new chapter in their lives, full of possibilities and hope for a brighter future.

Chapter 6

Venturing into Dargona

Given the choice, she would have taken to the skies, soaring through the expanse with Terri and Starlansha in tow. However, the pragmatic reality of their situation dictated otherwise, precluding her from utilizing her wings. The presence of Terri and Starlansha, both lacking her aerial advantage, necessitated more conventional modes of transportation, hence the reliance on horses.

While a semblance of anxiety lingered about potentially faltering during this venture, her desire to not appear incompetent propelled her forward, a hope that muscle memory would guide her. Freya's companionship was non-negotiable; the loyal canine would undoubtedly protest vehemently if relegated to the castle. The sigh that escaped her was accompanied by a wistful glance skyward, yearning for Shadick's presence to facilitate a shared journey.

The aching void left by his absence was profound, transcending expression. Thoughts of Managwa joined the mix, a pang of longing for their companionship reverberating through her. Suppressing these vulnerabilities, she bit her lower lip in contemplation, resolute in her determination to not display any perceived weaknesses during this critical juncture.

"Alex... are you feeling alright? You appear a touch pale," Starlansha inquired, her concern evident as she drew closer.

"I was merely lost in contemplation about the inception of my journey, my ventures to the Troll Caves, and the cascade of events that have unfolded since then," Alex swiftly fabricated, her words a veneer to conceal her true preoccupations.

"The recent years have been utterly surreal, and the circumstances of our initial meeting would likely sound implausible to those who weren't present at the time. The madness that ensued, coupled with the genesis of the Centaurs' conflict, is a narrative that defies belief," she continued, adeptly crafting a tale to divert attention from her actual thoughts.

"I reflect upon those countless years we dedicated to the arduous task of improving the world, even when the odds were overwhelmingly against us. It serves as a poignant reminder that, regardless of how bleak circumstances may appear, the potential for the world to thrive as a benevolent place persists. In the face of the Centaurs' tumultuous upheaval, there remains a glimmer of hope for a brighter future," she expressed, her voice imbued with a sense of optimism.

"At moments, the clarity becomes clouded, making it difficult to discern the multitude of genuinely good souls still among us. The landscape around us may be marred by destruction, yet if one looks closely enough, the triumph of goodness becomes apparent. Plants defying the parched earth to flourish, or animals venturing closer to Valencia than ever before – these instances underscore the resilience of positivity, even amid the darkest hours when all appears futile," Alex continued, seamlessly blending her narrative into the ongoing conversation.

"That's something I had also observed during my time with the Elementals," Alex chimed in. "The landscape was marked by ruins and desolation, an environment where survival was a formidable challenge. Here, nature demonstrates remarkable resilience, adapting and finding a way to thrive even in the face of adversity. While I can't say for certain about the current state of the Troll Caves, I envision nature reclaiming that space, as animals carve out their own habitat amidst the rocky terrain."

Terri interjected, her voice carrying a sense of mystery. "There's one location where nature's dominion was thwarted."

"Pray, which place might that be?" Starlansha queried, her astonishment evident.

"McLeod's..." Terri's voice carried a somber note, casting a shadow over the conversation. "I've been tirelessly attempting to gather information about the village where you spent much of your formative years, Alexandria. The tidings I've unearthed, however, are grim. A pall of despair seems to shroud the village, as it has succumbed to an invasion of ghosts and demons. Regrettably, my scouts were ill-fated enough to venture into the heart of that place. Only one returned, his visage forever scarred by the horrors he encountered. The others weren't as fortunate; they bore the marks of demon attacks, mere scratches that could have easily spelled their doom."

"Perhaps, it would be wise to abstain from further discussions about McLeod's."

"I genuinely appreciate your consideration, and I assure you that my feelings won't be wounded by any mention of McLeod's. You're right, dwelling on circumstances beyond one's control serves only to breed doubt and futility. It's a tiresome cycle that leads nowhere, despite the illusion of progress." A soft sigh escaped her lips as she reflected on Terri's observation. "I do recall the last time McLeod's was broached, or even its proximity. The anguish it stirred within me was undeniable."

"You needn't be concerned; I'm prepared to discuss the matter. As for McLeod's, it was a quaint village nestled amidst lush landscapes. Yet, it wasn't the physical beauty that left the deepest imprint, but rather the sense of community and camaraderie that flourished among its inhabitants. The bustling market square, the laughter-filled gatherings, and the spirit of cooperation were the hallmarks of daily life. But... time has a way of transforming even the most idyllic places."

"There's little else known about the village, except for the grim

72

reality that the Centaurs orchestrated its obliteration. It seems they made it their mission to deliver a devastating blow to the heart of the village, erasing all signs of its once-vibrant existence. Their efforts were not solely aimed at physical destruction, as they also cultivated a sinister delight in ensuring the place became infested with ghosts and demons. In their twisted perspective, it was a macabre fantasy to thwart any possibility of your return." Terri's expression was grave as he conveyed this disheartening information. "Before you inquire about the source of my knowledge, allow me to clarify. These insights are gleaned from what I managed to gather before aligning with your cause. The remainder of my understanding has been pieced together from fragments overheard from passing Centaur warriors."

"Your steadfast loyalty and unwavering support have saved me countless times, Terri. You've proven time and again that your trustworthiness knows no bounds. It's a testament to the remarkable friendship we've cultivated, and I'm genuinely glad you're a cherished part of our lives. The upheaval may have shattered the world we once knew, but it has also gifted us with unexpected and profound connections."

"I must confess, this period of my life has also been marked by profound happiness. There isn't a single day among my experiences with the Centaurs that holds a candle to the time I've spent here with all of you. Witnessing the humans and magical beings evolve from a state of enmity to a united front has been a marvel to behold. The transformation from animosity to collaboration, as though the hatred had never existed, is truly remarkable. I doubt it was a scenario Balditha had ever envisioned when he set this battle in motion."

"You haven't even seen Luanda since your return! If I remember correctly, you still wanted to tell her about how she came to receive her powers, before the battle started, of course, but it was completely waylaid with the attack on Amethyst," Starlansha said suddenly.

"I hope that nothing has happened to her while I have been gone?"

"No! Well... nothing untoward has happened to her at least. She and Michael got married, and they are expecting their first child."

"That's absolutely wonderful! I never thought that they wanted to have children in this world of chaos."

"It led to quite a few spirited debates between the two of them, as she adamantly maintained their lack of desire for children. However, her stance eventually shifted, and she revealed her readiness to embark on the journey of parenthood. The day he received this news ranks among the most joyous in his existence. He was a whirlwind of elation, racing through the village, exuberantly sharing his happiness and even engaging in spirited dances with the village children. A humorous interlude ensued when, in his jubilation, he attempted to coax an older lady into dancing, only to be met with a swift smack from her cane."

"Let me take a guess... she is one of those old and very proper ladies who find it an insult to be touched by anyone that isn't her husband?"

"Exactly! But it didn't dampen his spirits at all. The last couple of years, her visions have been getting stronger, which of course she has been sharing with Sachiel, seeing as Amethyst hasn't exactly been able to do much."

"I have no choice but to sit down with both Luanda and Michael when we return and inform her where she had gotten her powers from. Just so she also knows that her child will have abilities as well, so that they can be prepared."

"It will not be an easy conversation for you to have with her, but it is definitely one that has to happen," Terri agreed, "as long as you know that she might be upset with you because of her wanting to deny her true parentage. I know that some humans can be rather touchy about a subject that involves their mother or father, especially when it is something they might not want to hear."

"We have never been exactly the closest of friends, so it doesn't really matter if she is upset with me. We may have lived in the same village, but we barely had any real conversations. I wasn't exactly the most social of people when it got to the humans."

"As long as you are well aware that she may want to change that and to actually spend some time with you to get to know you, as well as talk about not just her abilities but yours as well," Starlansha said smiling.

"That bridge will be crossed when we get there… what exactly am I looking at?" she asked wide-eyed at the village ahead of them.

"This is the result of Astarte and her determination as to where she wanted the village to go, especially to make sure that not just the humans feel safe from the magical creatures, but anyone who might attack the village. It has come a long way since I was last here, and I really am impressed with the progress," Terri said, nodding happily. "I am very happy that the goal has been achieved."

"Who goes there?!" a voice shouted at them as they got closer to the village.

"We wish to have a few moments with Astarte and Chadromida; they are our friends. I assure you that we aren't here to cause any trouble!"

"It is as clear as day that you are a Centaur. And everyone knows that we cannot trust Centaurs!"

"Is this still something that we have to go through every time we meet new people?" she asked, sighing.

"I do, however, recognize the Mermalani and know that she is on our side… the other woman, though is not someone that I have ever seen, and from the look of those wings, I can tell that it can only mean trouble."

"Would you please call Astarte? Or even Chadromida?" Starlansha asked, stepping forward.

"The Dragons called Chadromida to the Mountains, the evening before last, and has not returned as of yet. Astarte, on the other hand, is too busy to be disturbed by those who only wish to waste her time."

"We have battled together more than once, so I can assure you that she will want to see us. We also know her brother, for goodness sake!" Terri told the guard angrily

"It is all too easy for you to be lying about all of this."

Alexandria put her right hand against her forehead, closing her eyes. Teleporting behind the gate, flicking the make-shift switch, and causing it to swing open, she quickly teleported behind the guard and loomed over him.

"All I ask is that you do not make me hurt you," she whispered.

"I will tell them that you overpowered me if you get me into trouble! They will take one look at you and know that it is a true story."

"I can assure you that you will get into even more trouble if you keep on delaying us. We are friends with both Astarte as well as Chad."

"Alex! He is just doing his job, so it would be for the best to not hurt him," Starlansha said, riding into the village, leading Alexandria's horse towards her. "It is a good thing that he did not just cave in and let us through the gates. Yes, he was being irritating, but he was doing what he thought was right."

"It would be admirable, if it weren't for the fact that we were some of the fighters responsible for the successful attacks against the Centaurs in the last two battles."

"Not everyone in this town was around back then, so not everyone would know who took part in the battle. I am sure that they only recently joined the village because of the attacks from the Centaurs," Terri said, glancing at the sweating guard.

"Do I look so odd and out of place that people believe I am in league with the Centaurs?! That was not aimed at you, Terri."

"The presence of wings can indeed be a staggering sight, particularly when it's an anomaly not commonly encountered. In a realm largely populated by humans, such a display would undoubtedly stand out," Starlansha acknowledged with a nod, her understanding evident. "It's fascinating how even though you bear a human resemblance, there's an inherent recognition of your distinctiveness. While they may need time to adjust and establish a sense of ease around you, it's heartening to know that they eventually find comfort in your presence, allowing their authentic selves to emerge."

"The wings aren't exactly something that I wanted, and I would be more than happy to withdraw them, but it would be a pain to keep doing it just to make the mass populous feel safe."

"There is no need to become defensive, as all I'm doing is commiserating with how you feel right now. To show you that you aren't the only one who feels as though they are always being judged."

"As thrilled as I am to have you here, my presence wasn't summoned to validate my trustworthiness. So, I presume you've managed to circumvent the gates," Astarte greeted with a wry smile. As her eyes fell upon Alexandria, she hardly wasted any time before rushing toward her, enfolding her in a heartfelt embrace. "Among all the possible occurrences this day might have brought, I can unequivocally say that your arrival is the most fortuitous. To see you standing here defies description; it's the best thing that could have transpired."

"Hi Astarte, it really is good to see you after so many years," she replied, smiling.

"From my perspective, those wings only enhance your beauty, adding a distinctive allure. They're a symbol of your formidable strength, a manifestation of your power that's impossible to overlook. You exude a commanding presence, even if you may be reluctant to acknowledge it. Embrace your uniqueness, for it suits you effortlessly, and there's no reason to conceal such a remarkable aspect of yourself."

"You're pregnant!" Starlansha squealed as she jumped off her horse. "How far along are you?"

"In fact, I'm nearly at the end of my pregnancy journey. There's only a week or two left before this little one enters the world. I'm looking forward to regaining my mobility and no longer being encumbered by a substantial baby bump."

"When we decided to come through for a visit, we did not expect to find you barefoot and pregnant. It is, however, nice to so people starting to move on and grow with each other and their own families."

"I really wanted to come through to Valencia so that we could catch up with each other, as well as informing you that the little one is on the way. Chad, however, forbade me to ride a horse."

"Have you gotten married without sending us an invitation?" Starlansha asked wide-eyed.

"I promise that we didn't get married without sending you invitations, especially seeing as no one in the village has the legality to marry us. The plan has been to go to Valencia once we have the little one around, and have Sachiel marry us. As much as it would have been a dream come true for Amethyst to marry us, I can only assume she is still in a coma?"

"A couple of times, there has been some movement, but other than that, she is still in a coma."

"Then I have absolute belief that she will come back to us faster than the blink of an eye. With you around, my hope grows stronger that we will see her up and about before too long."

"And what does Shadick have to say about his little sister not being married and very pregnant?" she asked Astarte, glancing around.

"When we told him initially, he was rather upset, but after a couple of days, he finally accepted it."

"Is there a chance that he is around?"

"No, he isn't, unfortunately... we haven't seen him in a couple of months. I am, however, expecting him to return at some point this week."

"Oh... of course."

"Your absence after the last battle had quite an effect on him. He seemed rather lost, caught in a state of inertia. It wasn't until he roused himself to seek the Glacier Sword that I truly felt a sense of relief. To be completely candid, it took nearly a year of persistent persuasion on my part to convince him. Managwa, on the other hand, was thoroughly displeased with Shadick's behavior. He maintained a steadfast silence for weeks on end, regardless of Shadick's attempts to bridge the gap. When Shadick finally reached out to him, signaling the start of their journey, the transformation in Managwa's demeanor was palpable. It was as if a newfound vitality had returned to his eyes,"

"One of the reasons that we decided to come through now is

that I was hoping he would be here," she said, sighing, Freya leaning against her side while she rubbed the wolf's head absent-mindedly.

"I am happy to see that the wolf is still attached to you and seems to be able to tell when you need support. That is a really good sign. As for Shadick... as I already said, he should be back soon enough. And I can assure you that he will be very happy to see you. I can just imagine his face if he were to walk into the village right now and see you! If I really think about it, he would completely ignore his pregnant sister and run straight towards you!"

"Perhaps we could spend some time in the village and wait for Shadick's return, then? Or is there something that we need to do in a hurry?" Starlansha asked, glancing at her.

"If Astarte will have us, I see no reason for us to not stay for a while. We can perhaps help around the village as there is nothing pressing requiring our assistance."

"Do you really have to ask whether you are welcome to stay? There is even space for you to sleep, so there is no need to worry about that."

"Alex has not been able to sleep much the last while, but I can assure you that Terri and I would appreciate it a lot," Starlansha said, laughing softly.

"Give me a couple of minutes, so that I can organize something for you to eat. I'm sure that you are starving after your trip!" Astarte said happily as she turned around, calling to people.

As Alexandria surveyed the village surroundings once more, a pang of disappointment crept into her heart. She had held a quiet hope that being amidst a community of individuals would instill a sense of belonging, a feeling of being at home.

Yet, it had become increasingly apparent that her expectations had been misplaced. The weight of this realization bore down on her, stirring an internal struggle between the desire for connection and the overwhelming urge to escape. A wave of restlessness and unease washed over her, igniting a yearning to flee, to distance herself from a place where she was known, understood, and potentially judged.

Chapter 7

Whispers and Tales

"Have you heard anything new from your grandparents in the last while, Star? From the reports that we have received, it seems to be rather quiet on that side," Astarte asked as they sat around the fire that evening.

"The latest correspondence I received from my Grandmother conveyed an assurance that there hasn't been an attack for a considerable span, at least a year," Starlansha recounted, a small smile touching her lips. "However, they're acutely aware that any sign of complacency could potentially be exploited by the enemy. Hence, the guards remain vigilant, patrolling the area as diligently as before, to ensure there's no opening for them to capitalize on."

Her smile took on a faintly amused tinge as she continued, "Now, my Grandfather, on the other hand, is a steadfast advocate for maintaining a heightened state of alertness. It's almost as if he's taken the role of guardian to heart, unwavering in his commitment to the cause. From the time we've spent getting to know him, it's been a consistent refrain – the guards must remain ready at all times. It seems lowering the guard isn't exactly in his repertoire," she concluded, her tone lighthearted.

"It would just be like them to wait for any kind of sign of weakness before attacking and making everyone's lives a living hell. These buggers have been working so hard to be smart and forward-thinking that they haven't realized we are numerous steps ahead of them."

"What I find truly disheartening is the way this conflict has severed the bonds of friendship and family," Starlansha concurred, her expression reflecting a deep sadness. "Lately, there's been a growing undercurrent of murmurs, with some sharing that they haven't laid eyes on or even exchanged words with their loved ones since the battles began. It's a troubling realization that raises questions about the very purpose for which Valencia was conceived – to safeguard families from such separation.

"Despite our intentions, circumstances have made it nearly impossible to gauge the extent of our success in keeping families intact. The danger is far too imminent for us to attempt any sort of intervention, and the unpredictability of attacks further compounds the challenge. We're caught in a relentless cycle where the next strike remains an enigma, making it a constant struggle to prevent further divisions among those we hold dear.

"I've had discussions with Sachiel as well, and he shares your sentiments, Starlansha," Terri interjected, nodding in agreement. "He's resolute in his determination to unite all factions of our people – those already residing within Valencia's sanctuary, as well as those who remain concealed in the shadows. It's a noble endeavor, one that aims to mend the fractures within families and communities. However, the ongoing onslaught of unpredictable attacks has created a formidable obstacle. We're confronted with a relentless threat that strikes at any given moment, leaving us unable to ascertain a safe window of opportunity. The last thing we wish to do is inadvertently exacerbate the pain of torn-apart families by misjudging the timing and making a grievous error. It's a delicate balance we're trying to strike, a weighty responsibility that we carry with the utmost gravity."

"That's a relief to hear," Astarte responded, her tone tinged with a mix of concern and reassurance. "The recent reports detailing minor attacks do show that there's been some activity, albeit not of a magnitude to induce significant alarm. It seems these incidents have mainly targeted travelers en route to Valencia or within our vicinity. While some have sustained injuries, we've managed to provide the necessary care to mend them. It does give me the impression that these attacks might be more of a diversionary tactic, a way to keep the Centaurs and their forces occupied and perhaps prevent any sense of monotony from setting in. Yet, the fact that certain individuals and creatures are being subjected to interrogations by the Centaurs adds a layer of complexity to the situation. Regrettably, the underlying motives behind these actions remain elusive, as I've been unable to discern any coherent pattern."

"They are waiting for my return," she said without warning, sitting up straight. "If you think about it, it makes sense. When I disappeared, the fighting just stopped. So to keep those under them happy, they were given permission to attack and question those whom they can, but they are not to harm them seriously. Also instructing them to find out anything and everything they can about me, and whether they knew whether I had returned yet or not. Promising them that the real fight will start soon."

"Don't you think that is a little far-fetched?"

"I'm sorry to say that she may have a point," Chadromida said from behind her, glancing at her and grinning. "It really is fantastic to see you after what has been too long! It was one of all of our fears that you had died when the explosion happened, but we always kept a little bit of hope inside of us."

"It is good to see you, Chadromida. You have no idea how much I mean it when I say that I have missed everyone here and am so happy to be back," she replied, hugging him.

"Why do you think that she may have a point?" Astarte demanded, frowning.

"The last couple of hours, the Dragons have been informing me of some rather disturbing events. These events were the reason they thought it fit to call me to Dargona Mountains, as they knew that I would want to hear about it. Some of the less powerful

Dragons have been attacked and questioned while in their worlds as well. They can't explain how they are getting into their worlds, as the only entrances that exist are those within the Mountains. And they have assured me that they have gone through the entire mountain and there has been no breach."

"Why do I get a feeling that this is your way of telling me that you will be with the Dragons the next couple of days?"

"They will try to do as much as possible without me there, as they know that the baby is due this week. So there is no reason for you to worry about me not being here for the birth of our baby."

"Even if they were to call him to the Mountains again, you don't have to worry. We will be staying here for a while to make sure that nothing goes wrong," Starlansha said, smiling.

"Has there been any news on my brother?! He knows that the baby will be here this week and that I would prefer to have him here as well!"

"Since the last message he sent us, I have not heard anything from him. And I know that you will ask this next, but the Dragons aren't sure where he is either, so they won't be able to help us locate him."

"Not once since my birth has he gone so long without at least sending me a message to let me know that he is alive and well. Even if he was busy with fighting, he would take a moment to write me so I knew he was okay."

"Then perhaps it would be for the best if you didn't lose contact with him for two years so that you could be sure you never lose him," she said, stepping away quickly while taking a deep breath, as she heard Starlansha quickly explaining.

"She is still feeling slightly disconnected from everyone since her return."

She ventured toward the edge of the tree line, leaping gracefully onto the sturdy branches of one of the massive trees. Settling down, she found herself swiftly engulfed by her own restless thoughts. Concerns swirled through her mind, a tumultuous mix of worries and uncertainties. Did she truly belong here after her extended absence, returning only to usher in a conflict that many had secretly hoped to avoid?

The cheers and displays of respect that had greeted her weren't necessarily indicative of genuine warmth – the chasm between a public show and genuine sentiment loomed large. With a heavy heart, Alexandria wrestled with her inner turmoil, grappling with the uncertainty of whether her return had truly been embraced by the people or merely acted out for the sake of appearances. The duality of perception weighed heavily upon her, and she found herself ensnared in a cascade of doubt and reflection.

"I never thought that you would be the kind of person to get lost in your own thoughts so much that you don't even hear when someone approaches," Chadromida said as he sat down next to her.

"I figured that it was one of the very few times that I would just be able to cut myself off and not have to worry about being attacked by anyone or anything," she replied, smiling slightly. "Besides, Freya would have growled if it had been someone she did not trust."

"You have a fair point there. Sometimes all we need is to just sit and try to sort out the thoughts that bother us most. So when the opportunity presents itself, then it should be embraced with both hands."

"Exactly…"

"Is there something on your mind that you would prefer to discuss with someone? Maybe a question you would like to ask before we actually start doing it? Something that could be dangerous if not life-threatening?"

"There is no reason for you to worry. I am not planning on going on a suicide mission. The last two years, as difficult as they had been, taught me that if you aren't ready to face something, then you will fail. So it is a good idea to make sure that you are strong enough to face it. That way, you don't have to worry about failing."

"I take it that no matter how bad it was, there was some good in what happened?"

"To put it in layman's terms, yes."

"I can assure you that Shadick is fine, if that is one of your worries. No, I have not heard anything from him for quite a while, but I saw the determination in his face before he left. He isn't going after the Glacier Sword for just himself or even his father... but to prove to you that he can do it. To show you that you weren't the only one who had stuff to do in the last two years, or even the only one who had to go through stuff. Most importantly, he is worthy of your love and affection.

"From what I have heard, he didn't go anywhere for the first couple of months."

"It was as though you had been his will to live, so he refused to go anywhere. Then the one morning, he woke up, mentioned something about how you had told him in his dream that he better not be slacking off, and from that day on, he threw himself into doing more research on the last known location of the Glacier Sword. It took him a couple of weeks, but as soon as he thought that he had a solid lead to where it might be, he would go there to see if he was successful.

"When it wasn't, he would come back here and would do even more research. Slowly narrowing it down, which is where he went about a month or so ago. No matter how many disappointments he received, he would not give up. He even started writing in a journal so that he could keep track of all the details and to make sure that he wasn't going to end up in the same place again. Some of the places in the journal were scratched out almost immediately, muttering that it wouldn't be there for some reason or another before returning to his mutterings, writings, and research."

"For some reason, I feel like I had a similar dream," she said, frowning. "I had gone to bed with him on my mind, wishing that I would be able to speak with him at least once to make me feel better. In this dream, I recall that he was just sitting around, not doing anything and just staring at everything going on around him, as though he didn't care whether the world was ending or not. I kissed him on the forehead and told him that slacking off wasn't going to help anyone and that he should get off his ass and do something. When I woke up the next morning, I just shrugged it off as being a dream... a very vivid dream, but a dream nonetheless."

"You astral projected!" Astarte shouted up to them excitedly.

"Close... it is called dream walking. Where one person is capable of entering into the dream of another. If you are well-versed in the ability, then you would be able to enter the other person's daydream," Terri said, bowing his head to Astarte slightly. "Whereas Astral projection is a premeditated out-of-body experience, a type of telepathy, if you will. It takes the form of a soul, or rather consciousness, called an 'astral body' that is completely separate from the physical body, and you are then capable of traveling outside of it throughout the universe, where it can interact with either other astral bodies or is used to implant thoughts into other people's minds. The Centaurs were determined to use it against those who dared stand up against them, hoping to end them that way."

"Well, at least I wasn't that far off..."

"I am impressed that you even know of Astral projection, as not a lot of people know what it means, never mind what it truly is."

"Well, whatever it was you did that night, it gave him the kick that he needed to start his mission, and I know that he is thankful for that. Even if it never crossed his mind that it was an actual event and not just a dream," Chadromida said, smiling.

"Then I am glad that I was able to get through to him, even when I thought that I had not succeeded," she replied seriously.

"If you would allow it, I have one question for you. I will not be asking you about what happened during the time that you were away, as I am sure that Sachiel has already drilled you on it. You are, however, free to tell us about it, if you wish to, but I don't expect you to."

"I really appreciate that, Chad. But you are more than welcome to ask your one question."

"Where in the world did those wings come from? Please don't misunderstand me, they're truly remarkable, and I must confess, a tinge of envy flares up within me as it's something I've always wished for. I distinctly remember you not possessing those wings when you vanished..."

"I've been making a conscious effort to refrain from asking

about the wings, though I did offer a compliment on them," Astarte chimed in with a nod.

"Very impressive indeed. But now, let's give Alexandria the floor so she can shed some light on the origin of these remarkable wings."

"I was, quite forcibly, I might add, granted these wings by the Master," Alexandria replied with a grimace.

"The Master?"

"That's what the Elementals referred to him as, and given the lack of further information, 'the Master' was the only term I could use. In truth, I took to calling him 'the bastard' out of sheer exasperation. From what I gathered, he holds a position of leadership in their realm – essentially their supreme authority,"

"What do you mean by 'forcefully given'?"

"When they transported me to their realm, the fiery wings were still aflame upon my back. At that moment, he emerged and casually mentioned that since I appeared to have a fondness for the wings, I could keep them. He reached out and touched the wings, an excruciating experience that left me screaming in agony. After what felt like an eternity, he withdrew his hand, and the wings were imprinted upon me permanently.

"I attempted to reason with him on multiple occasions, explaining that the fire wings had manifested involuntarily during a battle and weren't my desired choice. But he remained resolute in his silence, refusing to provide an explanation. Stranded far from home, I had to come to terms not only with the unfamiliar realm but also with the reality of having wings – a change he forced upon me. Despite my protests, he adamantly prevented my return, dismissing my pleas no matter how fervently I made them,"

"If you ask me, he sounds like a slight pain in the ass."

"Believe me when I say that wasn't even the worst of it."

"Do you have any idea what they are made of?

"Not really, no... the Elementals tried to figure out, but all they could tell me was that it looked as though it was made from molten lava combined with a lot of water, wind, and nature. And of course, most importantly, spirit."

"So all of the Elements then..."

"Indeed, I can assure you that it was not easy getting used to these things on my back. It wasn't made easier by the fact I had to do what they called training while still getting used to the wings, something I do not recommend."

"That sounds absolutely horrible!" Astarte said wide-eyed.

"From what the Elementals told me, that was nothing to what the Master was actually capable of doing, and apparently I was 'lucky' to get it so easy."

"Before Astarte gets all fired up and launches into an impassioned speech about administering a much-needed whipping to this 'master,'" Chadromida interjected with a wry smile, "I believe it's time for us to retire for the night and catch some well-deserved rest. Alexandria, you're welcome to use Shadick's makeshift resting spot, considering his current absence. Starlansha and Terri, the villagers have prepared accommodations for you, and Denisha over there will assist in guiding you to your designated sleeping spots."

"Thank you, Chad. Your understanding is truly appreciated," Alexandria responded, offering a grateful smile as she too descended and followed his lead towards her designated resting spot. "I completely understand; sometimes recounting the story makes it feel like a distant dream. Though I must confess, I have a feeling that I'll likely spend a good part of the night wandering around the village. It's been quite a while since I've been here, and I could use some time to reacquaint myself with everything."

"If there is anything that you might need during the night, our place is right next to this one. Just call my name, and I will be here in a matter of seconds to check up on you."

Alexandria embraced Chadromida tightly, expressing her gratitude before stepping into the room designated for her stay. With a mixture of nostalgia and comfort, she found herself surrounded by Shadick's belongings, small fragments of his presence that stirred emotions within her.

As the room enveloped her in a sense of belonging, Freya, her faithful companion, joined her in the room, reclining on the fur carpet with a watchful demeanor. Alexandria moved among the items, holding and inhaling his scent, the mix of emotions building within her. Gently clutching one of his shirts to her chest, her vulnerability surfaced, and tears flowed freely down her cheeks.

Overwhelmed by the flood of emotions, Alexandria eventually sank onto the bed, the soft fabric of the shirt cradling her as she succumbed to exhaustion and her emotions. The tears gradually subsided, replaced by a sense of solace as she drifted into slumber, the weight of her worries lifted, at least for a fleeting moment.

Chapter 8

Reunions Embrace

Startled from her slumber, Alexandria's senses snapped into high alert as a presence entered the room. Panic surged within her, a residue from her time surrounded by danger. She quickly assessed her surroundings, realizing her weapons were out of reach, and a surge of anxiety gripped her. Freya, sensing the intruder as well, was poised and protective, her growls filling the room. But then another sound joined the chorus, a familiar and distinct growl that stirred a recognition deep within Alexandria.

It was the unmistakable voice of Managwa, the wolf companion she had known for years. As realization washed over her, dispelling the initial fear, Alexandria's heart raced with a newfound anticipation. With an energy borne of a long-awaited reunion, she sprang into action, leaping from the bed and charging toward the figure in the doorway. A mixture of excitement, relief, and raw emotion propelled her forward as she sought the one who had been conspicuously absent from her life.

"Shadick!" she shouted excitedly.

"Will you get off of me, woman!" Shadick replied in irritation, but she refused to let go.

Amidst the flurry of emotions and the dimly lit room, the candles' soft glow illuminated the scene before them. Despite the temporary blindness caused by the sudden light, Alexandria's focus remained unwavering, her gaze locked onto the face before her – the face that had been etched into her heart and memory. Shadick, the man who had been both her anchor and her inspiration, stood there, a mixture of surprise, confusion, and possibly relief painted across his features.

In this fleeting moment, time seemed to stand still, and their connection remained unbreakable. Refusing to let go, Alexandria's grip tightened, her eyes searching his as if to reaffirm that this was not a dream, that he was truly here, in her arms. She held onto him, as if afraid that if she let go, he might slip away once more, back into the shadows that had kept them apart for far too long. Despite his attempts to free himself, she clung to him, unwilling to release him from her grasp after waiting for his return for so long.

"What in the blazes is going on in here?!" Chadromida's voice boomed, causing a momentary pause in the room's atmosphere. His eyes widened in surprise as he took in the scene before him, freezing in mid-step. "Well, this is certainly an unexpected surprise, Shadick. We didn't know when to expect you back, and we certainly didn't expect you to sneak back here in the middle of the night."

A mischievous grin tugged at Shadick's lips, his irritation momentarily forgotten. "I thought that I would surprise you lot! But as soon as I walked into my place, I noticed that you had given it away. And this woman is refusing to let me go!"

"And you know this so-called 'woman,' brother dearest," Chadromida's voice resonated with playful amusement, his eyes twinkling as he observed the unexpected reunion. Astarte and Starlansha, still rubbing sleep from their eyes, joined the gathering, their expressions shifting from bewilderment to realization.

"As awesome as it is to see you, brother, why are you standing as though you are being stalked when Alexandria is hugging you?" Astarte asked, arching her eyebrow.

"Lexie?" Shadick's voice wavered, a mixture of disbelief and joy in his tone. "Is it really you? You're here?"

"Yes, it really is me…" she whispered, smiling slightly.

"When… how… wings?!"

"That is a long story that she already had to relive only a couple of hours ago. Perhaps it would be best to give her a bit of a break before she is forced to tell the story again?" Starlansha said, shaking her head.

"Hi Star… long time no see."

"Tell me about it, stranger."

"Um… Shadick?" she asked, squirming in his arms.

"Yes, Lexie?"

"Could you please let me down? Besides, I think Freya is about ready to attack you, and I'm really not used to being held in the air like this anymore."

Shadick blinked, realizing that he had completely overlooked the presence of Freya. He quickly set Alexandria down and took a step back. "My apologies, Freya," he said, looking at the wolf. "I didn't mean to startle you. And of course, my apologies to you as well. It's just... seeing you here after all this time is quite unexpected."

"It has been 2 years, Shadick," Terri said from the doorway, "and as long as that has been, it is not forever."

"Is everyone here?" he asked, bending down to calm Freya down. "It's just me, girl, you can calm down."

"Why exactly did you scream, Alex?" Chadromida asked, frowning.

"I didn't expect to see someone silhouetted in the door, and I thought that maybe the Centaurs had somehow found out that I had returned and had come to kill me. But I then recognized Managwa's growl, which is when I realized that it was Shadick. I then flung myself at him and shouted his name," she explained, blushing slightly.

"That makes perfect sense!" Astarte said, nodding. "I would have had the exact same reaction if it had been me."

"Wow! Sister dearest, you are getting rather big," Shadick said wide-eyed.

"You are just in time to experience the birth of your niece or nephew, and if you had actually sent us a message, you would have known this."

"This explains why something has felt off and as though I was forgetting something!"

"I think that it would be a smart idea to leave the two of you alone, so that you can catch up. Besides, your sister needs to get back to bed before we force her to go into labor," Chadromida said, shaking his head. "As much as I want the little one to make their appearance, I don't want to force it to come early."

"We will talk more tomorrow, Shadick," Starlansha said as she and Terri disappeared from view.

"It really is good to have you back, brother," Astarte said, hugging Shadick quickly before being lightly pushed out of the room by Chadromida

Sitting down on the bed, Alexandria stared at Shadick with a mixture of emotions swirling within her. The moment felt surreal, as though if she touched him too much or too hard, he might vanish like a fleeting dream. Her heart was caught in a whirlwind of joy, disbelief, and an intense longing that she couldn't quite put into words. As Shadick closed the door with a quiet click, the room seemed to shrink, focusing all attention on him.

Freya, the ever-loyal companion, rested her head on Alexandria's lap, her eyes shifting between her and Shadick, almost as if she was sharing in the same emotions. There was an unspoken understanding between them, a connection forged through shared experiences and countless moments of companionship. In Freya's gaze, Alexandria could almost sense a playful accusation, as if the wolf was gently chiding Shadick and Managwa for the distance they had allowed.

As Alexandria met Shadick's gaze, a flood of memories washed over her – moments they had shared, battles fought side by side, and the countless times she had yearned for his presence during her time away. It was a mixture of joy and vulnerability, a reminder that no matter how powerful they had become, their emotions were still as raw and genuine as ever. With a sigh of relief, she let herself finally believe that he was here, present in the flesh, and not a figment of her imagination.

"I see that Freya is still attached to you even after all the time that you have been gone..." Shadick said, glancing down at them.

"I believe that the first time she saw me, all she wanted to do was attack me," Alexandria admitted with a soft chuckle, her gaze fond as she recalled that initial encounter. "Until she realized that it was me and not someone threatening her or those around her."

Managwa, the wise and vigilant wolf, seemed to confirm her words as he padded closer, his large frame settling down comfortably at her feet. The bond they shared was one built on trust and understanding, a testament to the deep connections that existed between humans and their animal companions. With a gentle smile, Alexandria reached down to stroke Managwa's fur, her touch a silent reassurance that she was here, and all was well.

In the quiet room, the presence of Freya and Managwa added a sense of warmth and comfort, grounding Alexandria in the reality of the moment. The reunion with Shadick was a whirlwind of emotions, yet the steadfast companionship of these two creatures served as a reminder of the strength and resilience that had carried her through countless trials. As she sat there, surrounded by the quiet presence of her friends, Alexandria felt a sense of peace settle over her, a welcome respite from the chaos and uncertainty that often defined their world.

"It would seem that even Managwa is just accepting that you are here, as though you never disappeared, or that you suddenly have wings!"

"It would seem that is everyone's first question, since my return."

"In case you haven't noticed, it is the first thing you notice now, Lexi. They are rather impressive, in case you weren't able to see them."

"Not to the wolves... they seem to be rather bored."

Without warning, Shadick stepped forward and pulled her up and wrapped his arms around her. Either not noticing or caring that tears had started to run down her face, but he refused to let go of her until a couple of minutes had passed.

"When I returned tonight, it was with the wish that I would see you in my bed. But I didn't really think that it would happen. I have been missing you so much the last 2 years, and every night it was with the wish you could be there, next to me. And sometimes, I would see you in my dreams. It felt so real that it made missing you even more unbearable. But this one night when I saw you in my dreams, it was motivation to keep going. Even when it felt like I wanted to give up."

"Well, it turns out that those times you saw me in your dreams, it felt so real. I was dream walking..."

"No wonder it felt as though you were really right here! It explains everything. Even that night you kissed my forehead and told me to get my ass into gear."

"Those weren't exactly the words I used that night, but yes it really was me. Although I didn't realize that I was dream walking. All I thought was that they were really vivid dreams."

"So who told you that you had been dream walking?"

"Terri... last night. When Chadromida was telling me about the one dream that gave you the motivation to get back to your mission."

"Trust the Centaur to know about dream walking."

"Were you able to find the Glacier sword?"

He nodded slowly before pulling a sword out and holding it out towards her. She let her fingers hover a few inches from the blade and shivered. Her eyes widened as she saw the colors of the hilt as well as the stones that adorned it.

"Are those…"

"As far as I have been able to tell, they are called Taaffeite. They are some of the rarest gems in existence. It looks like it is because of these stones that the blade is giving off that chill. Just like the stones, it is rare for any weapon to do that," he replied, grinning.

"Has there been an opportunity to use the sword yet?"

"No, not yet. But I can feel the power emanating from it and that it has a thirst for death."

"Thirsting for death isn't exactly something positive or even something to be proud of."

"Well, just think about it this way, you use a sword to fight and protect, so I don't think it's a bad trait to have."

"If you put it that way, I guess it makes a lot of sense. Then again, I'm still trying to make sense of a lot of things since I got back here."

"You must be absolutely exhausted! Perhaps it would be a good idea for us to get back into bed so that we can get some proper rest?"

"The last 2 years have been a constant not being able to sleep, and it still hasn't worn off. I'm hoping that one of these days my body will come to the realization that I'm back here and not in the other world anymore."

"Then what is it that you do when you aren't able to sleep?"

"Mostly I sit outside and stare at the stars."

"That seems to be a rather boring past time, especially as they don't change all that much."

"At least it is better than feigning sleep or even forcing oneself to sleep."

"Well, I know of at least one thing that will assure you will never get bored with, no matter how much the stars fascinate you," Shadick said, grinning cheekily.

"And what would that be exactly? You seem to be so assured of this fact."

As Alexandria and Shadick shared an intimate moment, lost in each other's embrace and kisses, an unexpected change began to unfold. Unbeknownst to them, her eyes flashed white, a subtle phenomenon that went unnoticed in the heat of the moment. Simultaneously, her wings, once adorned with fiery hues, started to twitch and transform, their color shifting to a pristine white. In the midst of their passionate encounter, a sudden cry escaped her lips, breaking the spell they had been under. The sound immediately caught the attention of the vigilant wolves, their growls resonating with concern.

As if guided by an unseen force, she levitated a few inches above the bed, defying gravity for a fleeting moment. Shadick's astonishment and worry were palpable as he reached out to steady her. However, before his hand could make contact, she descended back onto the bed, her body limp but seemingly unharmed. The commotion had attracted the attention of Chadromida and a contingent of guards, who rushed into the room to assess the situation.

Everyone's eyes were now fixed on Alexandria, her presence shrouded in an air of mystique and uncertainty. The room was filled with a mix of awe and trepidation as they awaited an explanation for this inexplicable event.

"Why did she scream this time around?" Chadromida asked impatiently.

"Astarte! Get to her side now, before it is too late!" she shouted at him before passing out.

Chapter 9

Kaedyn's Arrival

When she woke up in the morning, she was covered in a soft sheen of sweat, making her frown in confusion. As she looked around, there wasn't anything that seemed to be out of place. She sat up cautiously, biting her lip, trying to figure out what was going on and why she felt so twitchy.

"Slow down there, Alex," Starlansha said, sitting down next to her.

"Please tell me that Astarte is okay!" she asked, suddenly panicked.

"Thanks to you, yes she is, not to mention the baby is in the best health she could be."

"She had the baby then?"

"About an hour or so after your vision... warning... whatever it was."

"I'm not even sure what to call it, as it was the first time something like that happened."

"Baby Kaedyn is healthy, even when they saw that the umbilical cord was wrapped around her neck and was struggling to breathe. Chadromida was just doing a perimeter check with the guards when they heard your shout. When he stormed into your room, he was rather irritated, but at the mention of Astarte, he ran to her side. He got there just in time, to be honest. He was the one who caught the baby and removed the umbilical cord."

Kaedyn... I love the name. Where are they now, thought? Did I scare Shadick away?"

"You can relax, Alex. Chadromida and Astarte are currently trying their hardest to get some rest in while the village doctor is looking over Kaedyn. They aren't really needed for that, and as they are both exhausted, she gave them permission to sleep. Shadick was here until a couple of minutes ago. He thought that it would be a good idea to go and get some food and water, in case you woke up."

"He must feel so bad!"

"There is no need for him to be. His niece is in perfect health!"

"We were just getting... busy when the warning happened."

"I really doubt that he blames himself for any of that. In fact, I believe that he is very grateful to you for the warning about Astarte."

"I was in fact just waiting for you to wake up so that I could thank you," Shadick said from the doorway with a slight smile.

"As promised, she is perfectly fine."

"Except the fact that the food I'm smelling is reminding me of how starved I am," she whispered, biting her lip.

110

"That is the exact reason why I have temporarily brought the entire kitchen to you, so there is no need for you to get up!" he said, stepping to the side and allowing the villagers to put the food down near her. "Truthfully, it wasn't even difficult. They are all very thankful to you for making sure that their 'mayor' as well as her daughter is alive and well."

"Thank you!" one of the children said as he crawled towards her while staring at her, quickly dropping his head again.

"I'm just glad they are both healthy and that nothing bad happened," she replied as she watched the young boy crawl out, "and there really isn't any need for them to crawl around me."

"It is all out of respect for you, Lexie, and nothing else," Shadick told her and, sitting down, pulling her towards him. "What do you feel like eating? You have something of everything, right at your fingertips."

"I feel like… everything! The food in the other world had a rather weird taste to them, and there was nothing normal about it. It was honestly as though the animals had been fed something different, or as though they had planted the food in a different kind of soil. But I was never able to put my finger on what it was."

"Then it is a good thing that you are back home so you can have some of our normal and delicious food. The food that has been grown on proper ground and not the stuff that makes absolutely no sense," Starlansha said, smiling. "And after you saved

Astarte and Kaedyn, I am sure that they will make you anything you wish."

"I really don't want that much food! Just enough to keep me happy as well as to remind myself what proper food tastes like."

"Then we will make sure that you get as much food as you want," Shadick said nodding.

Silence fell as they all dug into their food. She kept glancing between Shadick and Starlansha as they ate, a small smile forming. It really was good to see them after such a long time not being able to speak to them, and she had truly missed both of them. Not even in the silence did it feel as though it was bad, more a relaxed kind of silence which was appreciated.

"You've been asked so many questions since your return, but no one thought to ask you, how are you so sure that you are actually back here? That after 2 years, you haven't completely lost it, and this is all just a dream you recreated?" Starlansha asked suddenly.

"Because the way I feel here is nothing compared to what I felt there. Back there, I could never relax, and nothing felt normal, as though I always needed the next thing to pop up. Whereas right now, I don't feel at peace, but I feel loved and cared for. As though the people around me actually give a damn about me. It is a feeling that can't really be explained properly," she replied simply.

"That explanation makes absolutely sense, so there isn't even a need to try and explain it more. Even during my journey to find the Glacier sword, I was never really at home and kept wishing that I could be next to you," Shadick agreed.

"I was constantly aware of the fact that I wasn't home and needed to get back as soon as I was able to. No matter how hard they tried, they were never able to change my mind that I wasn't home. The times that I tried getting back here, it all seemed as though it never worked."

"That sounds… horrible," Starlansha said wide-eyed.

"As horrible as it was, I was able to learn a lot while I was there, and I don't really regret any of it happening. Did I miss home and all of those that I left behind? Yes, I did. But I knew within my heart that it was all happening for a reason, that it would make me stronger than I already am, and that was a good thing."

"I can feel the energy flowing off of you, so I can understand that. The difference between how you were 2 years ago to the person I am sitting across from is huge. But I assure you that it is a good difference, in case you start worrying about that. Although I've noticed that you have gotten a lot slimmer and well-built," Shadick said in thought.

"It was absolutely horrid to be there, but I am glad that I went through some changes. Even when I got as lonely as I did."

"Did you see any creatures that you haven't seen before?" Starlansha asked

"No, not really... it was just mostly the Elementals that lived there. I saw a few horses... or I guess they were Pegasi, but it was never up close. I was also informed by the Elementals that they didn't trust anyone who hadn't earned their trust. That didn't stop me from trying a couple of times, but I failed every time."

"Perhaps it's just because the Magical creatures here are so approachable, but that seems rather strange. We have all been accepting of those who do not wish us any harm."

"Were there any Dragons?" Shadick asks.

"No... someone mentioned Wyverns a couple of times, but I was never able to see anything."

"I missed you more than I can ever tell you, to be honest. I will always miss my family when I'm not with them, but I know that I will see them all again. Whether that would be alive or dead. I guess almost like that time when you saw your parents in the Mountains. If it happens, it happens."

"That is a really good way to look at it! That you will truly see them again one day, even if it might take a while. To be honest, I never thought of it that way, perhaps because I lost my parents at a later stage in my life. To me, they were gone, and that was just it," Starlansha said.

"It was one of the best things that had ever happened to me when I saw my parents in the Caves that night. It was as though they gave me the courage I had lacked before, to make sure that I don't give up on my mission. They told me what I needed to know so that I would try even harder. It is one of the biggest things that kept me going in the other world. I knew there was a reason for all of the things happening to me, even when I didn't always know why they were happening to me. When it felt like I wanted to give up, I just pulled up the memory of their faces and how good it had made me feel," she replied, smiling happily. "They really gave me the strength to not give up. To keep working harder than I ever thought was possible."

"That really is some inspirational stuff, Alex," Chadromida said from the doorway, stretching. "Before any of you guys start panicking... Kaedyn is absolutely fine, the doctor just finished giving her the once over and she assures us that all is well. The fact that I was able to get the umbilical cord off as quickly as I did helped, so there was no damage done to her. She actually congratulated us on our quick responses and has asked me to tell you, Alex, that if you ever consider a position in the medical field, she would only be too happy to teach you the necessary skills."

"Uh... thank you?"

"Not only did you save me, but my niece as well! I knew that there was a reason for loving you as much as I do," Shadick said, beaming.

"Oh, is that why? And here I thought that you fell for my personality and not just for the actions that I have done."

"Oh, hush it! Stop complaining about the fact that people are giving you compliments! You have been in the right place and have been able to save so many people that you should be receiving some kind of award."

"I was rewarded... by being made Queen. I disappeared from this world shortly after the appointment, so it didn't last long."

"Everyone knows just how trustworthy you are, which is why they made you Queen. There hasn't been a day since you were made Queen that anyone questioned whether Amethyst had made a good or bad decision because they knew she wouldn't have left them with someone who would make their lives hell," Starlansha said, smiling.

"And I can assure you that the day Amethyst snaps out of it, she will be thankful to you. Not only did you save her life, but you made sure that Valencia wasn't taken over by either the Centaurs or even someone that would have caused more trouble than good," Shadick added nodding.

"I still have this fear in the back of my mind that she will never wake up again or that she will give my wings one look before passing out again into a shocked state, no matter how much she loves me," she sighed, "or that she will hate me for what happened."

"She is a strong enough person to handle it if that were to happen. Yes, it will be a huge shock for her to see you with wings, but she will be happy for you. She won't judge you for not being able to save her wings. I'm sure that she knows that it wasn't your fault that it happened."

"You shouldn't let something that is now a part of you get the best of you. They fit you rather well, and it must be really amazing to have the ability to fly. The freedom that it opens up for you."

"Chadromida! We have just received news from Valencia. The Centaurs have been spotted, and it is believed that they are gathering their forces together once again. From the report, they were seen walking towards us, but there is no solid proof of this," a guard shouted, storming into the room.

"Thank you for the information. You are free to return to your post. Please ensure that we send out some scouts, but ensure that they are very careful. As well as that, they need to report back to us as much information as they can," Chadromida said before swearing under his breath. "As much as I hate to say it, I think that Astarte needs to get to Valencia as soon as possible. If they are indeed on their way here, there is no way that we could fight them as well as make sure that Astarte and Kaedyn are not harmed."

"Then we are in agreement," Shadick said, frowning.

"Before you guys start a widespread panic, perhaps get some more information. If it comes down to the Centaurs attacking the village, I will teleport both Astarte and Kaedyn out of here and get back here. Besides, the only reason why the Centaurs would start attacking villages again is that they know that I am back. But we haven't run across anyone who was able to report back to them."

"Alexandria has a valid point. From the last report I was given, the Centaurs didn't have a mole within Valencia anymore. So, unless they actually saw her, there is no way that they could know. And from what they have told me, they killed the Orcs that did indeed see them. The more likely course is that they are moving back to the desert where they belong," Terri said, walking into the room as well. "There is no need to create a panic when there is no need for one. I am sure that you can just imagine the chaos it would create if you were to tell people they are marching to the walls and then find out that they aren't. We don't need people to start doubting our trustworthiness."

"Alright then, I will trust the two of you on this one. My scouts will go out to investigate, and once they have more information, they will come back to me with the news," Chadromida said, rubbing his forehead. "These last couple of days have been rough, and it is my sincerest wish that I could go on holiday."

"Would you prefer if I fly ahead to see if there is anything to worry about? If I stay high enough, they will just think that I am a bird." She asked smiling

"Thank you for the offer, but there is no real need for it."

"If you will please excuse us, I am taking Lexie for a walk and to get some fresh air. I think that after a very eventful morning, we

118

have all been stressing a little bit too much," Shadick said, pulling her up. "Perhaps I would be able to convince her to take me for a flight with her new wings."

Starlansha and Chadromida burst into laughter at the look on her face. Terri just shook his head before turning away from them and disappearing between the houses. She was, however, very happy to be able to hold Shadick's hand after what had been too long; there was no way that she would allow anything to get in their way again.

Chapter 10

Tears of Enchantment

A small smile curved on her lips as she watched Shadick and Terri disappearing into the village, Starlansha wandering off in search of Sachiel to inform him of the last month's activities. They had been gone from Valencia so long that she really needed to go and see Amethyst, to ensure herself that she was still well. She really had missed her best friend and wished that there was some way for them to communicate. She knew living in the past wasn't healthy for not just her but those around her. It had been one of her biggest hopes that she would be able to see her sister again. There was no reason for her to keep living in the past, as it would only allow new experiences and opportunities to appear.

As she reached Amethyst's room, she paused for a minute or so to remember her sister as she had been. It would truly be a dream if she could have her sister back to the way she had been before. Even if she wasn't the same as before, she would be happy. The important thing would be to have her sister back. She was still lost in thought when she walked into Amethyst's room and was suddenly engulfed in a hug, making her freeze. As far as she knew, there was no one in the room except for her sister. Taking a deep breath, she glanced down and gasped before wrapping her arms around Amethyst. Tears of happiness ran down her face as she allowed herself to see her sister.

"Alex! I was so sure that I wouldn't be able to see you again, even though I know it hasn't been that long. It was one of my biggest hopes that it would be you to walk through that door to come and greet me!" Amethyst babbled, still holding onto her tightly, "It feels like I haven't seen anyone in what feels like such a long time, which confused me because I'm in the hospital! Why am I in the hospital? Was I coming to see someone who had been hurt? I'm the Queen, but I haven't seen anyone. Isn't that just the most frustrating thing?"

"Could I please ask that you pinch me or something, Amethyst? Because surely I fell and hit my head," she whispers wide-eyed.

"Of course you didn't fall and hit your head, silly!"

"Nurse!" she shouted, making Amethyst flinch slightly. "Doctor?! Is anyone around?!"

"What seems to be the problem, my dear?" the doctor asked, walking into the room, dropping his pen and pad, "By the Gods! The Queen has returned to us! Nurses, get in here now so that we can ensure that all is well."

The nurses shuffled in, trying their best to move her out of the way, but Amethyst held onto her hand so tightly that they were unsuccessful. They worked around her while she kept her gaze on

Amethyst, still in shock. She wasn't sure whether it took them seconds, minutes, or hours to do their tests, but through it all, she refused to look away from her sister. Just in case it was just a very vivid dream.

Eventually, she got a little impatient as it felt as though they took their time while taking her pulse and blood pressure. She had to bite her lip to stop herself from shouting at them to hurry up so that they could assure her that it wasn't just a dream. Eventually, they all stepped back and nodded, smiling happily as though this was the best thing to have ever happened to them.

"Your Majesty," the doctor said before sinking to his knees, the nurses following suit, "from what we are able to tell, you are back to normal, and I have to admit that we are very happy about that!"

"There really is no need for you to bow before me, doctor," Amethyst said, smiling confusedly. "You are, however, dismissed for now. If there are any more tests that need to be done, they can be done later. When I have had some time to work through some things."

"I could never understand how you were able to make people jump only with a couple of words; being Queen really does have its uses," she said, watching everyone disappear.

"As flattering as that sounds, could you please inform me why it looks as though they just witnessed a miracle?"

"Because simply put, I believe we all did just experience a

miracle. Something that none of us thought would happen, even though we hoped that it would. Do you recall anything from the last time you saw me?"

"Not really, no, we were just walking in the forest when you were challenged by the water Elemental. You were able to defeat her, if I recall correctly. Not that I ever doubted you, of course.

"Am... do you honestly not recall what happened during that battle? Or even what happened after the battle?"

"I have to be honest, you are scaring me a little. So, can you please tell me what you are talking about before I scream and accidentally slap you? All I will say is that it feels as though I've been kinda out of it, but not for that long; my muscles feel a little stiff."

"Can we sit down, please? What I will be telling you now might be a little shocking," she asked Amethyst, who nodded, sitting down. "Uh... so the fight with the water Elemental was intense to say the least, but it was also more than 2 years ago. During the fight, you tried to help me by stepping in the way of one of her attacks. Unlike the other Elementals, however, she didn't stop. She destroyed your wings, not to mention that you got hurt quite badly. After I nearly killed the Elemental, I brought you back here, and I was able to heal you. I couldn't bring back your wings though, no matter how hard I tried. When you finally realized that your wings were gone, you went into a state of shock for the last couple of years, and we weren't sure if you would come back to us."

Amethyst looked at her wide-eyed before touching her back where her wings should have been, gulping softly as she realized that they were indeed in tatters and nowhere to be found. She closed her eyes and took a deep breath, indicating that she should continue with the story.

"Once everyone realized you were in a shocked state, they called the village to attention and declared me Queen; apparently, you had told them something claiming I was to take over. I delivered a speech and everything, and I believe that I did rather well. Anyway, shortly after that, we received reports that the Centaurs were on the battlefield and waiting for us to arrive. When the whole army was there, it was as though we were all just waiting for the other to make a move, but nothing happened.

"I eventually shouted at Balditha that we were waiting for him to make his move, but all he did was laugh. He got under my skin, I have to admit, which is when I turned into an eagle and plunged my sword into Diliante's heart," she said, ignoring Amethyst's shocked gasp. "It did, however, achieve what we had been waiting for; they started their attack. Shadick, Starlansha, and the rest of the group took out the Harpeas and Minotaurs while the guards and other warriors ran forward to attack the Centaurs and those creatures that had been hiding behind them.

"Both Balditha and Justren ignored everyone and ran straight towards me, and to be completely honest, our power levels were

124

about the same, and not one of us was able to get through the other's defenses. He started shouting things at me, which distracted him enough to give me the opportunity to call the Elementals.

"I don't remember all of this too well, as it seems that my memory had been wiped somehow. But from what I have been told, my daggers had turned into Water and Air while I sprouted Fire wings. Earth had turned into a new outfit for me while Spirit surrounded me like a shield. I attacked them again, and eventually, we were able to convince them that I was able to kill them all too easily, but was going easy on them.

"Justren was bleeding quite heavily at that point, and Shadick said something to Balditha, and they fell back, all the while calling to their warriors. We hadn't counted on Balditha being cowardly enough to queue an attack as soon as he was out of range. I used nature to create a vine shield around all of us, to ensure that we were not grievously harmed, if not killed. It took a lot of my energy, so I was left very vulnerable and weak. The Elementals then appeared in front of me and told everyone to back away from me as I was about to explode, which would harm them in the process. It might even have killed them, the Elementals, but they surrounded me and transported me to their world.

"It was there that I met their 'master'. From the word 'hi', he decided there was something he didn't like about me, but he refused to let me come back here. It took me what felt like 2 very long years to finally get back here. I don't regret any of it happening. Everything that happened to me there only made me stronger, and ensured that I was ready for what was thrown at me. From what Sachiel and Starlansha told me, you have been out of it since that day. There had not been a single hint that you were coming out of it. The doctors tried numerous methods, but no matter what they did, they were unsuccessful. So they made sure that you were fed and that if you came to, you would be healthy.

"Did you acquire your wings from that other world?" she whispered, her voice carrying a sense of wonder and curiosity.

"I had the wings initially due to the Fire element, but this Master thought they would make a fitting permanent addition."

"That seems as though it would hurt terribly!"

"I don't really think there is a way I can explain besides how it probably felt when you lost your wings."

"As you were talking about it, I recalled hearing and seeing things, but not enough to tell you for sure. I have to admit to seeing you in what I can only assume were my dreams."

"I recently found out that I was dream walking while in the other world. It wasn't just your dreams I had visited, but Shadick's as well. It didn't seem like much back then, but now I can see how it helped the ones I visited, and it makes my heart lighter."

"Now that you mentioned it, how has Shadick been doing? I can only imagine how terrible it had to be when you disappeared."

"From what he told me, he was just sitting around, not doing anything. That changed when I appeared in his dreams and told him to get his shit together and do what he needed."

"Alexandria! For some reason, the doctor ran to me and insisted..." Sachiel said as he rushed into the room, freezing in his footsteps as he saw Amethyst sitting up, "that Amethyst was responsive."

"The doctor wasn't wrong when he told you that I'm responsive. Alex has just been filling me in on some of the things that I missed while I was out of it. She was just getting to the part as to why you are here when you ran in here," Amethyst said, biting her lip.

"I moved myself as well as the other villagers here so that I could know that you are looked after. It was the only thought that ran through my mind when I heard what had happened. I knew that Alexandria had disappeared as well and knew that I had to run the village in your stead."

"There are no words to describe how much that means to me, that you were willing to give up your life there just to come and help me."

"There was no choice in the matter; the woman I love needed help."

"You flatter me, Sachiel. You will, however, need to catch me up on what has been happening over the last couple of years.

Alexandria briefly explained that she was in the otherworld, so she doesn't know what has been going on here."

Standing up, she kissed Amethyst on the top of the head before leaving the room and closing the door quietly with a small smile on her lips. She had her best friend and sister back, but Amethyst's feelings for Sachiel were still very much there. Once she realized that Adriata was here, she would spend some time with her so that they could get to know each other. She knew that they would get along well.

Everything had happened such a long time ago that it was truly time for them to put it all in the past. It was with a spring in her steps and a smile on her face that she walked out of the front doors, her heart lighter than it had been in years.

Chapter 11

Embracing Flightless Skies

"What on earth is going on? Did a Centaur just breathe fire? One of the nurses bolted out of the castle, yelling something about Amethyst, and then promptly passed out," Shadick exclaimed, his steps quickening as he ascended the stairs toward the front doors. "Fill me in, what's happened?!"

"Amethyst woke up! I walked into the room, and she practically bowled me over with a hug. I have no idea what triggered her to come out of it, and even the doctors are stumped," she exclaimed with a joyful smile, her excitement evident.

"As incredible as that news is... has she learned about her wings yet?" Terri asked, his expression marked by a hint of concern.

"Her recollection of the past two years was a blank canvas, prompting me to delicately piece together the puzzle for her. Prior to delving into recent events, I ensured she was aware of the newfound existence of her wings. With that crucial piece established, I began to unravel the tapestry of the past couple of years, weaving in the changes that had swept through the village and sharing fragments of my own narrative. Amidst the unveiling, a shadow of disappointment crossed her expression as she came to terms with the absence of her wings. However, I found solace in the fact that this revelation did not push her back into the depths of shock – a reassuring silver lining in the midst of our conversation."

"That's quite encouraging! How did she respond when she saw your wings?" Shadick inquired, observing her with keen interest.

"She inquired about it directly, and upon my explanation, her primary concern seemed to be whether the process of receiving the wings had been painful, rather than being overly distressed about the situation."

"Hmm..."

"Why does it seem as though you are doubting me?"

"It's not about doubting you; Shadick is simply attempting to grasp how she's coping with everything," Terri chimed in, lightly tapping Shadick's shoulder. "Considering the weight of losing her wings, the two-year comatose state – it's undoubtedly a tremendous amount for her to process. I can only imagine the mix of emotions she must be experiencing right now."

"When I brought up the topic of her lost wings, she instinctively reached back, her eyes revealing a blend of pain and astonishment. It seemed she had managed to come to terms with the reality to some extent, as much as one can under such circumstances. After a brief pause, she collected herself and continued our discussion. As I delved into the revelation of her two-year comatose state, I could discern a hint of resistance in her expression – a silent protest against the incredulous idea. Eventually, however, she acknowledged that fragments of memories resided within her, though they remained elusive in her grasp. During the conversation, she shared a heartening detail – the memory of encountering me on a few occasions. This recollection managed to conjure a smile, offering her a semblance of comfort and solace."

"Do you have any idea when we might have the opportunity to visit her?" Shadick inquired, his curiosity apparent.

"I didn't want to disrupt Sachiel while she was filling her in on all the village updates, especially considering some sensitive matters I can't discuss. I'm confident we can head back to her room, and you can see firsthand. However, it appears you have an option right now," she gestured with widened eyes, "they seem to have opted for a walk." Her explanation was punctuated with a subtle gesture towards the ongoing scenario.

"Amethyst! It's truly wonderful to lay eyes on you again after such a prolonged absence," Terri exclaimed, closing the distance between them and enveloping Amethyst in a heartfelt embrace.

"It's equally pleasant to see you too, Terri. Admittedly, with my memory gap spanning the past two years, I can't honestly claim that I've missed anyone," Amethyst responded with a warm smile. She then turned her attention to Shadick, her gaze settling on his transformed appearance. "Shadick, your changes are quite apparent! I would have been utterly bewildered if not for the update on the past two years. Those new scars tell quite a tale. And if I'm not mistaken, is that the Glacier sword resting on your back? You actually managed to locate it?" Her astonishment and curiosity were palpable.

"I was, yes. It was a very long search and what I must admit felt like more than a couple of years. After what felt like a lot of false starts, I was able to narrow it down to the place where it had been hidden," Shadick replied, also hugging Amethyst. "It really is good to see you up and about, Am. We have all missed you the last two years."

"That seems to be a recurring sentiment."

"You're allowing it to consume you, Am. Remember, we're all right here, standing by to back you up, regardless of the circumstances," she stated with an embrace that radiated sisterly warmth. "Our unwavering support never failed, just as it was before you were caught in that state of shock. Whether you're seeking a guiding hand to hold or a motivational push, count on us to deliver. By now, you should realize that whatever you desire or require, we'll provide in an instant."

"Indeed, our bond stretches back to our earliest days, and I trust you implicitly. For the moment, my focus rests on witnessing the villagers' happiness and ensuring they're aware of my return, ready to assist whenever they require aid. It's vital that they recognize my presence and understand my sincere regret for vanishing when they needed me most."

"Am, you need to pause and catch your breath. You don't have to shoulder the burden immediately. Taking a couple of days to restore your strength is more than acceptable. The villagers won't hold it against you if you give yourself the time you need before fully diving back into leading Valencia. They'll be overjoyed to know you're back, but they'll also comprehend if you don't leap into action right away. Sachiel has been at the helm for the past two years, so allow him to continue a bit longer while you prioritize your well-being and recovery."

"Sachiel will continue overseeing Valencia, and I'm here to provide assistance as well. I assure you, I won't rush into anything hastily. You're right; it's crucial for the villagers to hear about my return from a reliable source before any potentially misleading gossip takes root. Imagine if someone approached you with news of my comeback, but without substantial proof to confirm it. It's imperative to offer them certainty and reassurance."

"I don't want you to disappear again because you took on too much too soon. We just got you back, so you need to look after yourself. Promise me that you will not overtax yourself."

"You have my word that I won't let her take on too much too soon. I do agree, though, that the villagers deserve to see her presence firsthand," Sachiel confirmed. "On another note, I managed to persuade her that it's time for her to meet our daughter. It's been far too long for her to deny Adriata's existence. Our daughter is well aware of her mother and holds a deep desire to spend time with her, to forge her own connection and understanding."

"That's truly wonderful to hear, Am!"

"For the past half an hour or so, Sachiel managed to reason with me. He shed light on some crucial matters and ensured my comprehension. I have to admit, I've missed out on numerous milestones in her life."

"If only you had been more open about this before! I would have organized something long before any of this happened."

"Honestly, even before losing my wings, I had been contemplating the idea of finally meeting her and accepting her as my own. It's important for people to know that I have a daughter, one who is undeniably beautiful. I wouldn't have been fully prepared for everyone to be aware of her presence."

"Indeed, having a child carries immense responsibilities, making your perspective completely understandable! I've heard that you were quite young when you gave birth to her," Terri acknowledged with a nod.

"You're implying that she had no say in the matter!" she retorted, her expression turning into a frown.

"Alex... you, of all people, should grasp the reasons behind my decision to send her to Sachiel after she was born. Let's not allow a dispute to arise from something that transpired years ago," Amethyst implored, her hand coming to rest over her mouth. "You've been visiting her for years, and I'm aware of your dissatisfaction with me. Likewise, I haven't been pleased about your interactions with her, but I've chosen to remain silent on the matter. It was your decision, and you had the autonomy to make it."

"My sole concern is for you and having you back with us."

"Maybe it's time for you to ease up on the 'Miss Know-It-All' attitude, Lexie," Shadick murmured into her ear.

"Then we'll accompany you to demonstrate our continued support. I apologize if my words seemed a bit sharp; I'm still adjusting to being back here and not taking things too seriously."

"Your words mean everything to me, and I sincerely appreciate them. I understand your feelings, and I'm committed to rectifying my errors," Amethyst responded, taking a determined step toward the door and inhaling deeply to steady herself.

They entered through the grand doors, and the guards promptly formed an honorary path leading toward the town's center. With each step Amethyst took, the guards next in line would snap their weapons to attention in a salute, to which she acknowledged with a nod and a smile.

This ritual persisted throughout the procession to their intended destination. Observing her sister standing tall and content again brought a wave of happiness over her. It had been far too long since she could simply observe her sister and feel assured of her inner peace. As the group approached, Captain Davies summoned the village residents to gather at the central square. An air of curiosity and mild unease began to ripple through the crowd, evident in their nervous glances and hushed murmurs.

"I apologize for the abrupt interruption while you were occupied! But I assure you, it holds significance, and there's no need for concern," he called out to the assembled crowd. His gaze shifted to the protective line of guards encircling the area, a silent cue for them to gradually reveal Amethyst and the group accompanying her. A hushed silence descended upon the crowd, which swiftly transformed into joyful applause as they caught sight of her radiant smile, expressing their relief and happiness.

"I think that's your cue for a speech, Am," Shadick suggested with a grin.

"I'm at a loss for words!" she exclaimed, her hand instinctively reaching out for support.

"I'll accompany you to ensure you feel the backing of your family. Just speak from your heart," she responded, offering reassurance.

Captain Davies and the guards knelt before her, their gesture mirrored by the villagers without a moment's delay. Amethyst took a determined step forward, her sister's hand still clutched firmly in her grasp. Clearing her throat with a hint of nervousness, she exchanged a supportive squeeze before drawing a deep breath.

"I must extend my heartfelt apologies to each and every one of you for my absence over the past two years. It was never my intention, and I deeply regret any feelings of abandonment that may have arisen. I am, however, genuinely pleased that Sachiel stepped in during my absence and managed to fulfill my role. I am truly impressed by his accomplishments and the progress that has been made in the village and amongst its inhabitants. Observing the growth and resilience within this community warms my heart. The fact that you all stand here today, alive and thriving, is the most vital accomplishment.

"I can honestly say that I've missed each one of you tremendously, just as I'm aware that my absence has been felt. I wish to make a promise to you all today: I am wholeheartedly dedicated to not repeating the mistake of leaving again. Barring any circumstances beyond my control — such as, heaven forbid, my own demise — I am committed to being here for you all, supporting and guiding as best I can. Thank you for your understanding and your unwavering support."

Sachiel, sensing the need to offer his presence, took a step forward as a gentle murmur swept through the crowd, drawing a sigh from Amethyst. Sensing the need to regain order, Captain Davies stepped forward and emitted a sharp, attention-commanding whistle. The sudden sound prompted a collective flinch from the crowd before all eyes turned back to the focal point of Amethyst and her companions.

"Respectful silence is to be maintained while Her Majesty continues speaking!" he bellowed, reasserting the need for attentiveness.

"Thank you, Captain Davies. I recognize that the revelation I just shared might be considered unconventional, but I believe in addressing this directly rather than allowing rumors to spread unchecked."

"I echo Amethyst's sentiments wholeheartedly. Our daughter is a precious part of our lives, and despite not formalizing our union at the time of her birth, our love for her has never wavered. I understand that curiosity might arise, and if you seek more insight, I encourage you to approach those who are closest to us. I implore you to respect our decisions and understand that she was never abandoned; rather, I took on the responsibility of raising her with the support of a dedicated kitchen hand, who was promptly promoted to her caregiver. This caregiver remains an integral part of our daughter's life, especially during more challenging times.

"Our daughter is well-acquainted with her mother's identity and is eager to finally spend quality time together. In the spirit of understanding, I kindly request that if you happen upon Amethyst and our daughter, you grant them the space they deserve. Refrain from overwhelming them with countless questions. Your respectful consideration will mean a great deal to us. Is there anything else you would like to share, Your Majesty?" Sachiel concluded with a warm smile, leaving the floor open for any additional remarks from Amethyst.

"Thank you for addressing that, as I had the same intention. I am committed to rectifying the mistakes I've made, as I understand that none of us is without imperfections, even when we give our utmost efforts. I deeply appreciate each of you for gathering here today, providing me with the opportunity to speak directly with you. My absence was regrettable, and I extend my sincerest apologies for the time that has passed without communication. In the coming week, I plan to walk through the village to reconnect with all of you and to extend a warm welcome to any newcomers. I believe it's vital to forge these connections anew. With that said, you are now free to resume your previous activities. Thank you once again for your understanding and support."

As the applause filled the air, a chorus of support and understanding from the villagers, they gradually returned to their tasks, the atmosphere now infused with a renewed sense of unity. Amethyst released her sister's hand and took a step closer to Sachiel, their hushed whispers a testament to their shared determination and commitment. Shadick, on the other hand, approached Amethyst and took her hand in his, forming a circle of connection and solidarity. This marked the beginning of a promising journey for Amethyst and her family. It was an opportunity not only for her to forge a connection with her daughter but also to exemplify that personal growth and change were within the grasp of every individual. Amidst the backdrop of the bustling village, the promise of a brighter future unfolded, one where bonds were strengthened, pasts were transformed, and the power of second chances was embraced.

Chapter 12

Bloodlines of the Heart

"So," Starlansha began as she emerged from her room, a contemplative tone in her voice, "I've been wondering — do you have any plans for today? I've noticed how hectic things have been since your return, leaving you with little opportunity to simply catch your breath and unwind."

"I've been considering that it's about time for Luanda and me to have a conversation about the origins of her powers," she responded, her expression a mix of contemplation and concern, her lip caught between her teeth. "To be honest, I've been postponing this discussion ever since I discovered the truth. I kept convincing myself that there were valid reasons for the delay, but deep down, none of those excuses felt substantial enough to justify withholding it from her."

"That makes sense to me. I'm sure Luanda will be happy but likely shocked to discover the truth."

"I agree with you. I think Luanda might initially be in denial more than anything else. It's natural for children to view their parents as infallible and incapable of deception, especially when their true parentage is called into question."

"You're probably right. It's quite likely that she'll focus more on arguing about the idea of us being half-sisters than concerning herself with the origin of her powers,"

"I think you're absolutely right. She needs to hear this news from someone she trusts, especially from someone who has spent time with her and understands her feelings. She has a right to know her heritage, and it wouldn't be fair to keep it from her," Shadick chimed in as he walked over to join the conversation.

"In fact, Amethyst will be accompanying us. She has a letter from your father that can provide additional confirmation. With all of us there, offering support and reassurance, it might help her process the information more easily. Having us around could make it less overwhelming for her to accept."

"Agreed, there's no need to delay, so starting the day off by addressing this situation is the best approach. I've already cleared my schedule for this morning, so we're all set to proceed," Amethyst confirmed as she joined the conversation from behind them.

"We wouldn't want her to go into early labor, so I believe it would be best to wait until after she's given birth," Alexandria quickly replied, understanding the potential risks involved and prioritizing Luanda's health and well-being. She turned away from the front door.

"I have spoken to the doctor, and he has assured me that we

do not have to worry about that, but I've asked him to stay close by just in case. And to address your next question, yes, I did tell him the truth about what we'll be revealing to her. He deserves to know as well."

"So, based on our discussion, it's safe to say that we're all on board to support you while you reveal the truth to Luanda about her father and your relationship as sisters," Shadick summarized, gently leading her away from the door as they prepared to face this significant moment together.

"You managed to accept the truth about her being your half-sister, so there's hope that Luanda will come to terms with it as well. And you have evidence to back up your claims, which is more than just going into it blindly," Starlansha added cheerfully, her youthful energy evident as she bounced along behind them.

"I can understand that, but it took me nearly two years to come to terms with the fact that my father had an affair and that I have a half-sister. Trust in the magical community is still a challenge, even when they're aware that I'm a witch who's been actively assisting them."

"Luanda knows about your accomplishments, and she'll eventually realize that your words are trustworthy. Your consistent efforts have shown that you're dedicated to the betterment of all," Amethyst affirmed, linking her arm with Alexandria's for support. "And in case you haven't noticed, humans and magical beings have been living harmoniously for over two years now. They've become more receptive to the unfamiliar since it became a part of their daily lives."

"Speaking of which, I think it's time we consider reaching out to the Dargona village and discussing the possibility of them relocating to Valencia. Given their coexistence with not only the Dragons but also Chad and Shadick, I believe they might be more open to the idea than we initially think. While it might be daunting, it's essential for our safety that we come together instead of being scattered."

"Alex, you continue to show just how much we are like sisters! Ever since I woke up and started discussing matters with Sachiel and some of the villagers, I've been thinking about reaching out to Dargona village as well. However, that's a concern for another day."

"Indeed, no turning back now!" Shadick chimed in with a grin, his hand already on the door, ready to knock on Luanda and Michael's door

"Oh, is there a particular matter you all wanted to discuss?" Michael inquired, looking at the group gathered before him. "I realize I haven't been as active with my guard duties recently, but that's mainly because Luanda's due date is approaching. I can't quite comprehend why all of you have gathered here just to address this."

"No need to be concerned about that, Michael. Sachiel has already discussed the matter with me, and I've concurred with his decision to grant you a pardon during this time," Amethyst reassured as she entered the house. "Is Luanda up and around?"

"She wakes up even earlier than I do; she's sitting in the sun room."

"I think it would be a good idea for you to come with us. We're planning to have a serious conversation with her," Starlansha suggested, gently guiding Michael along with them. "Don't worry about her going into early labor; we've already spoken to the doctor about it."

"Even if the conversation were to trigger early labor, rest assured that the doctor is prepared for any situation," Shadick added, glancing back to reassure Michael.

"Amethyst? Alexandria? What's happening?" Luanda inquired, rising from her seat with a furrowed brow. "It's been a while since I had a vision, so I'm sure that's not the reason you've all gathered here."

"Alexandria has been wanting to discuss something significant with you for a while, but circumstances haven't allowed for it lately," Amethyst explained, assisting Luanda in sitting back down. "We decided to join her for moral support, both for you and for her, given the nature of the conversation."

"That does sound a bit daunting and unsettling, but I'm willing to hear what you have to say. Go ahead."

"Throughout your life, you've carried a curiosity about the

source of your powers. You've wondered if either your father or mother might have held back the truth from you," Alexandria began, her gaze shifting toward Shadick, who offered an encouraging nod. "Especially since the Centaur events began and you discovered others with unique abilities, you've been seeking answers and delving into research regarding your family's lineage and the roots of your powers."

"I've spent a considerable amount of time trying to uncover the origins of my powers, delving into research with little success. It's become apparent that my parents didn't possess any magical abilities, and I'm certain they wouldn't have concealed such information from me. This realization has weighed on me, but I eventually resigned myself to the idea that magic might have skipped them."

"Could I please ask that you don't interrupt me while I tell you what I do know? About how you received your ability to see the future."

"Very well, I will keep quiet."

"It was approximately four or five years ago, after I returned from my expedition to Sorceral Deep. I found myself at McLeod's, the place where I once called home. Among the chaos of that day, amidst encounters with ghosts and demons, I stumbled upon a photograph. The photograph depicted me at a tender age of three, nestled between my parents". She paused, allowing the weight of her words to settle. "What makes this photograph even more significant is what I discovered at the back of the frame – a necklace, accompanied by a note inscribed with a mysterious message: 'the twin is with blood.'

"It was clear to me that my father had written this note. Yet, amid the tumultuous events of those times, this revelation became overshadowed and faded from immediate thoughts. However, around two and a half years ago, during our time in Dargona Mountains, the significance of that note resurfaced. The pieces of this intricate puzzle began to fall into place, illuminating the truth about your parentage and the origins of your unique abilities.

"During my time in Dargona Mountains, a remarkable encounter occurred that provided even more clarity to the message behind the note. I had a profound experience where the ghosts of my parents appeared before me. It was in this moment that my father shared the truth behind the enigmatic message 'the twin is with blood.' He revealed that during the time when my mother was expectant with me, they faced a heated argument that led to a temporary separation lasting about five months.

"In the midst of his emotional turmoil, my father acted impulsively and had an affair with someone from the village. It was a decision born out of his deep sorrow and confusion. On my fourth birthday, you drew a picture depicting Centaurs and Faeries locked in a fierce battle. What stood out in this drawing was the presence of my parents, holding a child – me – in their arms among the chaos of the fight. Your mother recognized the significance of this drawing.

"She understood that my parents were witches, and the symbolism of their presence in the midst of that turmoil was a powerful revelation. She felt a deep conviction within her, a certainty that reached the core of her being, that you were indeed my father's daughter. Driven by this certainty, your mother approached my parents with the drawing and her conviction. She shared her belief that the drawing held a truth that couldn't be ignored, a connection that extended beyond the physical.

"In the midst of these revelations, your mother grappled with a complex decision. While she was certain of the connection and the truth that the drawing held, she also understood the potential implications and challenges that could arise from revealing this truth. In her wisdom and foresight, your mother chose a path of discretion. She believed that keeping this knowledge to herself would serve the greater good, both for your well-being and the well-being of my parents.

"By not openly sharing the revelation, she sought to avoid potential conflicts and protect the delicate balance of her marriage. Yet, in that same breath, she did communicate something of significance to my parents. You were my father's illegitimate daughter when he had the affair. Your mom informed them that you had been creating drawings of events that, at the time, seemed inexplicable but later manifested in reality. It was a subtle yet powerful confirmation, a gentle nod to the extraordinary abilities that were taking shape within you.

"In an effort to solidify the truth she carried, your mother took a profound step. She handed over the very drawings you had created, Luanda, to my parents. These drawings, depicting events that seemed enigmatic at the time, carried a potent weight of authenticity. As my mother examined the pictures, a realization dawned upon her – the images held a coherence, a pattern that couldn't be dismissed as mere chance.

"Among these drawings was one that portrayed my father spending a tranquil afternoon in our garden. While she initially chose to keep this particular drawing a secret from my father, deeming it a potential coincidence, the boundaries between reality and the supernatural began to blur. The moment arrived when she witnessed the garden scene you had drawn come to life before her very eyes, dispelling any doubts or skepticism.

"Despite the gradual realization and the mounting evidence, my parents still grappled with the weight of these revelations. It wasn't until a pivotal moment, a moment that intertwined our lives in ways we couldn't have foreseen, that their understanding shifted. The turning point came on a fateful day – a day that began with the drawing you had created, Luanda. This drawing depicted a scene where my parents and I were surrounded by Centaurs.

"Little did anyone know that this depiction would soon transform into a chilling reality. On that very day, as you and your parents set out to engage in a diplomatic dialogue with the Centaurs, an unforeseen turn of events unfolded. Out of nowhere, the Centaurs appeared, surrounding you all, and what began as a diplomatic mission swiftly escalated into a confrontation. Tragically, this encounter marked the day that I experienced a devastating loss, as I saw both of my parents taken from me in the midst of that chaotic encounter."

"So what you're telling me is that I'm your half sister?" Luanda asked wide-eyed.

"I want to assure you, Luanda, that this is a real revelation, even if it has come as a sudden and unexpected surprise. I can only imagine the range of emotions you must be feeling right now."

"And you genuinely anticipate me to simply embrace this without any reservations?"

"Absolutely not! I wouldn't for a moment assume that you'd readily take this at face value. I'm fully aware that I lack substantial evidence to unequivocally validate the veracity of my words," she remarked, her fingers delicately tracing the contours of the pendant hanging from her neck. "However, there is a singular element I possess that could potentially tip the scales in favor of credibility... perchance have you encountered a necklace akin to this one in your experiences?"

"Remarkably, that pendant seems to be an uncanny replica of the one adorning your own neck!" Michael exclaimed, extending his assistance as he gently aided her in removing it.

"When I was around 8 years old, my mother gifted me this very necklace," Luanda recounted, a slight furrow forming on her brow. "I distinctly recall her emphasizing that I would eventually discern the identity of the individual possessing its matching half. She spoke about the significance of family, unwaveringly asserting that no matter the trials we faced in the present, a sense of security would eventually envelop me."

"If my memory serves me right, Michael mentioned some time ago that your father subjected you to an abusive environment. Is that accurate?" she inquired

"Yes, indeed. Whenever I experienced one of my visions, he would essentially ostracize me for prolonged periods. Please, I implore you not to misconstrue his actions as physical harm; it was predominantly a form of psychological torment. I could never fathom why my own father would intermittently behave as though I were utterly inconsequential, and to this day, the rationale behind it eludes me."

"That form of emotional torment can indeed be more insidious than physical harm. I'm inclined to believe that your mother intended the necklace to imbue you with strength, just as my father did by bestowing it to you. Considering your father's complex nature, he might have found it arduous to express affection directly, especially considering the potential complications it could evoke.

"The necklace, I surmise, served as his way of silently conveying his enduring presence and support. I'm cognizant that my father yearned to share his wisdom and care with me, much like yours did with you, but my father's disposition posed significant challenges. If even the faintest inkling of your mother's fidelity had emerged, your father's response would have been ruthless and unyielding, potentially condemning you and your mother to dire circumstances."

"He was a very selfish man and would not have thought about leaving us twice. What confuses me is why you suddenly decided to tell me? I don't see why you needed to tell me any of this. It has been years since your parents' death as well as my own."

"My father fervently implored me to divulge this to you, though circumstances proved unfavorable until now due to the resurgence of conflict. Additionally, I held onto the belief that this revelation could offer you solace, providing insight into the origins of your unique capabilities. This knowledge could potentially bring a measure of comfort, particularly given my certainty that your upcoming child will also possess magical aptitude.

"I understand that learning about your mother's past actions and decisions has evoked a myriad of emotions, and I'm genuinely sorry for any distress it has caused. The revelation of such personal and complex matters can be incredibly challenging to process. It's natural for you to feel a sense of turmoil, and I deeply empathize with your struggle to find peace with this newfound knowledge. If there's anything I can do to support you through this difficult time, please know that I'm here to listen and offer whatever guidance or comfort you may seek."

"Oh yes, it is fantastic to hear that my mother had slept around and refused to tell anyone about it. Including me... how can I find peace knowing that?"

"Please excuse my wife, I think that hearing all of this is rather shocking, and she isn't sure how to respond to it," Michael said wide-eyed. "You have told me on numerous occasions that you wish you knew where you had gotten the powers from. Why now all of a sudden is it as though this is just another day? You now know that you have a half sister who was courageous enough to tell you this, as well as who your father is. Your real father and not the person that pretended to be, the one who mistreated you on a daily basis."

"As much as that man mistreated me, he is still the one that I believed was my father for years! He is also the one who raised me and made sure that I was fed and clothed. Who came home from a busy day at work to a wife he thought was loyal. She was the one who refused to tell him what happened."

153

"I have one question for you, Luanda," Shadick spoke up.

"And pray, what might that question entail?" she responded.

"Why does it seem like you're handling the news about your supposed father surprisingly well, but you're finding it tough to come to terms with the idea that your mother had an affair? What's causing this difference in your reactions?"

"The reason I'm seemingly more accepting of the truth about my supposed father not being biologically related to me is that, since I was old enough to understand, I've known that there wasn't any concrete proof of our biological connection. He didn't share physical traits like his eyes or blood type with me, yet he still treated me as his own. This suggests that he must have been aware, at some point during his life, that my mother had been unfaithful, and yet he chose to love and accept me regardless.

However, when it comes to my mother's affair, it's challenging for me to accept because it reveals a lack of honesty and transparency in our family. It feels like a betrayal that she couldn't be forthcoming with my supposed father about my true parentage, denying him the opportunity to have clarity and peace regarding my identity. This contrast in my reactions reflects the complicated mix of emotions tied to the different revelations about my family's history."

"Luanda, I comprehend that this news has been jarring, and you might have preferred not to have learned about it. Yet, the underlying truth is straightforward. It was essential for you to be aware, especially with the baby growing within you. Given the likelihood of magical abilities being passed down, the fact that you were conceived with magic as a component offers a substantial testament to the potency of magic in your lineage. At some juncture, you'll need to share this truth with your child.

"As daunting as this revelation may be, please consider that being aware of your magical nature is far better than existing in the dark, grappling with an undefined sense of uniqueness. It's a prospect that could have left you feeling like an outsider, navigating life without comprehending the true source of your abilities. Admit it, even if just privately to yourself, the revelation saves you from that potential isolation," she emphasized, taking a deep breath before continuing. "I realize the enormity of what this knowledge entails, and my intention is to support you as you grapple with its implications."

"Of course, I understand your point. It's evident that having this information earlier would have been much preferable. Unfortunately, circumstances didn't allow for that luxury... Now, if you could kindly give me some space and leave my house, I would greatly appreciate it," Luanda stated firmly, retreating back into her bedroom and leaving the others in the living room, bewildered by the unfolding emotions.

"She may come to terms with this more fully once she's had

time to process everything. For now, it might be best if you both take your leave. I'll be sure to keep you updated on her situation, including her state of mind and the progress of her pregnancy," Michael added with a bittersweet smile.

Shadick and Amethyst nodded in understanding, gently guiding Alexandria to her feet and escorting her out of the house, Starlansha trailing behind them in quiet contemplation. As the door closed behind them, the weight of the situation hung in the air, leaving a trail of uncertainty and reflection in its wake.

Chapter 13

Unconditional Bonds

A few weeks had passed since her conversation with Luanda, and she had to do her best not to run back to her and force her to accept everything that was being thrown in her face. It felt a little confusing that she didn't seem to care that she now knew who her father was, but was just shrugging it off as though it meant nothing.

"Alexandria! It is my daughter's birthday, would you be so kind as to get your thoughts back here so that we can figure out what to do to spoil her?" Amethyst demanded, fists on her lavender tulle-covered hips.

"You look like a carbon copy of her when you do that!" she giggled, falling back onto the bed. "The times I have seen her do that exact same move, it is so adorable!"

"Very funny... now, do you have any ideas that don't involve me making a fool of myself?"

"Maybe we should just spend a day with her, just you, me, and her. We can go for a walk in the forest that the Faeries have been working on and just take a bit of time to breathe."

"Hmm... that really isn't such a bad idea now that I think about it. And why is it that you didn't suggest it earlier?!"

"Because you only called me to your room, 5 minutes ago, and demanded that I had to help you. You never gave me an opportunity to help you figure the birthday gift out."

"Oh… right. Then I apologize that I had a little bit of an outburst. I'm just trying my best to make up for everything that I've missed since her birth."

"The past happened, you shouldn't try to make up for it, as it is already over and done with. She doesn't hate you for what you did. Not to mention, even though it's obvious, she still loves you even if you haven't been in her life."

"Of course, you're absolutely right. She loves me, I'm just letting me get to myself."

"She really does, she doesn't judge you either. I have known her for her entire life and learned really quick that if you put the effort forth to spend time with her, she will forgive and accept. If you show her that you care for her, then she is happy."

"I am still surprised at how much she already knows about me."

"She has been told about you, her mother, since she was a baby. Sachiel refused to let her grow up not knowing who her mother is. Whenever I had the opportunity to slip away to go and see her, she would make sure to ask about you. Asked me several times a day whether I didn't perhaps have a picture of you."

"I have been wondering more and more about whether I had done the right thing by giving her up."

"At the time, it was the right thing to do for you, and that is all that matters. There is nothing wrong with not wanting to be a mom so long ago. Nobody is keeping that against you."

"That's a relief to hear!"

"Aunty Lexa?" a soft voice asked from just outside. "Are you in there?"

"Come on in, sweetie! Your mommy and I are just talking a little."

They watched as she opened the door, a small smile on her lips as she curtsied to Amethyst. She ran straight towards her, hugging her tightly before crawling onto her lap and staring at her mother wide-eyed, a thousand questions running through her mind. She seemed unsure whether she should ask what she wanted to.

"Yes, hunny? Is there something that you would like to ask?" Amethyst asked, smiling. "You are my daughter and free to ask me whatever you want to."

"But... what if I'm scared that my question might hurt you?" Adriata whispered.

"I will be completely honest with you, just like you should be with me. If what you ask me does hurt me, I will tell you, and we will go on from there."

"I have seen some of the Faeries, and they all have wings. But I haven't seen your wings. Did something happen to them?"

"Adriata, that does hurt a little, but I also know that I need to talk about what happened so I can start accepting it. My wings were destroyed when I was attacked by someone. It hurt really bad, and I wasn't around for a really long time because of the pain and loss. But I have accepted it a little that I don't have wings anymore."

"Does it still hurt?"

"It doesn't hurt me physically anymore, but it does hurt that someone didn't care that they had hurt me this badly."

"Thank you for telling me the story; it really helps me understand things a little better."

"Anytime, hunny."

"Aunty Lexa… where did you get your wings from?"

"Oh, well, a very mean man gave them to me when he tried to punish me. He really thought that it would be a punishment to give me the wings, but he underestimated me," she replied, kissing the side of Adriata's head.

"And what did he punish you for?"

"He ignored me, not to mention refused to tell me, so I don't know."

"That wasn't nice of him at all!"

"No, no, it wasn't."

"If I'm a Faerie, why don't I have wings?"

"That is a really good question, sweetheart. Honestly, there is one of two reasons why that might be. The human part in you, which you got from your father, is so overwhelmingly strong that it is preventing the Faerie part from showing. Which of course means that you won't ever have wings."

"What is the other reason?"

"There have been a couple of cases where a Faerie only sprouts their wings at around the age of 14. Of course, others sprouted at a younger age. It really all depends."

"Do you think that I will grow wings?"

"I do not wish to lie to you or even promise you things that there is no way to be sure that it will actually happen. And for that reason, I cannot say whether you will get wings or not."

"There is no reason for you to let it get you down, sweetheart. Whether or not you have wings doesn't determine if you are a good or bad person," she promised Adriata, hugging her tightly.

"It's just that I don't know what it feels like to fit in, no matter where I go. All I see is either the Magical Creatures running around and giving me strange looks or the humans doing their best to avoid me. They all know that you are my mother, but I have not shown any sign of magical powers," Adriata replied, frowning.

"There is nothing weird at all with you! There is just no way for anyone to know how much of the Faerie gene you have in you, so please do not think like that," Amethyst said, shocked.

"Also, if anyone says anything to you, tell them that it is none of their business, and if they keep asking, then you come and get me," she replied, frowning. "If there are still whisperers, then I can tell them a couple of things that they may not want to find out about."

"That would be sinking to their level, and we don't want that, now do we?"

"Absolutely not! But I will not allow any of them to make Adriata feel bad about who her parents are. If she sprouts Faerie wings, then it will be fantastic! But if she doesn't? They have absolutely no right to make her feel like she doesn't belong."

"Thank you, Aunty Lexa! It means a lot to me that you are willing to stand up for me," Adriata said, smiling up at her. "I have been trying my best to not let them get to me; it was just getting difficult when the other children stared at me and didn't want to play with me."

"I think that is because you are a Princess. They aren't sure whether it is allowed or not, how they should be treating you, and what is accepted," Amethyst said, smiling. "There hasn't been a Royal child around for such a long time that people have forgotten how they should act. Add to that the fact that the humans aren't sure whether their rules apply to us or not. They look at you because I am your mother, but I can assure you that they do not look down on you."

"I really have tried being nice to them, but it is so discouraging when they look at me weirdly."

"They aren't looking at you, but at the guards who are always around you. When they see the guards, they get scared. Will they attack them if they were to get too close? Are they there just to watch over you? Perhaps Sachiel and you need to speak to the guards as well as the villagers. You need to explain to them that Adriata will be seen around the village and that they are free to include her in some of their activities. That the guards are just there to protect her, not to harm them." She said thoughtfully

"That sounds like a plan. There is absolutely no reason for them to exclude her. No one will harm you, except the Centaurs, naturally," Amethyst agreed.

"But I have been seeing a Centaur around the village, also around you, Aunty Lexa?" Adriata asked, frowning.

"Terri is one of the good guys; you've spent time with him before."

"I have overheard some of the village children talking about how he is actually a bad guy, just waiting for the right time to hurt us."

"Terri is a Centaur, yes. But he has something that the other Centaurs will never have."

"And what is that?"

"He truly cares about those around them. He has a heart that can actually love. And he doesn't go around believing that the world owes him everything."

Adriata nodded seriously, turning thoughtful for a moment as she processed the information she had just been told. Amethyst looked as though she was about to question her daughter, but she shook her head slightly at her sister, so as to not interrupt her. Amethyst bit her lip with a soft sigh, her eyes still on Adriata.

"That makes sense, Aunty Lexa. The next time I hear someone saying something against Terri, I will tell them that they shouldn't be judging someone just because of the way they look on the outside. It is how you look on the inside that matters," Adriata said, nodding thoughtfully.

"I never would have thought that my daughter would grow into such a wise, young girl!" Amethyst said breathlessly, eyes wide.

"She is truly her mother's child. I would expect nothing less from her," she replied, smiling.

"Perhaps we should get out of here for a bit and go for a walk in the village? We can ask the guards to make sure to give us some privacy. This way, the villagers will see us together, knowing that you are my daughter and that it would be okay for them to approach her."

"That would be really nice! I have been wanting to take a walk with you for the longest time now, mommy," Adriata whispered, blushing.

"Never in my life would I have said that I would like hearing that."

She smiled as Adriata jumped off her lap and into her mother's arms, both of them crying and laughing. When she heard a soft knock on the door, she quietly stood up to open the door, not wanting to interrupt their special moment.

"Is this a good time for us to have a talk?" Shadick asked, leaning against the wall.

"I am a little busy..." she replied, smiling.

"Then perhaps I should rather come back later?"

"That would be for the best... however, would you like to see something that will melt your heart?"

He frowned but nodded at her as she slowly opened the door again, enough for him to be able to see into the room. His eyes widened as he saw what was happening in the room, a slow grin spreading across his face.

"Is this the first time that they are hugging?"

"Yes, it is, and it only happened because Adriata called Amethyst her mommy."

"That's just great!"

"I agree with you there. Would you perhaps like to join us? We are planning on going for a walk around the village, making sure that the guards give us some privacy. Just so that they can see Adriata is in fact Amethyst's daughter, also that it is okay for them to approach them. It would seem that everyone has been treating her as though she is someone that shouldn't be approached."

"As long as it wouldn't be too much of a bother, I would love to join you."

"I can assure you that you aren't a bother."

"Then I will gladly join you," Shadick said, then frowned. "Why does it seem as though there is something on your mind?"

"It is just something that Adriata asked before all of the bonding happened."

"And what would that be?"

"Whether she will ever sprout wings. Of course, we told her that we wouldn't be able to tell her whether or not that will happen. I got the feeling however that she would be really upset if it didn't happen. It makes me want to assure her that she will definitely sprout wings, but it might just be lies."

"Unfortunately, there is no way for us to make sure that it will indeed happen, but there isn't."

"Alex? Are you ready to go for a walk?" Amethyst asked, suddenly getting up.

"But of course! I was even able to get us a guard that people have always loved," she said, smiling again.

"And who exactly would that be?"

"I also want to know who will be joining us!" Adriata said, standing on tiptoes.

"That would be everyone's favorite Wolfane," she said, stepping aside and revealing Shadick.

"I am here to serve," he said, grinning and taking a bow.

Adriata was staring at Shadick wide-eyed, seeming to be torn on what she would say next, biting her lip and glancing down at Managwa and Freya standing beside her. She glanced at Amethyst again before sighing.

"Would you like to come and give the wolves some love?" Shadick asked, kneeling next to the wolves.

"Yes, please. I have been wanting to touch them since I first got here, but I have always been too scared to approach them in case they bite me," Adriata admitted.

"Well, that isn't something you should be worrying about! They are very nice wolves. Besides, can I tell you a secret?" Shadick asked Adriata as she approached, nodding slightly. "They will protect you, just like they protect me and Lexie."

"Really?!"

"Definitely! They know that you mean a lot to us, so they won't let anything happen to you."

Adriata stopped and reached towards the wolves while they all stood there, watching her silently. It was only after a second's hesitation that Freya licked her face, causing Adriata to giggle before bending down and giving the wolves love.

Shadick grabbed her hand as they walked behind Amethyst and Adriata, watching the little talk as though her life depended on it. The wolves seemed happy with the occasional love Adriata decided to give them, and it seemed as though they accepted her as family as well. She saw some of the villagers pausing in what they were doing before going back to what they had been doing. After a couple of minutes as they were reaching a play area, Adriata slowed down and backed towards her eyes wide.

"Are these some of the children you've been wanting to join?" she asked, bending down next to Adriata.

"Yes, but they're so busy playing, and it feels as though they don't really see me," Adriata whispered, "I did try and approach them once or twice, but all they did was stare at me wide-eyed before running away because of the guards."

"Well, as I said earlier. Not only am I here, but your mom and Shadick as well, and everyone likes Shadick because of the wolves. Not that I can see why," she joked, making a face.

"Hey! That was mean." Shadick said shocked

"Would you like me to go with you and tell them that they don't have anything to worry about?" Amethyst asked, picking at her nails, "I'm sure if I talk to them, they will ask you to join you in their games."

"Can Uncle Shadick maybe go with me? I love you Mommy, but you might scare them as well," Adriata whispered.

"Oh..."

"It would be the biggest of pleasures!" Shadick said, taking Adriata's hand and walking towards the other children.

"Don't take it personally, Amey. She is still new to having you around and asking you for stuff, even if it's just to talk to kids she doesn't want to bother you. You are the Queen after all," she whispered, putting her arm through Amethyst's.

"I don't want her to be scared to ask me for things, I'm her mom, not just the Queen," Amethyst replied softly, biting her bottom lip. "It doesn't even feel right that she curtsies to me and calls me Your Majesty. I'm her mom, and she doesn't need to do that!"

"You haven't told her any of this; she doesn't know what she should or shouldn't do around you. Once you spend more time with you, you can start telling her to not curtsy when she sees you. That she can ask you for anything, within reason of course, and you won't hold it against her or judge her. Sachiel has raised her right so she knows what is expected of her when there are people around she doesn't know, not to mention when she doesn't know someone that she needs to be careful when she doesn't know that person.

"He made sure to tell her about you and that she knows you, but obviously there hasn't been much time for you guys to spend time together. When you told me to take her to Sachiel, it was a difficult decision, one I saw you regret on numerous occasions. I never pushed you though because you did what you did because it was right for you. And no one judges you for that."

They watched as Shadick and Adriata bent down in front of the other children. It seemed as though they asked Shadick a couple of questions to which he replied before taking Adriata's hand and pulling her closer a little. At first, they seemed uncomfortable and unsure of what to do, but slowly they started including her with their games, giggling filling the air.

"I don't know if I would ever be as brave as you were back then, letting go of something as precious as her. That night, when I was taking her to Sachiel, I didn't want to let her go. I thought that perhaps I should take her and raise her, but I knew it would be impossible for me to do that, as I was still around you all the time. Once she's older and understands things a bit more, you can tell her why you decided to give her to her dad and not be in her life, and you will see that she won't blame you."

"When I found out about her, I felt so confused, and in the back of my mind, I was happy about it. Then I realized I was just made Queen and wouldn't be able to keep her, so I would have to send her to her dad to be raised. I thought that it was better that he raise her than a stranger who might abuse and hurt her. It crossed my mind so many times that the Faeries would help me raise her, just as the other magical creatures.

"On the other hand, I didn't want her to be raised in a place where she would always be in danger, which we always have been because of all the deaths that had happened. Not sure if my mom would have been proud of me, not when I made the decision I did."

"She would have tried to convince you to keep her, but would have accepted if you kept insisting that you wanted to give her up. It isn't as though you just abandoned her; you made sure that she would be safe. Can you imagine how spoiled she would have been if your mom were still alive?"

"Considering how much she spoiled us, she would have been a little monster!"

"We weren't that spoiled. She made sure it was the perfect middle ground. When you were too much of a spoiled Princess, she would put you in your place, and you know it."

"I was only a spoiled Princess cause she gave you all of the attention!"

"No, she wasn't, she was just trying to make me not as depressed as I was because my parents had died. It just felt like she was giving me more attention because the attention wasn't just on you."

"It seems to be going well, not just with Adriata and the other children but the two of you as well," Shadick said, walking towards them. "What's the topic to make the two of you smile like this?"

"Reminiscing about the past," she said with a smile.

"I'm glad they asked her to join them!" Amethyst said, resting her head on her sister's shoulder.

"It was easy, I just told them that even though she's a Princess, they are still more than welcome to ask her to join them while they play games," Shadick said with a nod. "At first, they said they weren't allowed to, but I made sure to let them know it is. As long as they don't play too rough."

"Thank you, Shadick. It means a lot that you went out of your way to talk to them."

"It was no problem at all. I will do it again in a heartbeat."

Chapter 14

Seeking Blessings

"It feels as though we never get a chance to just have some time to ourselves? To be able to take a walk and not have to worry about anything?" Shadick asked as they slowly walked through the village outskirts.

"Because our lives have been rather busy the last while. What with me needing to go and do some ridiculous training while you'd gone on a crazy adventure to find a sword? A sword, if I can remind you, everyone had believed had just been a legend."

"It really has been a rather busy last couple of months... I mean, years. I have to admit, though that I'm hoping that we will have some quiet for at least the next couple of months."

"I wouldn't get my hopes up on that one, unfortunately. If we were to go with everything that's happened the last couple of years, it won't take too long for everything to blow up in our faces."

"You make a fair point, I do have a question for you though, and if you don't want to answer, then you don't have to."

"Surely you know by now that I will answer any and all of your questions."

"It seems as though you're okay with everyone staring at you?"

"When I first got back here, and I saw how everyone had been staring at me, all I wanted to do was to just disappear. Starlansha was the one who pulled me aside the one night and told me that they had to get used to me being back not to mention the fact that I now have wings, not to mention there is no reason for me to keep them out the entire time as I'm able to withdraw them but it's just too uncomfortable to do it so I'd rather not do it. So it was decided that I should stop trying to make everyone happy by making myself uncomfortable for the simple fact of them not being accepting."

"That is a really good and positive way to look at things."

"Adriata is one of my biggest supporters, and she is one of the people who I have to thank in regards to that. It's all in the way she has accepted the fact that I changed. I am still the aunt that she grew up with and who she loves, so there wasn't even any hesitation about treating me differently."

"It is clear as daylight that she loves you and will do all that she can to stand up for you if she had to."

"I have to agree with Shadick on this one. Ever since her birth, she has cared about you a lot. She knew who you were from the very first moment that you brought her to me, as she knew you for what you are, a protector. Not to mention one of her biggest supporters," Sachiel said as he walked towards them. "Although I do have to admit that sometimes you put me to shame when it comes to that little girl, and I'm her father. There is no doubt in my mind that if you were to tell her something, she would believe it without hesitation."

"I haven't had the opportunity to spend a lot of time with her, but I have to agree on that; she worships you."

"For some reason, I have the strangest feeling that I will be replaced soon. Amethyst has been doing her best to make amends for the years that she wasn't around," she replied, biting her lips. "Although I'm still trying to convince her it isn't needed."

"I have been telling her the same thing, but she is rather stubborn and refuses to listen to what I have to say. Starlansha mentioned to me that even she had been trying to remind Amethyst that she had to do what she did for a reason," Sachiel sighed, shaking his head.

"Valencia had made sure that we knew the difference between right and wrong. Not to mention, when she found out that she was expecting Adriata, there was no doubt in her mind that she had to send her to you when she was born. It had been for the best, but in her heart, she believed it was right. There wasn't a day since then that I didn't see how much it hurt her, even when she acted as though she was strong, yet I could see the longing in her eyes."

"Which is why I had always done my best to make sure that I was loved from the start, I'm not just talking about myself, naturally. I need her to understand that the moment Adriata was old enough to comprehend the world around her, I told her who her mother was and how, even though she wasn't with us, she still loved her. As far as she knew, her mother was only absent as she had a lot to do."

"You are a great father by doing that, so you shouldn't have to let that worry you," Shadick told him, grinning. "So tell us, what exactly is this idea you had?"

"The moment I met Amethyst, I always knew that I wanted to marry her. No matter what happened in our lives, I knew that I wanted to marry her even if it got delayed by a couple of years," Sachiel said, turning towards her. "I have already gone to Adriata and asked whether she would be happy as well as approve of me asking her mom to marry me. To say my hearing is still returning would be an understatement."

"So that's the screams I heard earlier this morning?" she asked, smiling.

"It was indeed, it was her way to show me how happy she is with my decision. Her screams were so loud that some of the guards stormed into the room, swords drawn, ready to deal with the 'threat'. Not to mention her keeper also gave her a scolding for giving everyone a scare before giving her a lecture that she was a Princess and she shouldn't be so loud."

"A Princess has every right to be as loud or even as soft, as she pleases, and no one has a right to tell her differently. It is especially accepted when something exciting happens."

176

"And with those words, you have proved just how much Adriata listens to you."

"What do you mean?"

"Those were the exact words that she decided to use."

"You two have completely derailed yourselves from how this conversation started. Personally, I think it's fantastic that you wish to ask Amethyst for her hand in marriage!" Shadick said laughing

"There are two reasons I need to speak to Alexandria about before I put my plans into action."

"You're the king! You don't have to ask me for permission about anything!" she squeals wide-eyed.

"If this were normal circumstances, I would have to traditionally have to ask the parents permission for Amethyst's hand in marriage. Unfortunately, I can't do that as she is no longer around. So in my mind, I have to ask you for that permission as you are her sister."

"That is rather convoluted, but it really means a lot that you have come to me. I know that ever since she returned to us, her feelings towards you have been getting stronger. She would be ecstatic to be your wife. I do, however, ask you not to tell her I told you I ever spoke those words."

"Then you have made me one of the happiest men alive by simply giving me your permission. I would also like to ask you for your advice on my next move, as you are the one person who has known her the longest and knows what she likes and hates."

"Go on then, you have my attention."

"I want to ask her somewhere where she won't expect it, but a place that would make her happy and make the memory of me asking her, unforgettable."

"That is really a question for me to answer, as she had instructed some of the builders to work on a waterfall not too far from the Castle. She has been determined to make a place so she could remember where we grew up, and even though she has been telling everyone that it would be a good place to just go and relax. It is a case that she misses the waterfall so much and wants a little bit of the past close by."

"I will ensure some of the guards go to your old home to see if they can get some things to bring back. So thank you for telling me, I am happy that I decided to ask you for ideas."

"To not make her suspicious, it would be for the best to tell her you are just going for a walk instead of asking her on a date. Assure her that it is just so you can get away from the madness going on around us and just relax for a couple of minutes. Once you're there, it will be up to you to know when the best moment would be to ask her."

"Shadick, I feel sorry for you when you finally ask her, as it will be a very difficult task to surprise Alex."

"I can assure you that she will be none the wiser when that day comes," Shadick replies with a grin.

"The mere fact that you asked Adriata for permission truly means a lot. All she has wanted was to feel that she was included in your lives," she replied, rolling her eyes. "For the first time in her short life, she has the opportunity to see the two of her parents together, and it will give her the reassurance that you are a family."

"And that right there is one of the biggest reasons I believe I should involve her in my decision. As you know, it was one of the things I always ensured she knew, honesty is one of the most important things we can give people. Some of the times, I would approach her to ask what she thought about certain decisions before going through with them."

"She may not be my blood, but I'm happy with the way you brought her up. You were strict with her, but you gave her the opportunities to just be a child and not just a Princess. Her keeper, as well as yourself, has made sure that she knows she is a Princess and the responsibilities that come with that title, and how the time might appear she would need to be there for people."

"I have always had this fear that she wouldn't get a chance to just be a child. That day Iva stepped forward to help me was one of the happiest moments in my life as she ensured that Adriata had the best of both worlds."

"If you want tonight to be perfect, you'd better get going so you know everything will be to your liking, and you both will be happy," Shadick said, patting Sachiel on the back. "You will only regret it if you were to forget something, so it would be best to start early."

Sachiel nodded, shooting a smile at Shadick before turning towards Alexandria, giving her a hug, before rushing off towards the castle. His personal guard looked between herself and Shadick, frowning before rushing after Sachiel, shaking their heads as though they were frustrated.

She had found a spot in a nearby tree not too far away from the waterfall, so she could watch the proposal happen. There was no doubt in her mind that Amethyst would be torn between two minds on her watching it all happen, and it made her heart squeeze. As she glanced around, there was no doubt in her mind that Sachiel had chosen the time correctly. It was Amethyst's favorite time of day, twilight. Chewing her lip, she thought about how her sister had been denying it for a couple of months now, but this was one of her biggest dreams. To officially be a family, not just for them but for Adriata, to be united through love and honesty.

Showing everyone that the magical and human worlds could get along and that there would be no judgment. When they were children, she had told no one about Adriata as she hadn't wanted to cause trouble. Those long nights when Amethyst had been inconsolable had been some of the worst they had gotten through.

It had been those moments where they had been truly alone, and she had been able to just let go of her emotions and actually feel what she didn't want anyone to experience.

"There is a meeting room in the castle for a reason, which would have made talking so much easier. I really don't see the need for you to drag me out here to have a talk," Amethyst grumbled, making her grin.

"You love the waterfall, and everyone knows it; it is your small place of escape for when things get a little too much. And that is what I wanted, for you to actually stop and take a couple of minutes to just relax." Sachiel replied

"When I told the builders to do this for me, I didn't know just how much of a place of solace this would become. It reminds me of my home, not that I mean the village isn't home!"

"I don't see why there is a reason for you to explain yourself. No one has ever questioned the fact that you had been raised in Antithia. Everyone also knows that the Unicorns and Fae called it home before everyone had been chased out and made to live with those who had been wary of themselves. There is no doubt in anyone's mind that this waterfall was inspired by Antithia, and it makes everyone smile, to know they get to experience even a moment of where you had grown up."

"I have to thank you for always being so understanding, as there have not been any words for me to explain to anyone in the village how I truly have been feeling. To just have a place where I can remember when I still had my family, not even to mention when I still had my wings," Amethyst whispered, stepping to the water's edge. "There have been too many nights when I wake up screaming for my wings. You really don't know what you have until they're gone, do you?"

"Your wings were something that's been a part of you since you were a young girl, so I don't see a reason for you to apologize. I believe it's a good idea to remember the things that have brought us happiness. If we were to forget those things that bring us happiness, we might forget why we are fighting so hard, and it would only make us become like the Centaurs. Disappointed and completely void of love."

"Sometimes I forget how good you are with words, and why people have no issues with listening to what you have to say."

Shifting slightly in the tree with a small smile on her lips, it really had been too long since she last saw Amethyst smile as much as the last couple of months. She had faked so many smiles just to ensure people around them didn't notice how brittle her smile was. Her acceptance of losing her wings had nearly destroyed her at first, but with the help of Adriata, she had started to feel a little more normal.

"I do have a rather important question I would like to ask you, which is why I thought this would be the best place to come and talk more privately, as there is no doubt in anyone's mind to not bother you when you are here," Sachiel said as he stepped closer to Amethyst.

Lightly biting her lip, Alexandria decided it was time to leave them to their peace so she wouldn't spoil the moment for her sister. There was no doubt in her mind that the answer to his question would be yes. Initially, she would be surprised, and she wouldn't be sure if it was all a joke, but she would slowly realize that it was what she had been dreaming of. If it hadn't been for Amethyst convincing herself that it was the right thing, she would never have let Sachiel or Adriata go. Protocol however, had demanded that she put herself second and do what was best for the creatures that looked towards her for guidance.

It had been one of the biggest lessons that had been drilled into both of them from a very young age. This would really be good for everyone, as they would finally realize it is okay to get along with each other. It had been one of her biggest beliefs that her mother would not have approved of them, and no matter how hard she had tried to tell her that Valencia would not have held it against her or even judged her, she had made up her mind, and nothing could change her mind.

Flying over the forest towards a place she knew Shadick would be waiting, lost in her thoughts of the past. As much as she had watched some of the creatures get married or declare themselves as being together, she had never really realized what marriage truly meant until now. Nor had it ever been one of her wishes to find someone she cared enough about to consider getting married. It had always been her mission to make sure no harm would come to the magical creatures, and they were happy. Hearing Freya howling up at her caused her to freeze mid-flight, quickly glancing around. A strong wind suddenly picked up, causing the trees to bow in the breeze. A shiver ran down her back as the feathers on her wings ruffled in the wind, making her frown. Quickly turning around, she saw a dark cloud approaching the village, making her gasp softly.

"Lexi?!" Shadick shouted up at her. "Is everything okay?"

She glanced down to where Shadick was standing, watching her closely with Managwa and Freya sitting next to him quietly, noticing Freya also looking not up at her but towards the horizon where the dark clouds were. Whipping around back towards the clouds, her eyes widened as she realized the clouds had disappeared and she could no longer see them.

Chapter 15

Preparing for Forever

"Is Amethyst driving you that crazy? Enough for you to do guard duty?" Starlansha shouted up at Alexandria. "Surely there are better things to do?"

Alexandria let out a sigh, running a hand through her hair. "Yes, I did ask her," she replied to Starlansha's question. "She said it's because her mom isn't here to help her, and she knows how much their mother would've enjoyed being a part of the wedding preparations. She thinks I can fill that void, and I understand where she's coming from, but it's been overwhelming."

Starlansha nodded in understanding. "I can see how that would be a lot of pressure for you. But you know Amethyst; she's passionate and determined, especially when it comes to something she cares about."

"That's true," Alexandria admitted with a small smile. "She's always been like that, and I love her for it. But sometimes, I wish she would understand that I have my own responsibilities and struggles to deal with."

Starlansha placed a reassuring hand on Alexandria's shoulder. "She'll come around. Just give her some time. In the meantime, it's good that you found some solace in the sky. We all need a break from time to time."

"I agree," Alexandria said, feeling grateful for Starlansha's understanding. "Flying helps clear my mind and gives me a sense of freedom."

"Well, just make sure you don't fly away and leave us all behind," Starlansha teased, trying to lighten the mood.

Alexandria chuckled. "Don't worry. I'm not going anywhere. The whole wedding thing hasn't been helping with everything between me and Shadick."

"Does that mean Shadick is going to ask you to marry him?"

"Doubtful... he mentioned it, very jokingly, I might add, to Sachiel when he asked me for permission to ask Amethyst."

Starlansha nodded in understanding. "Ah, I understand. It doesn't seem as though he is very eager to take that step as of yet. Not that it's a bad thing, of course! It will happen when both of you are ready."

Alexandria sighed, her face tinged with uncertainty. "Don't worry about it, I'm not sure if we'll ever be ready to take that step. It isn't really something we've discussed, whether that's because we just haven't had an opportunity to talk about it or if it's because we just don't want that for us."

Starlansha, ever supportive, probed gently, "Have you ever thought about bringing it up?"

186

"Considering what has been happening the last couple of years? Not even a little bit," replied Alexandria, her shoulders slumping under the weight of their complicated circumstances.

"When you put it like that, I guess it makes sense," Starlansha acknowledged, trying to empathize with her friend's situation.

Their conversation was interrupted as Captain Davies approached them. "Your highness? The Queen has been looking for you and asked me to come find you."

"Well, that didn't last long," Starlansha muttered, a hint of disappointment in her voice. She then took to the skies, saying, "I guess you can tell Amethyst you only found me and not Alexandria. I am, however, more than willing to help if she wants me to."

"She won't be too happy about my not being able to find her. I will, however, inform her of your offer and let you know if she decides to take you up on it."

With a soft sigh, Alexandria landed on the Castle's roof, stretching her arms. As much as she loved Amethyst, her sister had a habit of making things seem worse than they actually were. If she were perfectly honest, she still felt like she didn't belong there. Months had gone by, and she continued to feel as though she should take to the skies and not look back.

However, she knew that wouldn't solve anything; it would only cause stress to her friends and family. Starlansha's mention of her getting married to Shadick made her feel disconnected from everyone around her. Getting married was not something that had ever crossed her mind, not because she didn't think it would happen, but because it wasn't in her future. From the training fields, she could hear and see Freya playing with Adriata, bringing a smile to her face.

The wolves had adopted the little girl as though they had known her their entire life. Manangwa sometimes stared between herself and Adriata before lying down at her feet. On some days, it felt as though Shadick knew she just wanted to disappear. He would be nowhere to be found for hours on end, and when asked what he had been doing, he would just shrug or make a joke out of it.

On more than one occasion, she had wondered if it was something she had been doing wrong. The nights had grown lonely as Shadick would only go to bed after midnight. For a couple of nights, he would wake her up to make love, but even those nights had stopped. With a sigh, Alexandria stood up and jumped off the roof, allowing the wind to catch her wings, carrying her to the field where Adriata was still playing.

"Aunty Lexa! I've been missing you. Freya has been keeping me company, though," Adriata said, throwing herself into Alexandria's arms.

"I'm sorry, baby girl. Your mommy has been keeping me busy the last couple of weeks. I will, however, make sure to remind her to spend some time with you," she replied with a frown, giving

Adriata a hug. "She really shouldn't let the wedding plans become more important than you."

"That would be nice! Although it is going to be a big day because my mommy and daddy are getting married. Mommy is going to look so pretty! She's also getting me a pretty dress."

"You're going to be the prettiest little Princess there has ever been!" Shadick said from behind her.

"Hi, Uncle Shadick! Aunty Lexa, I'm going to go and play with Freya before Iva finds me again," Adriata chimed in.

"Be careful, Adriata!" Alexandria yelled after her. "I swear she's worse than what Amethyst was at that age."

"I'm glad I finally found you," Shadick said, "I was looking all over for you. Even ran into a very stressed-looking Amethyst, followed by a local woman with material in her arms, both looking very harried."

"She's going to send that poor woman into an early grave. According to Amethyst, she's just not getting the idea of her dress."

"Could we maybe go somewhere to talk?" Shadick asked.

"Of course! I know we haven't had much time to talk the last while," Alexandria replied.

He lightly grabbed her hand and pulled her towards the horse stalls, smiling as the workers scattered. They were always there, ready to clean, but as soon as they thought they might get in the way, they disappeared. Shadick lightly pushed her into one of the stalls, making her laugh softly. He started pulling on her clothes as he lightly slammed his mouth on hers in a deep kiss. She lifted her arms, allowing him to pull her shirt off.

"I could have sworn you wanted to talk," she whispered, lying on his chest after they were done. "But what we did is most definitely not talking, not that I'm complaining or anything."

"It started off with just wanting us to talk, but my mind was changed when we walked in here, and the stall hands just disappeared, which made me believe it was meant to be."

"What did you want to talk to me about?"

"Well, I know that everyone has noticed how I haven't really been around the last while. But it's not because I'm ignoring anyone."

"Alexandria! Get your ass out of here; now!" Amethyst yelled. "The stall hands have told me how they scattered when you and Shadick walked in here."

"Amey, could you not give us like 30 minutes?" she asked with a sigh.

"No! You know that I need your help right now, and it feels as though I'm going to lose it."

"Just give us one moment, Amethyst," Shadick said, standing up, getting dressed, and holding out her clothes. "Guess we'll have to talk later."

"Do you have any idea how stressed that poor human woman is because she doesn't understand me properly?"

"She does understand you properly, Am. What she doesn't understand is how you want it to be done in the amount of time she's been given. You can't expect someone to make a Faerie-perfect gown in less than a month," she replied, walking out of the barn with Shadick slipping out behind her. "Why don't we sit down and talk about what is possible and within reason? You don't really want a full-on ball gown, but wedding fever has you thinking it's your biggest dream. Even when we were young girls, you never talked about how you wanted a big dress. It was always something light, girly, and definitely not floor-length."

"Why haven't you said this before?!" Amethyst questioned, frustration evident in her voice.

"We have!" Shana shouted, stomping her foot in annoyance.

"Because, sister dearest, you haven't given me much chance to give my opinion. Now that my mind is a little clearer, we can let Mrs. Henderson know she can take a breath and come back to discuss the dress tomorrow," Alexandria said, smiling and waving the other Faeries away. "For now, it is time for us to spend some time with your daughter. You know, the one that you've been neglecting the last couple of days because you've been so obsessed with getting your wedding to be perfect."

"I haven't been concentrating on the wedding for that long,"

Amethyst protested.

"It has been almost a month, Am. Adriata has been doing her best to not bother you, but she misses you."

"Oh my! Where is she?!" Amethyst exclaimed.

"She was playing in the one training field around the corner with Freya. Unless Iva found her in the last hour or two, she should still be there," Alexandria replied, leading Amethyst towards the mentioned field. They could hear Adriata's giggles as well as Freya's soft howls as she was chased through the field. As they turned a corner, they noticed Freya pretending to be taken down by Adriata, making the little girl giggle even more.

"I'm a terrible mom, aren't I?" Amethyst whispered, her voice filled with guilt.

"No, you're not; you're a person who got excited about marrying the man of her dreams. A person who temporarily lost sight of their daughter because of a future you have wanted for more than just a couple of years. You do, however, have me to remind you of what is important. Yes, I have been lacking in that department lately. Adriata reminded me that she is more important than something that happens, hopefully, only once in someone's life," Alexandria reassured her.

"Mommy! I'm so glad that Aunty Lexa was able to find you. I've been missing you so much," Adriata said, running towards them. Amethyst picked her up, and Adriata continued, "Freya has been keeping me company though, sometimes even Manangwa allows me to play with his fur."

"Of course, I found her. I did make you a promise after all," Alexandria reassured Adriata.

"Adriata, I have to say sorry for not spending enough time with you the last couple of weeks. It isn't something I should have done; I should have, in fact, asked you to help me plan the wedding. Alex has reminded me that you are more important, and I will right my wrongs by asking you for some advice." Amethyst said apologetically.

"Advice?" Adriata asked, curious.

"Oh, absolutely! I haven't been able to decide on the colors for things like the dresses, the flowers, and all of those things."

Alexandria followed behind them as they started walking back towards the Castle, with Freya walking beside her. She ran her fingers absently through the wolf's fur as she listened to Adriata enthusiastically talk about all the colors she loved. Shadick had found her so they could talk, and it had made her hopeful, but they got distracted and were interrupted.

She knew if she went looking for him, she wouldn't find him. There was a reason he had walked away after getting dressed – to avoid dealing with things that weren't on his mind. It wasn't always that way; he used to go out of his way to at least show some kind of interest, even if it had been faked. It bothered her that he thought he had to deal with these things on his own, but she could never find the right words to tell him. Before she knew it, time had passed, and something else had happened. One of these days, they would sit down and talk about what was going on, but today was not that day.

Chapter 16

Forever United

"Aunty Lexa!" Adriata screamed as she excitedly ran towards her, "It's finally the day my mommy and daddy get ma... ma... married! But Iva has been scolding me the entire morning cause I've been dancing around my room in happiness."

"You're right, it's their wedding day. Although I do believe Iva is right, you really need to slow down a little and take a deep breath, honey," she replied, picking her up. "You wouldn't want to fall asleep before you could even take the rings to them. Nor do we want you to get overexcited that you pass out."

"I've been wondering if we're going to be helping mommy to get ready?"

"No, darling. She has her ladies in waiting who will be helping her. Besides, we need to make sure that you are ready as well."

"So I will really be able to wear that pretty dress mommy had gotten for me?"

"Of course you do! You and your mommy will be the prettiest ladies at the wedding. Everyone will be blown away by how beautiful you are."

"But I don't want everyone to be blown away; so wouldn't that be a bad thing, Aunty Lexa?

"I do apologize for the interruption, your majesty, but the Queen has requested your presence in her quarters," one of Amethyst's ladies said with a curtsy. "I have ensured your dresses have been moved to her room so you can get ready there as well."

"Mommy needs our help to get ready, I just knew that she would ask us to help her!"

"Adriata, as for your question whether it would be a bad thing for everyone to be blown away, if you were to do that, it only means that you look really nice, and that is a good thing. It would be because they really like what you're wearing, or even if you did something really nice. But most importantly, it would be because they love you," she replied, smiling at Adriata. "If you were to blow someone away in violence, then and only then would it not be very nice."

"I really have been trying to make the children like me, so I play games with them when Daddy visits the townspeople. And of course, daddy likes asking me questions on what I would do if it were in my hands, but I can't always understand him because I don't understand what he's asking."

"You playing with the other children is a really nice thing to do."

"Announcing, the Princess Adriata and her majesty Alexandria!" one of the guards called as they got to Amethyst's door

"Thank goodness that you're finally here! I was getting worried when you didn't join me first thing this morning," Amethyst said, rushing towards them, looking harried.

"It was my belief that your ladies maids would be helping you to prepare?" she asked, tilting her head. "Please don't tell me you sent them away?"

"Only temporarily! I have asked them to go and find some more flowers as I am a Faerie after all, and it just wouldn't be right to be seen at my own wedding with an abysmal amount of flowers."

"Uh... Amey, in case you didn't actually listen to yourself. You are a Faerie, the Queen of the Faeries, in fact, and it is in your power to just summon as many flowers as your heart desires."

"Oh, right, I knew that I was forgetting something important."

"How can you ever forget that you're a Faerie, mommy? All the other Faeries curtsy when they see you!" Adriata asked with a cute frown. "Even though you don't have wings anymore, it doesn't make you more or less of a Faerie."

"Those are such wise words from a young Princess! And I really have to thank you for reminding me of that very important fact."

She put a squirming Adriata down, watching as she ran towards her mother to give her a hug. As new as it was, Amethyst wasn't able to get enough of it. As much as she had regretted giving Adriata up all those years ago, it was one of her biggest missions to make sure nothing went wrong. To prove that she was loved and would never abandon them again. In a flurry, the ladies' maids walked through the doors, quickly walking towards where they had put their dresses. Sighing softly before following them, knowing that it was going to be a long day with Amethyst forcing her to wear a dress, not to mention she had to promise not to have her swords on her person.

She stood in front of one of the picturesque windows with a deep frown. In all of her years, she had always done her best to not wear a dress, using the excuse that she wouldn't be able to fight if s fight were to break out. Reasoning that pants just made a lot more sense as they weren't only comfortable, but she was able to keep her weapons close by. She was still fuming at the fact that Amethyst had bullied her into this, which was why she was now wearing a mint forest green, silk dress with a lighter green see-through material falling over the dress, which ended just above her knees.

The corset they had forced her into was the same color as the underskirt, decorated with pearly white beads in the shape of flowers. The shoes on her feet were pure black, covered in forest green beading with a thin ribbon winding around her lower legs, stopping just below her knees. Amethyst had of course also insisted that her hair had to be curled slightly and hanging loose. She had offered to withdraw her wings so they wouldn't get in her way, but Amethyst had insisted that the dressmaker had made the outfit with her wings in mind.

"You look absolutely gorgeous, Lexi!" Shadick whispered, making her spin towards him. "I truly had no idea what Amethyst had planned for your outfit, but I have to admit she had done a really good job!"

"Isn't it too much, though?" she asked, fidgeting.

"Not even a little bit, it is absolutely perfect and suits you perfectly."

"There is no need for you to try and sweet-talk me, Shadick. You have proved more than once that you like me, from the very first moment we met; stalking me from the trees."

"Once it started bleeding into one, I lost track of time; not to mention I have completely forgotten the fact that I had followed you from the trees. Are Amethyst and Adriata ready for their big day?"

"For one, I had to tell Adriata to take a deep breath and calm down as she was getting overexcited and on the verge of passing out way before the ceremony could even start. As for Amethyst, I had to remind her that she is the Faerie Queen and had the ability to create flowers when she sent her ladies maids to find more flowers."

"I take it that she is still adjusting to the fact that she no longer has wings anymore and feeling like a human?"

"She has mostly accepted it a while ago, and with Adriata

around, it has helped her so much."

"Then I assume she has been a good influence?"

"In a way, yes she has been. Amethyst has been watching Adriata and made sure to notice how much it's getting to her that she doesn't have wings, as well as feeling different from the other children. In an attempt to make her feel more relaxed and normal, Amethyst stopped being so upset about the loss of her wings. And as twisted as that sounds, she has accepted that they won't return. This time however, it was more a case of being so excited about getting married to her long-time love and forgetting something like being in control of magic."

"I can tell the two of you now that you'd better get a move on and get to the waterfall before Amethyst beats us all there. If I'm not mistaken, she will either start without you or stop the entire thing to send a search party to find you," Sachiel said, rushing towards them.

"She is more than likely to come and find us herself. Not to mention we're not important enough for her to remember us above yourself," Shadick said with a laugh.

"You have that completely wrong; I am only the third most important person that will be there, just after Adriata and barely ahead of Alexandria."

"Of course! I've forgotten about our beloved Princess, which makes me curious as to where she's gotten to," she said, glancing around.

"From the last report I received, she is still with Amethyst, getting ready."

"Adriata has been very determined to be one of the first ones to see Amethyst in her wedding dress, which is why I left them to it."

"It was only because I knew that mommy would look really pretty, but I had to also make sure that daddy looked pretty as well," Adriata said, skipping towards them, holding Iva's hand. "I have to say that mommy really does look very pretty."

"Adriata?! Am I really looking at my baby girl?" Sachiel asked, pretending to clutch his chest.

"You are indeed, your majesty. When she walked out of her mother's room, I was just as surprised that she was looking like the perfect little lady!" Iva said seriously. "One of these days, we will have to lock her up in a tower because she will be the prettiest girl here and bossing us around."

"If you were to think about it, she is already the prettiest girl here and has been bossing around."

"Aunty Lexa! Would you please tell all of them that I'm right here and that I've also not been bossing anyone around because I'm only 6 years old," Adriata said, pouting.

"You definitely got your mother's way around words," she said before quickly adding, "I really have to agree with you, though, that you've never bossed anyone around because you're still a young girl."

"I reckon the most important thing right this minute is that we all get to the waterfall and take our seats, just in case the Queen really does show up before us while we're just standing around here chatting," Iva said with a glint in her eyes. "Now Adriata, you need to remember that you will need to go down the aisle before your mother; it really will be an amazing sight with the prettiest women in Valencia."

Bending down next to Adriata as the others slowly drifted away to find their spots around the waterfall. Sachiel looked as though he was a bit nervous, pacing up and down with the priest just standing there watching everyone. Adriata was staring at everyone and everything around her, doing her best to take it all in.

There was no doubt in her mind that she just wanted to run around to explore as much as she was able to; there were so many things that had been added for the evening that it looked as though they had traveled to a different place. It made her smile to see her family and how they would finally be able to be together the way they were supposed to have been from the start.

Yes, them not being together earlier had been Amethyst's doing, but she had a very valid reason as to why she had done the things in the way that she had, and it was about time that they were united. A sudden noise from behind her made her glance back, her eyes widening in shock.

Amethyst was standing there in the perfect dress for her, with her hair, light makeup only adding to what was already the perfect picture. The dress was the color of olives, decorated with tiny beading. The top part was cut into a V-neck with the edges rising past her shoulders, while the bottom of the dress was loose-fitting and flowing, reaching just below her knees. Her shoes were the same ones she was wearing, although she had to admit hers paled in comparison. There would be no questioning that it truly was her sister's big day and that she was the center of attention.

"Please tell me that it isn't too much?! I have been arguing with the other Faeries the entire morning that it's all just too much," Amethyst said, pulling on her dress softly.

"There is absolutely nothing to worry about, Am. You are truly looking absolutely amazing!" she replied with a smile. "Don't you agree with me, Adriata?"

"I know I saw you earlier, but it looks as though you just stepped out of one of my dreams, mommy. A very nice dream where everyone is happy," Adriata replied wide-eyed.

"Thank you so much, my darling. I really have to admit, though, that you are giving me quite a run for my money. You look just as pretty as I'm feeling," Amethyst said, bending down to hug Adriata tightly, "even though I never imagined myself in this position, I'm happy that I have the two of you next to me."

"Are you really still in the mindset that you don't deserve this?" she asked.

"No, I've known that this was how it has always meant to be, the very second he asked me. That our little family is finally becoming one after what has been a really long time."

"Before you decide to storm out there and spoil what has been considered a tradition for many years, it would be for the best that we get this ball rolling and get you married."

She shot her sister a smile before quickly hugging Amethyst, stepping away slightly so she could give the musicians the sign to start. From the first note of the song, a hush fell over everyone. They had chosen a song that had meant a lot to them ever since they had been little girls.

Winking at Adriata, lightly pushing her to walk down the aisle, gasps ran through the crowd as they watched her walk to the front. It truly looked as though she was flying across the pathway, blinking with a frown as she saw a soft flash of light flowing from Adriata's back before a small smile appeared on her lips.

"Amey, move a little closer to me so you can watch Adriata," she whispered to her sister. "Your beautiful daughter is finally getting the wings she has been wishing for."

"And that on my wedding day! We really couldn't have planned for this day to turn out any more perfectly," Amethyst said as she glanced down the aisle.

A small gasp ran through everyone again as it only confirmed that the wings were visible to everyone and in fact glowing brighter and more visible. Sachiel's eyes widened before a grin broke across his face, rushing towards his daughter, picking her up, spinning her around, making her giggle happily. He quickly whispered something in her ear as they rushed to the back to where the priest was still waiting, staring at them, shocked.

Lightly squeezing Amethyst's hand as the song changed to show it was their turn. Walking around the corner and into full view of the people who turned towards them as they watched them closely.

A lot of the people were doing their best to find something they were able to judge, but they weren't able to find anything. They walked in time with the music, slowly proceeding enough for everyone to get a good look at Amethyst and herself, but fast enough that they would reach their destination soon.

When they finally stopped in front of Sachiel and Adriata, she kissed her sister's cheek, giving her a big hug, before moving to the side where the planner had been frantically indicating for her to stand as she turned to watch the ceremony in silence.

Chapter 17

Dreamscapes

The reception started shortly after the main ceremony; the area had been cleared of all the chairs as well as the altar, so there was enough space for a dance floor to be summoned. Glancing around, she could only see smiles and people happily talking to each other; it was something that they hadn't seen in a couple of months, as everyone had been worried about the oncoming war without a proper chance to relax.

She was glad that this was a night that was giving them a chance to just breathe and step away from the worries of the world. Her gaze fell on Luanda and her small family, glad that her sister looked relaxed and that she even had a slight smile as their gazes clashed. A frown slowly formed as she realized something seemed to be off about her, quickly decided, however, that it would be for the best not to say anything, as it was more than likely some of the stress that lingered.

There could have been numerous reasons for her to worry, even if she had done her best to not cause herself any stress. The palace workers, not to mention everyone who ran the stalls in the village, knew that Luanda and her family didn't have to pay for anything they needed. It was something she considered something small she could do to help her sister. After what had happened the last time they had gotten together, she had been hesitant to approach her again, but she had hope that once the war was over, they would get their chance to sit down to get to know each other. To attempt to have a normal sibling relationship, whatever that consisted of.

"It would seem that I always find you hiding in a corner all by yourself, as though you were staring at people, doing your best to find any kind of dangerous weapons that might need to be removed," Shadick asked, walking towards her.

"Simply because that's the type of person I am, I observe more than participate. You would be surprised at how much I've learned about people by simply watching them, and actually having a conversation with them," she replied with a small smile.

"When you talk to a person, there is a bigger chance that you actually get to know them, so I have to disagree with you on that. You are able to actually watch them closely and react to the things they do and take it from there."

"My mom had always called me her little observer when I was still a young girl. Not to mention, I'm more comfortable in the corner than actually having to talk to people."

"The last couple of years really have changed you quite a bit; you have to at least admit that. Don't get me wrong, as I don't mean it as a bad thing."

"Considering everything that we have been through the last couple of years, everyone has changed in some ways."

"As I've already said, it isn't a bad thing. It was a simple observation, as you said, but there is no need for us to keep hammering on the subject. I must admit though, that as I was walking over here, I noticed that you were looking at Luanda with concern. Is there something bothering you about her?"

"It's just something I've noticed in her aura, as though something is wrong, but she's doing her best to keep quiet and not make anyone worry. Or it might be a case that she doesn't even realize something is wrong."

"She does look a little pale, but I was thinking it might just be a new mother thing as I've not been around a lot of children. It's only ever been with my sister and Adriata the last while."

"That's also something that crossed my mind, but there is something that keeps telling me that it isn't just that."

"Then wouldn't it be a good idea for you to go and talk to her to find out how she's feeling?"

Nodding, taking a deep breath, taking a step towards where Luanda was sitting, just as Michael noticed just how pale she looked, glancing around, looking panicked and worried, making her pick up her pace until she stood next to them.

"I take it that she's about to have a vision?" she asked,

spreading her wings to give them some privacy from those around them. "I thought that she looked a little pale and rushed over here."

"Yes! But she doesn't really like it when there are people around her when it happens, but I don't see a way to get her out of the public eye before it completely takes over her," he replied, picking up their daughter.

"Take your daughter and enjoy a dance, pretend as though nothing is wrong, and I will take care of Luanda."

"But..."

"Michael, you have long enough, so please know that I am doing this out of the goodness of my heart and worry about my sister. So please take your daughter to dance," she whispered, still staring at her before nodding, walking away, his shoulders sagging a little.

Turning back to Luanda, touching her shoulder lightly, she bent down next to her. "If you can hear me, this is going to feel like a slight pull around your navel area. But all I'm doing is teleporting us a short way just so we can be away from people and give us a bit of privacy."

Luanda seemed to breathe a sigh of relief as the cold air surrounded them, but there was no way for her to know what had happened as her eyes were still closed. But she refused to leave because she could just sense Luanda needed someone close by. Just as some kind of invisible support system, biting her lip, she sat down next to her sister, lightly taking her hand in her own.

"So I've never been around when you had one of these visions, and I'm not sure what I'm supposed to do exactly. I can however talk to you and try to distract you a little from what is happening. I've made Michael dance with your daughter as though she's a big girl; she is absolutely loving it and can't stop smiling," she said before pausing. "The way that I told you we were related shouldn't have happened the way that it did. The way I decided to tell you was wrong, and I should ask you to forgive me, even if you don't accept it. When I found that letter and realized that you were actually my sister, I was so shocked that any and all reasoning went out of the window.

"Then, when I spoke to the ghosts of my parents, and they confirmed it, I was completely shattered. My father had always been the person I had looked up to all of my life, and he'd cheated on my mom. She had been the one person that he had promised to never hurt. It was then that I had a hard time getting over it; there was still a little bit of pain in my heart, but he was also the one who assured me it hadn't been planned. It was after that that I decided it was time to talk to you. It would have been better if I had actually sat down to think what the best way to tell you instead of just blurting it out. I'm not blaming anyone, of course, but I had Amethyst, Shadick, and Starlansha who insisted that I tell you as well.

"I should have stood my ground and told them I wasn't ready to tell you yet, but I caved and went to your place. Not to mention, I dropped this huge bomb on you while you were heavily pregnant, which may have caused a lot of trouble. If it helps even a little, I can tell you about my, I mean our father, just so you don't think too badly of him.

"He loved horses and would make sure that he raised me in the best way, so that I would love horses as well. We had a family horse, the most beautiful colt I had ever seen. My mom, of course, thought that I had been too young to ride a horse. She thought that about my bow and sword as well, but whenever he had a chance, he would sneak me into the forest and teach me everything he knew.

"The day she found out that he had been teaching me without her knowledge and permission, she almost slapped him. She however, admitted that it was probably a good idea that I knew how to handle weapons. I was a very young girl when they were killed; although I do remember my father telling me how they would always love me no matter what happened. At the time, I thought that it was such a strange thing to say; it was as though he knew what was going to happen to them. Now that I think about it, he probably did know that something was going to happen. He also knew that if they were to change it, things would only get worse. Wait... Dad also had visions, and that is where your gift comes from!"

"As weird as this might sound, you may not be that far off," Luanda whispered, "especially after the vision I had."

"Am I to assume that it was something really bad?"

"It wasn't exactly bad; although it was a mixture of the past, present, and future. For now, I have to thank you for trying to make all of this better. It really has been one of the best reactions there's been to me having a vision."

"In all honesty, I wasn't sure what I should do, so I just babbled."

"For the past part of the vision, I saw your... I mean our father with your mother. I think that it may have been the day they died, they were arguing while you were not too far from them, playing. Your mom looked very worried and kept trying to convince father that they couldn't just leave you alone. It was at that point that it jumped to the future, where you stabbed not just Justren but Balditha as well.

"I had this really strong feeling that it had to be you to do it, as too many others would have died in the attempt. The vision then shifted to the present, where I saw everyone happy and smiling and not worrying about anything. They are celebrating life and not just crying over death, which was when it panned to you, and I heard your voice as though from a distance."

"Do your visions normally jump the way that this one did?"

"This was a first; normally, they are straightforward and to the point."

"Then we can only assume there is a reason as to why the vision happened the way that it did."

"Personally, the reason for that is clear, and there is no reason for you to seem so surprised. While you were away being tortured or training or whatever, I was working on figuring out what my visions mean, and I have to say I've gotten rather good at it and they've been very accurate."

"I'm glad that you were able to work on that and actually succeeded in doing what you wanted to do."

"I can feel the curiosity seeping out of you," Luanda said, laughing softly. "Right, the past showed that father had known of their coming deaths, your mother was against actually going through with it, but as we both know, he convinced her of it eventually. Jumping to the future just proves where the importance lies, and that would be of you taking them out and no one else, just so those vile creatures don't take anyone else down. It is war, unfortunately, and there will always be death as well as casualties, but not all of them have to die.

"It was clear though, you are the one who has to kill Balditha and Justren. You will be the one who has to take their lives to finally end all of this. As for me, seeing the present means that there will be happiness after the war. People will go back to being happy, to being able to spend time together with friends and family."

"Since the start, there had always been an inkling in the back of my mind that I would have to be the one to end them; it's the same way I knew that I had to kill Diliante when I did. If I hadn't killed her, things would only have gotten worse. It seemed as though Balditha was the one who was in charge of causing the war, but I believe it was she who was whispering in his ear as well," she replies, shaking her head sadly.

"Are you two ladies doing okay back here?" Sachiel asked as he kneeled in front of the., "Michael approached me and told me that you had moved your sister to a more secluded spot as she was having a vision, so I thought that it would be for the best to leave you in peace until I thought it was done as I didn't want you to feel overwhelmed, Luanda."

"I do appreciate the consideration, your majesty. The vision was very informative with so many details, and I have already spoken to Alexandria about it. And we are in agreement as to what the vision means, as well as the fact that it's aimed at her specifically. I do believe, however, that it would be for the best to discuss this in the morning. It is, after all, your wedding evening, and that is more important than anything else," Luanda said seriously, standing up with a smile, "and that reminds me; I haven't congratulated you yet. I know that you and Amethyst will have a great life going forward."

"Thank you so much! Your good wishing really is appreciated."

"Would you stop looking so shocked, Sachiel? My sister has already made up her mind, and it's never a good idea to argue with either of us," she said with a grin.

"Very well then, Alexandria. Your Faerie sister has requested that you go and have a dance with her. It is also one of the reasons why I came over here to check up on you."

"Are you feeling better?"

"Yes, I am, thank you for your concern. Having someone to talk to or at least listen to what happened in the vision was rather comforting, so I'm so thankful. Now go, before the Queen decides to have your head," Luanda replied, surprising her with a hug, whispering in her ear. "Your niece's name is Demiane, in remembrance of her true Grandfather."

It was in that moment that she knew there was a chance to actually have a relationship with her sister, and it would be great. Giving Luanda a smile, quickly walking towards the dance floor where Amethyst was waiting for her.

Chapter 18

Chronicles of Discovery

She was sitting in one of the largest trees in the forest, its branches reaching towards the sky as though wishing they could be free. Unless someone knew that she was sitting there, no one would be the wiser. So much had happened the previous couple of weeks with no explanation as to why she was feeling the way that she had been, as though she was under constant scrutiny. It constantly felt as though they were either expecting her to have a breakdown and destroy everything or just waiting for her to finally start the war. Everyone, however, kept assuring her that she was just imagining things, which is why she had vanished into the forest to temporarily disappear.

She had been determined to get to know not just Luanda but Demaine as well, and had been spending a lot of time with them. When she had first knocked on the door, it had been rather awkward as they had been unsure how to just relax to get to know each other, which had left them to sit there watching Demaine.

It had only changed when the little girl had stumbled and had grabbed onto one of her wings to catch her fall that they had burst into laughter. They had started sharing stories from the past couple of years, as well as the things that had always bothered them about people and things that had happened.

"Alex! I really don't know why you insist on my traveling into the forest just so I can speak to you," Amethyst muttered in frustration. "We haven't had a proper conversation in two weeks with absolutely no explanation from you as to why! Even if Shadick has told me that everything is okay, you are making me worry."

"We are still living in the same Castle, Am. It really isn't that difficult for you to just walk across the hallways to get to my room," she replied, closing her eyes.

"You are making it sound as though I am the only one responsible for everything that goes on around here. You are a Princess and have just as much, I mean less, responsibility than I have."

"I don't really want those responsibilities when it seems as though people are just waiting to turn around and say 'I told you so'."

"You are just imagining things. I can assure you no one is looking at you. Could you please just come down here? In case it slipped your mind, I no longer have wings and am not able to fly into trees. Not to mention it would be very un-Queenly for me to climb a tree while wearing a dress."

"Do not make it sound as though a dress or the fact that you're a Queen has ever stopped you."

Amethyst muttered softly before she heard the sound of her dress material, making her aware that her sister was climbing the tree. Glancing at her bare feet, she noticed her shoes lying on the ground before looking back at her sister as she continued scaling the tree. Barely 2 minutes later, Amethyst was sitting across from her with a smug smirk on her face.

"I have to admit, I'm impressed you chose a tree that isn't noticeable to everyone and can confidently say even the magical creatures would have a difficult time finding you. You really do have this uncanny ability to find the one place that everyone always seems to overlook, giving you a small place of peace," Amethyst said as she straightened her dress.

"Adriata would have been in absolute hysterics if she had been here to witness you climbing this tree," she commented with a smile. "Speaking of, how has she been handling her new Faerie wings?"

"It has been coming along, albeit slowly. It's happened on numerous occasions now that I noticed her wanting to try something only to pause as though she's afraid or that she would hurt my feelings."

"It's only natural for her to keep your feelings in mind, as she saw how much it hurt you when you lost your wings. Or rather, the result of you losing your wings."

"Watching her trying to figure out how to fly has been rather sweet. Once she gets the knack for it, poor Iva will be pulling her hair out of her head, wishing her Princess hadn't gotten her wings. The other Faeries have been super excited and helpful as they have been determined to teach her how to work with her wings. If I'm not mistaken, they had already been talking about how once she's mastered flying, they will be teaching her how to go into her mini-form."

"Would that even be in the scope of her abilities?"

"Your guess is as good as ours! From what everyone has been able to figure out, she is the only half-Fae, half-human to have ever existed. Which makes it rather difficult to guess what kind of powers she will have. Remember when we thought she wouldn't even get her wings? She has truly been missing you the last couple of weeks, not to mention she feels as though she would only be a bother if she were to try and speak to you."

"Is the only reason you came to talk to me, to make me feel even worse than I already am? Because I'm not spending enough time with either of you?"

"Get off your high horse, that hadn't been my intention at all, thank you very much," Amethyst huffed. "Now that things have calmed down slightly, I believe it is time to go and talk to Chadromida and Astarte. We are too divided, and it will only give Balditha more opportunity to attack when we don't expect it. Them being next to Dargona Mountains and us all the way over here also means that we wouldn't be able to just send help within a couple of minutes; by the time reinforcements were to reach them, it would be too late."

"I agree with you, what does it have to do with me? There isn't really much need for me to go with you."

"Well, that is a really difficult question to answer. You are the only one able to teleport us there. I am the Queen after all, not to mention a mother, and I'm unable to just leave my Queendom."

"Hmm, I see what you did there. It's an official command that no one, even I, would be able to say no to."

"Nice try; as you are my sister, I know better than anyone that it wouldn't work on you. Besides, you know too many of my weaknesses, not to mention you love me."

"And because I'm your sister, you also know that I will truly do just about anything for you to ensure you're happy."

"Basically, yes."

"If that is what you want, I will take you without questioning it; it would also give me a moment to just have a little bit of a breather to get away from here."

"That's the spirit! You can think of it as a small, couple-of-hours holiday," Amethyst said, giggling.

"Marriage really has made you a very happy person," she replied. "I can't decide whether I like the change or not."

"You know you like it, but I do have to agree though, it has changed me. Marriage has always been something we have both dreamed of since we initially met each other, so finally being given the opportunity to do so has made the world seem not so dark. It's as though wrongs had been fixed, if that makes any sense."

"Yes, it does make sense. You have been feeling as though you're broken and missing something for a really long time. Now that you and Sachiel got married, it finally feels as though all the pieces of your souls have been healed. The change I see in you is good; for myself, however, I'm not sure whether the change is a good thing."

"That's the Alex that I know and love! The one who's always been ever hopeful of love and what it can bring us. It's as though we're still wee little girls running around and driving my mom up the walls. Change is something that will happen to all of us whether we want it to or not. We may not always believe it is something good, and it might feel bad, but in the end, it is how we decide to see it that decides it. And with all of the things you have been through the last couple of years, it's no wonder that you have changed. Change is something that will happen to all of us whether we want it to or not.

"We may not always believe it is something good, and it might feel bad, but in the end, it is how we decide to see it that decides it. I was in a coma for two and a half years, and I sure as Valencia changed! Everything we go through, not to mention how we handle it, is what makes or breaks us. Ever since that very first journey you took with Justren, it was all up to you whether you wanted to keep going or not. You had the option to at any point say no and turn your back on everyone.

"There is no way for us to know what would have happened if you had changed your mind about the journey. You knew however what the right path was to take, and it has brought us on the road we are on right now. Not to mention, you know how much I trust you, especially considering you hold my daughter's fate in your hands. I'm telling you this, not to pressure you but to prove just how loved you are as well as trusted by those around you," Amethyst said touching her cheek with a smile. "All you need to do is believe in yourself and know that no matter your decision, it is the one that feels right to you and the little voice in your head."

"Thank you, Am. I can't tell you enough how much that means to me."

"Of course; now, how do you propose we get down from here? Or do you want me to climb down again?"

"I'll teleport us to the Castle; it will just make things so much easier for us to quickly grab whatever we need so we can get going to Dargona Village," she said, standing up, pulling Amethyst with her, and giving her a tight hug. "You are indeed right about how I will do absolutely anything for you. No matter what anyone says, you are my sister even though it isn't by blood."

"Well, you know my mom always insisted that we should treat each other like family."

"As always, she got what she wanted," she whispered as she teleported to the main entrance.

"Could I please ask who will be going with you, just so I know you will be safe and I will have some kind of peace?" Sachiel asked, walking towards them.

"Alex will be going, obviously, as she will be taking me there. Shadick has insisted on going as he would like to spend some time with his sister and their new baby. Starlansha has expressed her wishes to come with as she would like to find out what the newest development is, not to mention she is part of the trio. It was one of Adriata's biggest wishes to come with us so she could meet the Dragons. I however informed her that she will have plenty of opportunities to meet them as they will be moving here. It isn't the right time for her to travel to a new place, especially as we are planning to be back before it gets too late," Amethyst replied, squeezing his hand. "You won't be going with us as we can't leave the village without a leader."

"As sweet as that is of you, honey, it would be rather nice if you were to leave someone who can actually have an adult conversation with me, not just a little girl."

"But I did! Iva will be running around the Castle, doing some things Adriata has 'commanded' of her."

"I mean no offense to Iva, but I would much rather have Shadick or even Starlansha around to talk to, it would give me a chance to have a conversation I will actually enjoy, not forced small talk."

"And as I have already said, we are planning on being back by nightfall. If something were to happen that would keep us there longer, I will make sure to let you know. Not just for your peace of mind but to ensure you let the chef know to prepare dinner for us or not."

"If that is your wish, your majesty."

"Besides, you know you will have to deal with some of the queries that have been streaming in from the villagers. So perhaps it would be a good time to go for a walk and talk to some of the villagers."

"You mention queries; what exactly are you making me deal with?"

"Some of the families have expressed their need to expand their homes, or they would rather move to a new place because it's either too big or too small. I know that one of the farmers has also expressed his wishes to expand his land. So please don't pretend as though you don't know what you're doing, darling, as you've been doing this a lot longer than I have."

"You've been a Queen a lot longer than I have been King."

"It is one of my greatest wishes that my mother were still alive so she could look after the Kingdom, but it doesn't seem as though it's in the cards."

"I'm sorry, my love. I have become used to having you around on a daily basis, and us making the decisions together."

"Sachiel, you really are underestimating yourself. I have been keeping an eye on you, and you really do have a way of dealing with the villagers that shows how much you care for them." She told him with a smile

"Of course, you're right, and it was rather selfish of me. The villagers of Dargona Village really do need to be brought here, and it will be one of the biggest jobs there is, not to mention I believe that you will be able to convince Chadromida of the plan as well. He will see how right it is to even if it's temporarily combine the villages."

"My sister had mentioned moving everyone this side for a really long time, if it makes you feel better. At the time, however she was pregnant, and the planning was put on hold." Shadick said, stepping out of the Castle, "Chad was close to tying her down in the hope of getting her to stop moving too much."

"From all of the stories I've been told, your sister really is a force of nature once she decides on something," Amethyst said with a smile

"After giving birth, she was given strict instructions to take it easy and not move unless absolutely necessary. She told the doctor where to shove it and was up after a couple of hours' sleep, commanding people to do things."

"I really can't wait to meet Kaedyn!"

"The last time we saw her, she was so tiny. It felt as though I could hold her with only one of my hands."

"You really are making it sound worse than it is, as you weren't able to hold her in just one of your hands, even when you tried," she replied, rolling her eyes with a smile.

"It isn't as though I've had much opportunity to be around a lot of babies! But I guess she would have been the same size as any other baby her age."

"Perhaps one of these days you will have the opportunity to have your own babies," Sachiel said, slapping Shadick's shoulder as his frown deepened in confusion. "You will eventually realize what that means, my friend. I can assure you, you don't have to worry about that."

"If we keep standing around talking, we won't get back here by nightfall. So is everyone ready?" she asked with a stretch of her wings.

"All present and accounted for," Starlansha said as she stepped forward, glancing at her wings. "I still say that there is some kind of gold mixed in your wings, I swear I just saw a glint of it when you stretched."

"It feels as though they keep changing every time I look in the mirror, so I can't argue with you as I'm not even sure."

Amethyst kissed Sachiel's cheek before grabbing her hand as well as Starlansha's. Shadick stepped closer, grabbing her other hand as Managwa and Freya moved between their legs, ensuring they were touching them. Shooting Sachiel a smile, closing her eyes, concentrating on where they were going, the wind picked up around them before they all disappeared, reappearing within seconds in front of the gates of Dargona village.

Chapter 19

Ever-changing Paths

Starlansha covering her nose as she sneezed, while Managwa shook his coat as though the wind from the teleportation had messed up his fur. Amethyst touched her hair as though to insure it was still in perfect condition, Shadick rolling his neck until it cracks. Freya standing there just watching them in silent judgment and their inability to travel by teleportation.

"I'm not sure if I will ever get used to teleportation." Shadick said frowning

"If it means anything; I've gotten used to it." She replied tilting her head slightly "I doubt that you aimed that at me though."

"Of course I was talking to you! You're the one that's been teleporting longer than any of us, although I have no doubt that it feels differently for you than to those that teleport with you."

"I believe that it is different for each person, so you can't really compare your experiences against someone else's experience." Amethyst said quickly hugging her "oh look! Astarte!"

They watched as Astarte froze mid-step, and glanced towards them. A couple of seconds passed by as she stared at them before squealing and rushing towards the guards, holding Kaedyn in her

228

arms with a happy smile on her face making the little girl giggle at her mother

"Open the gates! If you idiots didn't realize, that's my brother." She shouted at the surprised looking guards "not to mention the Queen of Faeries!"

"Astarte, you are going to make your poor daughter burst into tears with the way you're going on right now." Shadick commented smiling "you really have been the one to get overly excited about anything and everything."

"Oh shut your mouth, brother! If you keep going I might just get the guards to lock you up in the stockades."

"I would pay to be able to see that!" Starlansha said stepping towards them "could you perhaps organize it as a part of a show?"

"I have to agree, that sounds like it would be a fantastic show! And I could definitely have it organized."

"Typical, we've barely arrived and I'm being bullied by my younger sister." Shadick said shaking his head

"We should ensure that he's tied up while in the stockades so that people have the opportunity to throw water at him." She suggested waving at Kaedyn

"I give up; I'm being ganged up on by three women! Where is Chad, as there doesn't seem there is any way for me to win today. I know for a fact that he will give me backup in all of this."

"As per his usual habit, he is walking around the village talking to some of the guards as well as the villagers. Don't ask me about what as I've not been informed." Astarte replied shrugging "he spends time with Kaedyn and myself but at times he gets into this mood where he's unable to get any rest and just starts walking around, muttering under his breath about security."

"That is actually one of the reasons why we decided to give you guys a visit." Amethyst interjected quickly "we've been wanting to speak to yourself and Chadromida about the villagers and moving everyone away from here. It has been something we've been wanting to discuss for a couple of months now; but with everything was kind of forgotten when Sachiel proposed and with us needing to organize the wedding."

"When is the wedding?!"

"If I remember correctly it was about two weeks ago. I really can't tell you for sure when it was, the day and everything that happened has been feeling a little blurry."

"Congratulations! If we had only known, we would have been there without a second's hesitation."

"I really did want to invite you guys but it just didn't feel like the right time to invite you to the wedding when there is just so much other things that needs to be discussed."

"Please don't feel bad about not inviting us! Once Chadromida and I finally take that step we can all have a big celebration in honor of all of us. Before you say anything, brother dearest. We are planning on getting married especially now that Kaedyn is in our lives and has made our little family complete."

"I can't tell you how happy it makes me to hear you say that, otherwise it may have been high time for us to have a very serious conversation about where he wants this relationship to go." Shadick said giving her a hug "now if you would please hand over my niece so I can teach her all of the bad things, I know you will refuse to teach her, it would be appreciated."

"Seeing as Shadick and Kaedyn is being entertained, I think it's a good time to go speak to the cooks about what we would like for dinner. I'm sure you understand that we won't be able to stay for too long." Starlansha said linking arms with Astarte

"I'm sure you understand our need to get back to Valencia before it gets too late? But as I've already said, we really need to discuss some rather urgent matters that can't be put off for that much longer." Amethyst said as they followed behind them

"Then I do believe it would be for the best to have one of the guards run and find Chad. If it really is as serious as you're making it sound he really needs to be there as well." Astarte said "Alex, will you be joining us in the meeting? You have been so quiet that I was starting to wonder if you wanted to perhaps join some of the guards."

"Of course I'll be joining you, my mind had just wandered to what needs to happen while you were talking. The discussion we're going to have really will be of the utmost importance." She replied smiling

Astarte led the way towards the dining room tossing a glance at Shadick who was holding Kaedyn rather awkwardly. Amethyst was talking to Astarte in hushed voices about their children both serious as they discuss what they each had to do recently for their children. From what she could over hear it all seemed scary yet exciting all rolled into one. It made her wonder if she would be ready if it had been her, and knew that the time was not right for her. As much time as she had spent with Adriata since her birth, it had never been her own child she had to constantly think about. Surely if it was your own it was a completely different experience? Naturally it would be with an added bonus of the excitement of experiencing all the firsts.

Perhaps if she were to stop thinking about it so hard it could bring happiness as well, she bit her lip looking at Shadick and the happiness clear on his face as he played with Kaedyn. Did he want children of his own? It hadn't exactly been something she had been considering especially not the last couple of years, but not having Shadick around had been lonely. Was those emotions enough to considering spending the rest of their lives together? No matter how much she though about it she honestly didn't have a answer to those thoughts and perhaps it made how she was feeling even worse. Did she have a fear of commitment which was why she was being so hesitant? Her parents had been together for years and had died together, so her role models had always been good choices. Even Valencia had been with her husband until his untimely death. Perhaps there really was just something wrong with her.

"How can time be passing so quickly when you have children in your life? The day she sat up by herself it felt as though my heart had learned how to fly in excitement and disbelief." She heard Astarte gush

"Rest assured that you are at least there for all of those milestones! When I was expectant with Adriata, I unfortunately made all of the wrong decisions. If there had been anyway for me to do it over again I would never have let her go just so I could be there for her during all of those milestones. I have to admit that I am happy that I was there when she received her Faerie wings as it had been one of the greatest feelings." Amethyst replied

"Your reasonings behind not raising her, yourself has always been very valid. No one has the right to judge you for the decisions you've made, and if someone does say something about your choices they should perhaps have a look at their own lives before attempting to judge someone else's."

"I have no reason to disagree with you on that statement, there is no way of going back and changing it even if I sometimes wish it was in my power to change those things. Not that I believe I even would have changed it as I've learned so many things throughout the years. Things I may not have learned if I had Adriata to look after."

"Being a parent really does change a person, never in my life would I have thought I would need to tell another person that they need to cut their meat into smaller pieces so as to not choke."

"That sounds like it could be a lot of fun; I guess." Starlansha said frowning "wanting to tell an adult just how to eat properly, there has been numerous of times where I wanted to shout at someone just to eat a little neater and not just gulp down their food as though they're starving dogs. I realized rather early in my life just how important chewing is while eating."

"Then just wait until the day you have your own children as that feeling will only double."

Manangwa ran up to them making her frown as she glanced down at him, she had not even noticed that he had disappeared from the group. Not even 5 minutes later, realizing that he had gone to find Chadromida making her smile and scratching the wolf's ears. Chadromida was looking very unhappy for some reason as he glanced between their group.

"Here I was telling Astarte just this morning that I was wondering when we will be seeing the three of you again. Now just look, we have the four of you in front of us." Chadromida said as he hugged Shadick "I see that you've had an opportunity to get acquainted with your niece."

234

"She really is such a little star! I was truly expecting her to be hesitant to be around me because she doesn't know me, but she has accepted me as though she's seen me around since she was born." Shadick replied grinning

"The only reason for that is I'm ensuring she knows all about her crazy uncle Shadick." Astarte said rolling her eyes "now if you'll give me a couple of minutes while I go to discuss the menu for tonight with the chef."

Chadromida pulled them towards the dining hall as Astarte disappeared around a corner, ushering them into seats around the table. Everyone started talking to each other at the same time, Starlansha was giggling at something Amethyst was telling her while wiggling her fingers towards Kaedyn causing lights to glide over to the little girl. Shadick and Chadromida talking about the latest news from the dragons as they watched the little girl clapping her hands at the lights. Sighing softly while chewing her lip, feeling rather disconnected from everything that was happening around her.

"So tell us, what is it exactly that you wished to speak to us about?" Astarte asked as she took her place next to Chadromida "it has to be important enough if we get a visit from the Faerie Queen."

"This subject has been brought up before it had been kind of waylaid however when the previous fight started not to mention everything that happened ever since." Amethyst started with a frown

"Well; please feel free to continue, we're listening." Chadromida said nodding

"With the war looming in front of us, I believe that it is time for the two villages to combine, it would make things a lot easier if we knew everyone was together and we didn't have to worry about the other being attacked. The thought of the villages being separated makes me rather panicky as one might be attacked and there would be no quick way to get to each other. Life has been difficult the last couple of years but all of us have done marvelously at keeping it all together. A lot of things however has changed since we last sat down to discuss this, what with the unification of the Magical creatures and the humans.

That was after all one of the biggest things that have happened the last couple of years as we have been separated for centuries. I had some of the scribes go over the notes and scrolls that is in our possession and there is no record of why it happened in the first place. My mother used to tell us that there had been some kind of misunderstanding between the two which had caused them to make the decision that it would be for the best to part ways. It had always been one of my mother's biggest dreams to finally reunite everyone, she sadly passed and unable to experience all of her work coming to fruition. When the Centaurs finally decided to reveal it had been them causing the latest strife I just knew we had to take the opportunity to get everyone reunited."

"After so many years pretending as though the others don't exist, I agree with your statement wholeheartedly. The problem laying in front of us right now is that we have no idea what the Centaurs are planning. What if we were to decide to move within this week only to be attacked on the journey there? I don't see how we would be able to defend everyone when in a convoy."

"Sachiel and I have spoken about this in details and have agreed to send some of our fighters so they can help with the move, that way we can rest assured we would have enough to defend the innocents. A couple of the Faeries will be with you guys as well just in case there is an attack. If there is any sign of danger one of them would come and warn us so we could send more men to fight."

"You have already mentioned that there may not be enough time for either of our armies to get to the other group."

"The moment one of the Faeries were to alert us of an attack, I will teleport to help. Shadick, Starlansha as well as some of the other fighters will be standing close by in the unlikelihood you get attacked. But I do not believe that the fighters would be needed as the Centaurs won't want to risk taking any of us on, especially as they are planning something much bigger. My sister had a vision the night of the wedding which just proves that we have nothing to worry about." She replied smiling

"Your sister?" Astarte asked frowning "from what I understood you and Amethyst are sisters, even if it weren't by blood."

"We are sisters, yes. But I found out kind of recently that I actually have a half sister."

"Then I guess congratulations would be in order then?"

"Thank you, we had a bit of a rough start. When I had to break the news to her it went absolutely horrid and we had quite a bad argument. After the wedding though, things changed and we have been able to spend quite a bit of time together."

"You mentioned that she had a vision during the wedding?" Chadromida asked sitting up straighter

"The vision appeared to her in three parts, the middle part of the vision is the one which is important right now and we need to concentrate on that. The vision showed her a big battle, in the middle of a big open field with both sides fighting hard with absolutely not sign of backing down. The most important part is that I killed both Justren as well as Balditha, it will be because of those actions that we will be able to end the war. It is as we have suspected from the beginning and it is because of those two that the Centaurs and other creatures are still fighting. If not for those two, there would be no war."

"How can you be so assure about that fact? There is no way for us to know that there wouldn't still be a war if it wasn't for them."

"There is no doubt in my mind about it is because of them that

238

we have to go through this. Not to mention Luanda's visions had been very helpful to us so far so there is no doubt in my mind that they will stay useful, if you're doubting me you are welcome to ask Amethyst that they have come true."

"There is no reason for us to suddenly doubt her visions, especially seeing as how useful they've been from the very start. If she is saying that Alexandria is to be the one that will end this war then I without a doubt know that it will happen in the way she saw it. As much as I hate that Alexandria will be in danger, I also know that nothing any of us do will change the future she's seen. The very moment this war started we all knew that it would end this way, that it would be up to Alexandria to end it all.

It all started when Justren started his ploy to make us all like him and ensuring he travels with her. They had been hoping that he would be able to seduce her so she would be distracted when they started their first steps. It was also her parents that had been murdered by the Centaurs. Not to mention it was also Alex that killed Diliante, which was the catalyst for the start of the second war a couple of years ago."

"The last time I was able to speak to my grandparents, even they were in agreement that it was all pointing to Alexandria ending this. He has heard all of the whispers from his guards not to mention he has seen everything that has happened in Trilantica which just proves to him even more that this is all about her."

Starlansha said sadly "if my grandfather had it in his powers, he would have done his best for there to not be any casualties."

"If I have anything to do with it she won't get killed!" Shadick said loudly scaring Kaedyn who immediately started crying "I'm so sorry, angel! Uncle Shadick didn't mean to scare you."

"Hand her to me, brother dearest. If I'm not mistaken it is time for her dinner and then she needs to go straight to bed." Astarte said standing up grabbing her daughter "once I have put her to bed I will be back, so please don't stop just because I'm not here."

"I don't have the same confidence as you guys do in moving the villagers. We would still have a huge target on our backs even if the Dragons were to stay close to us during the journey. You can't give me the promise that there wouldn't be any stragglers thirsty for bloodshed." Chadromida said with a shake of his head

"Then perhaps if I were to put it to you this way; would you consider it to be better or worse being ready for an attack that may or may not happen while moving your people to Valencia? Or would you feel better if the village was to be attacked at any moment when no one is expecting it? As I have already told you, I will have Alex ready to teleport some of Valencia's best warriors here so they can travel with you and they will be alert at all times during the move."

"I don't see why Alex doesn't just teleport the village then?"

"Unfortunately it is not in my power to teleport a large group of people, even if I were to do it in smaller groups it is a very draining thing to do. So if I were to do it numerous of times, it would be dangerous for my wellbeing." She replied

"Then you can do the teleportation over a couple of days and it would make it easier for yourself."

"Chad, could you please just get it through your head that it is draining on Lexie's energy. I have seen how bad it can get, so there is no way that I will allow her to do it. Not only because it isn't good for her health in the long run but because we need her to be at her strongest for when the fighting actually starts." Shadick told his friend "if there had been any way for us to safely teleport everyone to Valencia, I would have been all for it."

"If you're so sure about that, teleportation isn't something we will consider and I won't keep harking on the subject. I do however believe we need to discuss a better way to move the people."

"Then why do you not consider asking the Dragons for help? Surely they would be more than capable to transport a couple of humans on their backs and not have any issues."

"Dragons aren't know to exactly be the friendliest of creatures in existence. I have spent most of my years with them and we still have arguments about things, so there is no way they would allow strangers to ride them."

"Do you perhaps now realize just how difficult it is to come up with a solution to all of this? You need to realize I have been thinking about how to move the villagers on numerous of occasions, all the way from teleportation to me using my magic. Unfortunately the latter isn't possible either as my magic hasn't exactly been the most stable ever since I woke up." Amethyst said before closing her eyes "no matter which scenario I have come up with, this one will be the safest, fastest as well as most reliable option. I know that the villagers will be in danger but even the villagers in Valencia is in danger. Everyone is for that matter until we stop those two Centaurs who has been causing so much loss for all of us. We can keep arguing over this matter until we turn blue in the face yet the point remains the same. The move has to happen one way or another."

"Apologies if I am the only person in this room to point out everything that could go wrong during the move. I do however think that everyone needs to be aware that an attack is possible even if we were to pray to the gods that it didn't happen." Chadromida said seriously

"Chad..." Astarte said from the doorway "we really do need to get our people out of here, a day hasn't gone by where a group of Centaurs or other creatures weren't passing by the village and it's become a game to some of the guards how many they can see, so the fact remains we are a target. Especially considering those who doesn't want to wait for the fighting to actually start. I've had some of the guards approach me to tell me that they have started to

242

notice some stragglers seeming to group together. They are planning something and only waiting for the moment they know we would be our weakest."

"And why is it that no one has deemed it worthy enough to come tell me about it?"

"As you have been spending all your time with the Dragons the last while, they decided that it would be for the best to come to me with the information. The thought had crossed their minds to tell you, but when you returned from your last trip you had been furious so they decided against it. They didn't want to be the ones to make you get upset with them."

"Then why is it that you decided to tell me this information now?"

"Because I'm scare for the wellbeing of our daughter! I do not want her to end up on the list of humans or creatures to be killed or even have worse happening to her! She deserves a better upbringing than having to worry over stupid things like that. I want her... no, need her to have a long and happy life."

Shadick jumped up quickly wrapping his arms around his sister, whispering in her ear. For a couple of seconds she thought that she was going to fight her brother but her shoulders sagged before nodding slowly. Letting go of her, taking a step back towards the chair he had abandoned glaring at Chadromida.

"I have to agree with Astarte, but it isn't only just because of

Kaedyn. There are a lot more children in both villages that doesn't deserve to lose their parents in this war. Or even worse losing their own lives because of someone being too stubborn to listen to those around them. If it is your wish, Astarte. I will teleport yourself as well as Kaedyn to Valencia with us tonight. We have already prepared a suite for you so there is no need for you to worry about getting in the way. When Chadromida finally decides he can stand to leave his village, he can send us word." She said standing up moving out from behind the table, her wings turning to fire "now if you will please excuse me, I need to go get some fresh air before we return."

All of their eyes were on her back as she walked out of the room but no one stood up or said anything. Amethyst was the only one that noticed Chadromida's hand turning into a fist in anger, while she tried her best to ignore everything going on around her. Astarte was shaking like a leaf next to her making her worry, but she knew that the other woman had taken a deep breath before leaving the room as well. Sighing softly as she thought about how it hadn't meant to go the way that it did.

Chapter 20

The Redemption's Embrace

It wasn't long after their return from Dargona village that Sachiel called a town meeting. He felt that it was important as he knew the people were getting restless and was worried about all that had happened over the last while. They had heard the whispers and rumors of the people saying that they were just sitting ducks for when the Centaurs finally decided to make their move. Alexandria had been close on more than one occasion to shouting at people that there was nothing to worry about. She had decided against it, though, as she was already being looked at differently.

They watched as of the villagers moved closer to the Castle's courtyard. Some of them were whispering excitedly, while others were quiet and unsure of what was going to be said. If her parents had been around, they would have been walking among the people, reassuring them that there was nothing to worry about. She, however, did not have the energy required to do that, getting a little impatient and wanting it to be done with. It all felt as though this was all unnecessary; there was no real reason for them to worry about an incoming attack. They were well protected behind the walls, and the guards were ready.

"I understand your frustration, but this is something that needs to be done. Glaring at the people as though they are only ants that get in your way doesn't help," Astarte said, stepping up next to her. "We need to make sure that the people, and more importantly, the fighters, know what is going on exactly. Some of them only took on the position as guardsmen and have no idea what is going to happen next."

"Do you regret your decision to come with us that night?" she asked, tilting her head.

"No, I don't regret it. I miss Chadromida, as does Kaylee. But we both know that he will be here before the end of the month. We all know that it was one of the biggest reasons that he finally decided to move the Dargonian villagers."

"He was just being a complete idiot, arguing for them to stay there when he knew all along that it was for the best," Shadick said with a shake of his head. "Then again... he has always been the stubborn one who never wanted to listen to those around him. To be completely honest with you, I have no idea how the Dragons put up with it."

"When he is around the Dragons, he is a completely different person. I was taken aback when I went with him the one time, when I saw how much he changes around them. It was in that moment that I wondered where the man was that I fell in love with."

"Is the change in attitude that severe?"

"Worse..."

"What do you mean when you say it is worse?" she asked

"It isn't just that his attitude changes when he's around the Dragons; it is as though his personality changes completely. He is a different person than what he normally is. And to be completely honest with you, there is no way to explain it properly."

"And have you spoken to him about this? About the differences when he's with them and when he's with you?"

"I have, and he doesn't believe it. It is one of the main reasons why the guards have been coming to me about things, more than they do to him. They don't wish to see the anger in his eyes if he considers their fear as stupid. I have even gone as far as keeping Kaylee away from him until he has come to the realization that he isn't with the Dragons anymore. The one time it was for almost a week until he came back to himself."

"Then perhaps it would be a good time to have a conversation with him, especially if he changes that much without realizing it. He is putting his family in jeopardy this way, and anything might happen to not just you but the villagers as well. He might be shrugging it off as nothing when, in all honesty, it is something serious," Shadick said, shaking his head.

"I'm not even sure if he would listen to you, not if he doesn't even listen to me the last couple of months. I have seen how some of the villagers move out of his way whenever they see him getting close. I think that they are more scared of him than the Centaurs, and I don't hold them at fault for that attitude."

"Then I think that it really is a good thing that we decided to do the move now, before it is too late," Sachiel said as he joined them. "It is never a good thing when your people are more scared of you than what they trust you. I will never take over the rule of your village, but perhaps it would be for the best and make them feel more at ease to listen to someone else."

"There is no doubt in my mind that you will never take over as the leader of my village. I do agree, however, that you should take over, even if it is just temporarily. Just so we can make sure that they relax a bit more and don't have to worry about their 'leader' going evil on them. Please also just assure them that they are still to come to me if they need to."

"I think that once they arrive and have settled down a bit, we should have another meeting. Just so that we can inform them of the temporary change. I agree that they need to know that they are still more than welcome to go to you if needed. But they need to know that Chadromida is to be left alone until further notice."

They all turned and watched the last couple of people walking into the courtyard, silence falling over everyone. It was as though they knew exactly why they had been called to a meeting but wanted some reassurance nonetheless.

"I would like to first thank you for taking some time out of your busy days to come and listen to what I have to say," Sachiel said, stepping forward. "I know that all of us have things that need to be done, and I will do my best to not let this drag on for too long. This is however something that needs to be discussed, so I ask for your patience.

"From the very first day that we all moved here, everyone knew that a battle wouldn't be too far away. Alexandria, of course, has had a big role in the village as well as the battles. In her absence, it felt as though peace had finally followed. We however ignored the whisperers of the attacks that were happening in the other villages that did not want to join us. We ignored what was happening around us because it was not something that we wanted to happen to us. And more importantly, we ignored the threats that seemed to creep closer to our walls on a weekly basis. Ever since her return, those threats have become more and more noticeable, and there is no way that we can keep ignoring them.

"Before the month ends, there will be more people joining us here in Valencia. That is nothing to worry yourselves over, as it is something good that has to be accepted. Everyone can rest well knowing that their homes will not be taken from them or destroyed for something else. We have been waiting for this to happen since the beginning, so there is enough space for everyone. We do ask that you be welcoming and kind to the new arrivals. Most of those that will be joining us will be fighting by our sides and have more than likely already fought by your side.

"I know that everyone has been worrying about when the final battle with start. And this may be difficult to hear, but it will be happening sooner than any of us might like. One of your fellow villagers had a vision of the final battle and has confirmed that it will start within the next month. It might feel to you that there isn't enough time for us to prepare, but I can assure you that there is enough time.

"Our fighters, even those who have not joined the guards, have been training. They have been making sure that they are in top form for when the battle does start. You may not have seen these preparations as they happened very early in the morning and sometimes late at night when everyone was fast asleep. We organized it that way so that there would be no interruptions to the people going about their normal lives.

"It is true that we have no idea what the Centaurs have been doing or which new creatures they have on their sides since the last battle, and no matter how worrying this is, we have prepared for anything that they might be throwing at us. It is an unfortunate fact of war that there will be loss of lives. And no matter how hard we try not to let this happen, it will. It is not something that any of us want, and we will of course be trying our best to stop as many deaths as we can."

A whisper ran through the crowds as his words reached them. Some of the people looked shocked, but the majority nodded sadly. Amethyst quickly stepped up to Sachiel, laid a hand on his arm, and whispered something in his ear.

"I have personally spoken to King Sachiel and have told him that we need to give people the choice whether they want to partake in the war or not. We will be sending some of the guards to each of your homes to take note of those who wish to take part and those who do not. There will be absolutely no judgment from anyone if it is your decision to rather not take part in the war. A lot of you have new families that you may not wish to leave. Or you are perhaps too old and would rather spend the time with your family. Whatever the reasoning behind your decision, there will not be any judgment." Amethyst said smiling

She noticed that some of the families immediately hugged each other with tears of relief in their eyes. She wasn't able to see how this would work, but it had not been up to her. Amethyst had tried to remind her of how it had been in the past and how people had been forced to fight and had lost their lives. If her parents had still been alive, they would have tried their hardest to not have her take part in the war.

"If there is anything that any of you might need, there will be guards situated throughout the city. Just approach one of them, and they will be more than happy to assist you in the best way they can. If they are unable to help you, they will come to one of us, and it will be taken from there. The warriors who do choose to join us will slowly be moved to the battlefield just so everything is at the ready. We have a suspicion that Balditha will be doing the same and do not wish to be caught off guard."

"I noticed that you haven't mentioned Alexandria all that much! And we have all been wondering if she will be amongst those that will be hiding behind closed doors!" one of the villagers shouted.

"Then you are sorely mistaken. I will be on the front lines during the war. There is no way that I will not be fighting, and I will be doing my damnedest to try and keep people safe. My main mission however will be to take out their leaders, but on my way there, I will be taking down any Centaurs or any other monsters that get in my way. So there is no need for you to worry about that," she said, glaring at the man. "It would be for the best if you stop pretending that I am as much of a coward as you are. I have been part of all of this since it all started, more than even you know, so do not just assume."

"We will not be judging each other! Most of the Castle will be taking part in the war. Only those who have not fought a day in their lives, and the children, will not be taking part. Just in case that was going to be your next question. But for now, that is all that we needed to be discussed. You can all return to your daily business. If there is anything else that needs to be shared, the guards will be sent around to make sure everyone is informed," Sachiel said angrily before turning his back on the crowd and storming off to the Castle.

"It was not how I wanted it all to end. Everything was going so well until that one guy decided to question the obvious. How can anyone believe that you wouldn't take part in the war? From the very first day, it was you on the front lines. Justren was the one manipulating us and making sure that he was traveling with you to keep you off track. Trying to win your loyalty. You were the one who had to go through all of the fighting and training. And most of it you didn't even have a choice in!" Amethyst said, pacing up and down. "We should have had him flogged right then and there."

"You will then have a line all around the Castle with every single person who was more than likely thinking the exact same thing. There is no use in your letting them upset you as much as they did," she replied, shrugging. "People will always think the worst about another person, most of them just won't say anything about it."

"Amethyst is right that it was out of line and shouldn't even have been questioned," Starlansha added. "Most of them have been around since the first battle and have been told of what you have gone through."

"But they haven't seen me around the village, doing things that would make them feel more reassured. I haven't been interacting with the guards, nor have I been talking to the people in the village."

"There is no reason for you to have to do that! You aren't the one responsible for making people happy or even reassuring them of anything," Amethyst insisted.

"That exit Sachiel and the rest of you made, sure has the village talking," Luanda said, walking into the room.

"Really?"

"On my way here, all I heard was how shocked everyone was at the audacity of the guy who spoke up. And it would seem that no one recognizes him from the village. I have asked some of the guards to go with Michael so that they can find out who he is before he causes more trouble. And yes, I know that it isn't my place to order anyone around. I did however figure that it would be for the best."

"I appreciate that you did that, and I agree that we need to find out who he is and why he thought it appropriate to put it out there."

"Do you perhaps think that he could be someone that Balditha sent to spread doubt? Just like he sent Justren?" Starlansha asked.

"I don't think that he would risk it. He is desperate to know more, but not enough to send someone on what would be a suicide

254

mission. He would know that if we were to find one of his amongst us, they wouldn't live for long," she said, biting her lip.

"Why does it seem as though you are unsure about that?"

"It's not that I'm unsure. I am just wondering if he had perhaps gotten to some of the villagers without it being noticed."

"How would that even be possible? It doesn't matter if you are a magical creature or human; everyone is scared of Balditha."

"He could have kidnapped the man's family and said that if he didn't as demanded of him, he would kill his family."

"I think that it is more plausible for him to have found some kind of wizard that would be able to project himself here or even hide his true identity," Amethyst said, thoughtfully. "My mother used to tell us that we had to be careful of people like that."

"Just sitting here and speculating won't do any of you any good. All that this is doing is working ourselves up for nothing. There really is no need for that. Luanda has already made sure that people have been sent out to find out more about this guy. Once they find out anything, they will return here and inform us of what they were able to find out," Shadick said as he walked into the room. "The more important thing right now is to start organizing the armies for the move. I think that the swordsmen should be moved first as they will be on the front lines."

"You have a point, Shadick. There really is no need for all of this worrying, as there are bigger things that we need to concentrate on," Amethyst said, stopping next to him. "I am in agreement that the swordsmen go to the field first. After them, it should be the spearmen and lastly the archers. I have been thinking that it might be a good idea to give the archers a form of melee weapon as well. Just in case there is a need for it."

"I have to agree that it would be for the best. I think along with the swordsmen, the Giants should go to the field as well. They are bigger, but we know that most of them like to be in the battle as soon as it starts. They wouldn't like to stand at the back just throwing things at the enemy," she said, seriously. "Sachiel has already gone outside, speaking to some of the guards and asking their opinion. This way, he can make sure that he has a couple of different opinions and see if it can be worked into the plan."

"He truly is a King in every sense of the word."

"Alex...? Is there any possibility that we could maybe talk in private?" Luanda asked. "I don't mean to step on anyone's toes, so if you can't, that's okay."

"All you have to do is ask," she replied, smiling. "You go ahead, I'll catch up with you guys later."

Luanda smiled in apology as the others left the room, a soft frown creasing her forehead as she turned back towards her sister. She watched her closely, knowing that it never did anyone good to be rushed on while gathering their thoughts.

"What I have to say might be best when not overheard by the

256

rest of the group, hence me asking whether we can speak in private," Luanda said, still frowning. "It's just that I have been getting a feeling the last while that there are going to be a couple of casualties that we have not been expecting."

"Were you able to tell who it was exactly?"

"Not in detail, no. It wasn't exactly a vision or something like that. It was just a strong feeling that there would be a lot of sadness around all of us. I also think that there will be some bad news for Starlansha, something that might cause her to lose her cool. Especially when it happens before or during battle."

"Are you saying that they have Roslata?"

"I just don't know!" Luanda replied, frustrated. "I have been doing everything I could think of to try and get more details out of these feelings, but it's like I hit an invisible wall. Michael had to force me out of a meditation the other night because I was going too deep."

"Is Starlansha the only one that we need to worry about, or is there someone else that we need to look out for?"

"I can't tell you who it is exactly, but there is someone else. All I can say for sure is that it will be rough on everyone involved. And it will be very unexpected."

"It really means a lot to me that you are trying to keep an eye out for everyone, and thank you for bringing this to my attention. It isn't good for your health, so I ask that you please look after yourself. And it isn't good for Demiane to see you worrying like this. Go and spend some time with Michael and your daughter, before he has to leave to help with the fighting."

"How did you know he would be joining in the battle?"

"Because I know not only you but him as well; he wouldn't be happy unless he was right there making sure that he does his best."

"I honestly forget at times that we have known each other for so much longer than just the last couple of years. Although, back then, we didn't know that we were sisters. If we had known, things would have been very different. We actually would have spent time together rather than just greeting each other when passing each other in the market."

"Besides the fact that I would've had someone to talk to and who would know that I was different. It would have been completely different if we had been closer back then. Don't get me wrong when I say that Amethyst didn't listen, but it would have been on another level."

"I'm sure that father did what he did for a reason, even if we don't necessarily understand it. Or is it just me trying to be overly positive for no reason?"

"No, you aren't, and I don't blame our parents for keeping us from each other. Not with the kind of man your stepfather had been. No offense."

"No offense taken... he was a horrible man. And I realized just

258

how much after our initial conversation, I tried to deny it, though. I believed that I only ever saw the good, but when I actually sat down to think about it, I realized how he had abused my mother.

"I understand why it would feel as though it was just stories when I told you."

"I suggest that we keep the family reunion for a later stage… Amethyst asked that I please come and make sure that you were on your way, "Shadick said, leaning against the door frame.

"Surely you didn't leave that long ago?

"Not that long ago. But it has been long enough for Amethyst to get impatient, and we both know that it's never a good idea to keep her waiting."

"I should get back to my daughter. There is no doubt in my mind that she is making the nanny's life a living hell," Luanda said quickly, hugging her before disappearing.

"Was it truly necessary for her to ask to talk to you on your own?"

"I do not blame her for wanting to make sure that only I hear what she has to say. The information she has given me was rather disturbing and very worrying," she replied with a shrug.

"Would it then not be best for everyone to know what she told you?"

"For now…there is no need for anyone to worry."

Chapter 21

Embers of Fury

"When I said that it would cause confusion and difficulty trying to get everyone settled, I didn't expect it to cause it to be so chaotic," Sachiel said, frowning as people streamed around them.

"It hadn't exactly been in our plan to move people to the battlefield while still welcoming the people from Dargona. Clearly, our plans aren't going as well as we had wished," she replied. "We should perhaps rather look at the fact that they weren't attacked while traveling here. We both know that Chadromida would have been furious if we had been wrong about that."

"It seems as though he has been getting mad too easily the last while. From what I've heard from those who ran into him, I have not had any opportunity to spend much time with him since their arrival."

"If you remember, my sister has already discussed this with us. Whenever he gets anywhere close to the Dragons, his entire demeanor changes. But I do still want to talk to him about his behavior," Shadick said as he joined them.

"That conversation should be put on hold until we have been able to settle down this confusion and chaos. He really won't be willing to listen unless he is sure that his people have settled down and are safe. I will send a couple of guards around to the new arrivals to find out who will be joining us in the war and who isn't. That way, we don't have to worry about it later," Sachiel said, calling a guard to his side and giving whispering orders. "We don't want it to be said that we are forcing people to battle."

"So it is really happening, isn't it?" she whispered.

"As much as we don't like any of this, yes it is. The fighters have been preparing for this for quite some time now, so they are as ready as they can be. There is no doubt in my mind that they are wishing for this to be over and done with so that they don't have anything to worry about," Shadick told her.

"I can only imagine how difficult it has to be for not just them but their families as well. Having to watch them march onto the battlefield, with no assurance whether they will return or not."

"You are overthinking things again, Alex," Sachiel said. "As I have said already, death is part of war, whether it is something we want or not. That doesn't however, mean that any of us should go into this war believing that everyone will die. Luanda has already told you, you will be the one to end all of this. And we know that it won't be easy."

"Right; all I have to do is get past the Centaurs, Minotaurs, Harpeia, and who knows what else just so I can kill not just Balditha but Justren as well. That will be as easy as making pudding pie."

"If there was only some way for us to go back in time, to where he had still been pretending to be a good guy, so that I could kill Justren when I wanted to. The days when I knew something was off, but I didn't want to push the subject," Shadick said, frustrated.

"Changing the past will change the future, and that might have made things even more difficult for you during these troubled times," Necron said as he appeared next to them.

"Welcome, Necron. I didn't expect to see you or any of the others around here until the battle started," she replied, barely glancing at him.

"What would have given you that impression?"

"Only the fact that you had to sneak me out of your boss's home, without the knowledge of most of your kin."

"Oh, that? That was nothing! Sure... neither they nor my 'boss' was very happy about what I had done. But there was nothing for them to do as it had already happened. It is not in his power to pull you back there again."

"Then that is something positive to come out of all of this."

"And what did he do to you when he finally came to the conclusion that you were behind her escape?" Shadick asked suddenly. "Beat you? Take your powers? Maybe tortured you?"

"None of the above, but thank you for your concern, though," Necron said, frowning at Shadick.

"And what exactly brings you here?" she asked, smiling. "I

really hope that it isn't more bad news."

"For now, there is no bad news for me to deliver. Although I do have to admit that I overheard the conversation with your sister not too long ago. Which makes me think that it might be better for us to go somewhere a little more private?"

"If there is anything you want to say to her, you may as well include me in the conversation. It isn't as though she won't just tell me what was discussed," Shadick said, standing straight.

"Shadick, go find Chadromida and talk to him, as I know he is still up in arms about the move. There is a reason why Necron wishes to talk to me in private, so if you will excuse us," she said, quickly turning her back on them and walking away. "I do apologize if I was snappy back there. I have no idea as to why he has been so short-tempered the last while. He has been refusing to talk about what is going on, and it has been getting rather frustrating. But that is neither here nor there. What is it that you wish to discuss?"

"You and your sister were discussing how your friend Starlansha will get distracted on the battlefield, and I have to agree that you will need to keep a close eye on her. As for the person who will die, it is not going to be good, and a lot of bridges will be burned because of it."

"Not going to be good in what way, exactly?"

"For everyone involved, it will only cause heartbreak."

"Could you disclose the identity to me, or are you once again going to respond with 'I'm uncertain'?"

"To be entirely transparent, my perspective on this matter is a blend of uncertainty and intuition. While I have a distinct impression about the potential individual involved, I must admit my certainty is limited. This explains my reluctance to disclose my suspicions, as such an act could potentially escalate panic and exacerbate the situation for all parties involved.

"In my view, it is paramount for everyone's focus to be directed towards the ongoing struggle, rather than diverting attention to monitoring the well-being of a specific individual whose fate remains uncertain."

"Once again, I must ask: is there an implicit guideline dictating the extent to which you can divulge information to me?"

"For individuals in normal circumstances, indeed, there exists such a guideline. However, in your case, there are no such constraints. You have traversed our existence and become intimately acquainted with us as well as our surroundings. The elements are woven into your essence just as they are to us. It would be unwise for us to withhold information from you, provided it lies within our capabilities."

"At least on this occasion, I'm feeling a little more reassured that you aren't intentionally shrouding things in ambiguity."

"Since our first encounter, I've held the belief that complete transparency with you would yield the most favorable outcomes.

264

Regrettably, circumstances have occasionally been preventing us from divulging every piece of information, all to the detriment of everyone involved."

A gentle smile adorned her lips as she silently acknowledged his words. Necron extended his arms, inviting her into a tight embrace. After a brief moment of hesitation, she stepped into his embrace, drawing in a deep, calming breath. Within that hug, she was able to find a space to release some of the burdens of stress and concern that weighed upon her shoulders.

Little did they realize, Shadick's gaze was fixed upon them, his brows furrowing in a subtle expression of disquiet. It had been quite some time since she had experienced a hug like this, and the sensation was comforting, soothing. While she had always cherished Shadick's embraces, recent times had left her questioning the intention behind his hugs, as if a sense of forced obligation had been woven into them. The distinction between reality and her own thoughts remained elusive, leaving her in a state of uncertainty, unsure if she was exacerbating matters within her own mind.

"Thank you for being such a strong person in my life. I might not always find the words to express it, but your support really does mean a lot to me," she murmured with heartfelt appreciation.

"I would have been here sooner, but a minor disagreement amongst us caused a delay," he explained.

"Is it something that I should be concerned about on my part?"

"It has absolutely nothing to do with you."

"Then it is a relief to know that not everything is my fault."

"You've been reminded of this on numerous occasions – it's crucial to get out of the belief that you're accountable for every misfortune in the world."

"I understand, and I acknowledge your repeated advice. You've given me that speech countless times. Will you also be present on the battlefield?"

"If it is in my power, then yes, I will be. But I do not want to make empty promises."

"That makes me feel a little better, that you will try."

"Is my being here a bother to the two of you?" Amethyst inquired as she rounded the corner. "I had thought you were with Shadick and Sachiel, overseeing the organization of the armies. Yet, I find you here. Could I ask what the reason is behind this embrace with an Elementiel?"

"I was helping them, but Necron wished to speak to me. I sent Shadick off to go talk to Chadromida about what has been going on for the last couple of years. Sachiel was talking to some of the other guards about making a list of those fighters who will be joining us."

"Then I don't really see the reasoning for you to hug each other?"

"Oh, right! My apologies." Necron said, jumping away from her.

"Is the reason you're here to take my sister away again? Has your boss ordered this because he found out that she is no longer in her cell?"

"He realized that the same day that we helped her escape. But it isn't in his power to force her to go back there, so there is no need for him to try."

"She is an important part in this war, so that is good to hear. We really do need her to fight alongside us, giving us her strength."

"I will be there, Am! There is no need for you to worry about me running away. There is no way that I will allow you guys to go into this war without me," she said, frowning. "What's wrong with you? You were fine earlier."

"I think that the stress is getting to me. And the fact that I have to make sure to keep a happy face for Adriata has been very difficult the last couple of days. As well as the fact that I have been feeling a little under the weather."

"You need to take some real time to breathe. Adriata will be understanding if you don't spend every single minute with her."

"That isn't what I meant!"

"I believe it might be more suitable for me to return at a later time," Necron remarked before fading from view.

"What is wrong with you, Am?" she asked, stepping closer to her sister. "I have never in all of our years together seen you reacting this way."

"You didn't witness Shadick's expression as he hurried past me.

He seemed utterly shattered by something and disregarded my attempts at conversation. I couldn't comprehend it until I turned the corner and came upon you embracing that being!" Amethyst's words were laced with frustration and anger.

"Nothing is going on between me and Necron! We are friends, and he was hoping that giving me a hug would make me feel better. Just like you, I have been worrying. I just haven't said anything because everyone looks to me for strength. It is also not anyone else's problem if I have worries."

"Has Shadick been informed that it was merely a hug between friends?"

"No, as I was unaware of his presence, nor did I have any knowledge that he was nearby. Had he taken a moment to approach and ask, I would have readily clarified the situation."

"Why on earth are the two of you quarreling?!" Starlansha exclaimed as she hurried toward them. "Your voices could be heard all the way to my room."

"I apologize if our voices became overly loud. We were engaged in a heated conversation about certain matters where our opinions differ, and it appears that things escalated," she explained with a conciliatory tone.

"Then perhaps this isn't the best place to have this conversation. There is no doubt in my mind that if I could hear you, then some of the villagers would have overheard as well."

"Once again... I do apologize."

"Apologies, Alex, but that's not what needs addressing. We're dealing with larger issues than a mere disagreement between us," Amethyst retorted, her hands firmly planted on her hips.

"Could either of you provide me with an explanation of what happened? I'm quite confused. The last I was aware, everyone here seemed content and resilient against the pressures," Starlansha inquired, her confusion evident.

"Then please ask Alex who I just caught hugging."

"Since when has it been a sin to hug someone, Am?!" she asked loudly.

"Uh... who were you hugging, Alex?" Starlansha asked hesitantly.

"Well, Necron was just here, and he was just giving me a hug. And it was only a hug. Amethyst is freaking out about it because apparently, Shadick saw it and then stormed off."

"Please call me dumb or something, but since when is receiving a hug a bad thing?"

"That has been my question the entire time!"

"Then why were you alone with Necron if there was nothing more to it?" Amethyst's eyes narrowed as she questioned, her suspicion apparent. "Shadick could have accompanied you if it were genuinely as innocent as you claim."

"Because he asked to speak to me privately about what Luanda had told me, something that neither of them wanted other people to overhear, because it would only upset everyone! So they thought that it would be for the best to talk to me alone, because I am the one who is the least likely to freak out about what might happen."

"She does raise a valid point, Amethyst. We tend to react strongly when we hear potentially unsettling information, so it's plausible that he requested a private conversation," Starlansha conceded, her expression contorted with concern. "However, the question remains: Why would Shadick become so agitated if it truly was just an embrace?"

"I'm completely at a loss! I instructed him to talk to Chadromida, aiming to understand his significant transformation while interacting with the Dragons. It never crossed my mind that he'd be lurking around corners. Had I known, I would have invited him to join us, rather than him secluding himself before erupting in anger. Why am I being cast as the villain when all I was offered was a hug? Would the response be identical if it were Sachiel? Or even Michael?" she exclaimed with a mixture of frustration and bewilderment.

"Breathe, Alex, breathe. You are working yourself up a little, and to be honest, the fire wings are slightly scary."

She shut her eyes, drawing in a deep breath, and let her soul settle, determined not to let the turmoil engulf her. The perplexity remained: why were certain individuals so plagued by insecurities over someone else's actions? Embracing a friend couldn't possibly be deemed a transgression of such magnitude. It wasn't as if they had clandestinely retreated to a separate room to disrobe.

"I apologize if my response was more than it should have been. It might have been an overreaction on my part. Yet, witnessing Shadick's distressed expression back there profoundly affected me and stirred my emotions. Especially when he departed without offering any insight into his vexation. However, I now comprehend that there was a misinterpretation between him and the circumstances," Amethyst confessed, placing a reassuring hand on her shoulder. "Occasionally, I do have rather intense reactions when I perceive my friends in distress."

"I should probably have explained the situation before just jumping down your throat," she replied, slowly opening her eyes. "On the positive side, this hasn't been our biggest disagreement. When we were younger, they had been way worse."

"Don't remind me! The Faeries always feared that we would flatten the entire forest when we got into one of our fights. But after an hour or so, we would be laughing afterwards as though nothing had happened."

"I really miss those days. The days when we had absolutely nothing to worry about, except what we would be doing the next day. When the only thing that truly mattered was the tricks that we played on each other."

"Those seem almost like the days when my sister and I were still living by ourselves. Even when my parents had been alive, we would play tricks on one another, and my mother or father would end up spoiling it without even realizing that they had." Starlansha said, smiling. "It's times like these that I really miss her."

"We will go and find your sister once we've beaten the Centaurs. More than likely, she will be at home, waiting for you. Or perhaps she is with your Grandparents and helping them with the fighting that's happening there."

"My grandmother would have said something if she had been there, but from the last communication I received, there had been nothing of the sort. She even sent some of the guardsmen to go and have a look at the place on the beach, but there had been nothing."

"There is nothing to worry about, we will find her," Amethyst said, hugging her.

"Here I thought that Necron and Alex had something important to discuss; instead, there is some kind of hug fest happening here," Sachiel said as he walked into the room.

"Necron left a while back, as the necessary conversation had been finished. Disagreements arose when Amethyst entered the scene while he was hugging me. Amidst this dispute, my wings unexpectedly ignited, prompting me to take a calming breath to prevent any escalation. The topic then shifted to our childhood, reminiscing about the pranks we used to play on one another.

272

Furthermore, Necron left before Amethyst could deliver a potential blow to his face," she summarized, providing a comprehensive account of recent events.

"I'm not sure if I want to know why she almost smacked him."

"On my way here, I walked past a very angry-looking Shadick. I tried to ask him what was going on, but he completely ignored me and kept walking. As I walked around the corner, however, I saw the hugging that was happening. And I simply overreacted like he seemed to have done."

"As I have already said, I don't think I want to know."

"Have you been able to work out a proper battle plan?"

"I've dispatched a contingent of guards to maintain order amid the chaos and gather a comprehensive roster of all fighters present. Unfortunately, a few of the Dragons made the dubious choice to touch down among the populace and are adamantly resisting any attempts to relocate them, resulting in a degree of disorder.

"As we all know, engaging in discourse with a Dragon is a futile endeavor; it could culminate in being devoured whole or met with absolute indifference. My intention in venturing here was to locate Shadick, ideally either among the assembly or inside conversing with Alex, as I hoped we could convene with Chadromida for a discussion," she elaborated, adding more depth to the description of the current situation and her motivations.

"I think that he either went to our room or to the forest to give himself a chance to clear his mind. I can also still see Managwa in the grounds, so he didn't go very far. The wolf is almost permanently attached to his side," she said, craning her head and looking at the wolf. "Do you want me to go and talk to him about this? It will also give me the opportunity to explain all of this."

"No, don't worry about it. I will try and find him myself later, or I will go and talk to Chadromida alone about the Dragons. We will have to see which one comes first. I do believe that you need to go and talk to him in any case."

"There really is no need for you to look so scared, honey. The Dragons know that we are the good guys and won't hurt us, especially with Chadromida running around," Amethyst said, giving him a hug. "Perhaps we need to go and see what our little one is up to?"

They walked out of the room, and she watched them until they were out of sight. She took another deep breath, trying to relax. It wasn't that much better, but she knew that she was on edge the entire time. Why had Shadick reacted the way that he had? Had her hugging another guy been such a big deal?

"Star…" she whispered

"What's up, Alex?" her friend replied.

"Was it really so wrong of me to hug a friend?"

"I don't see why it should be such a bad thing. But maybe he saw it and thought that kissing had preceded the hug? I've not known Shadick to be the kind of person to get jealous easily, so I honestly can't say."

"It's just been feeling as though I have to be super careful around everyone this last year or so... no, even longer than that to be honest with you."

"The notion that you're compelled to tread cautiously is unjust. Your moments with friends and loved ones should be a haven of tranquility, not a realm of scrutiny for something as straightforward as hugging a friend. And it's not even that; the aspiration to be free from judgment just for being yourself. There exists absolutely no cause for you to alter your essence. It's universally acknowledged that you embody an affable spirit, someone who genuinely cares for those in her midst," Starlansha affirmed with earnestness, imbuing the sentiment with a deeper emotional resonance.

"It hasn't been feeling like that; it's as though they haven't been understanding me. It feels as though I am being judged for things that I have absolutely no control over."

"We will get through this, we always do. Especially if we continue supporting each other and refusing to let others get to us or to let them get us down. As long as we make sure to motivate each other, there shouldn't be a problem.

"Thank you, Star. It truly means a lot to me when you say that. And I meant every word when I said earlier that we will go and find your sister. We need to make sure that the two of you get back together, as I know how much you've been missing her."

"The way you say it makes it seem as though we're a couple or something."

"I just know that she means the world to you, so it was not how I meant it. I know that even if you were to find her and she is safe, you might just go off on your own again. It is the fact that you don't know whether she is safe that is truly bothering you."

"I appreciate that you understand that, I'm not sure whether other people actually understand it."

"Perhaps they don't belong in your life, which is why they don't wish to understand any of it."

Starlansha offered a grateful smile before departing the room at a leisurely pace. As she walked toward the window, her gaze shifted outward, observing the ebb and flow of daily life below. Despite the reassurances from those around her, an unshakable sense of unease remained.

Shadick's reaction had left her wondering as to why he had responded in the way that he had. She shook off the puzzlement and nimbly climbed onto the windowsill. With a purposeful leap, she surrendered herself to the currents of wind, her wings gracefully unfurling and propelling her above the bustling cityscape.

The ingenuity of Sachiel's creation never ceased to amaze her, how there always seemed to be space for more people, each corner meticulously designed. While Amethyst had a role in the village's planning, Sachiel had woven her visionary ideas into a reality. A swell of pride engulfed her as she considered her connection to this thriving community, nurtured by the contributions she had made, even amid her numerous departures that often occurred without prior notice.

The fact that they had continued to welcome her back, harboring no resentment for her transient nature, was both surprising and heartening. Their patience and non-judgmental acceptance in the face of her ever-changing nature spoke volumes. Witnessing the unity within Amethyst's newfound family was a source of joy, and the radiant happiness that now graced not only Amethyst's countenance but Adriata's as well was a testament to the bonds they had cultivated.

Strolling through the encampment, she positioned herself not too far from the impending battlefield, a silent observer of the warriors as they made their final preparations for what promised to be their most significant clash yet. She keenly noted the diverse array of emotions that painted the faces of the fighters. Some exuded palpable nerves, their apprehension tangible, while others radiated an eager anticipation, their readiness palpable.

Lost in contemplation, she briefly wondered under which category she would fall if she were among the ranks – the anxious or the battle-ready. A twitch of jumpiness betrayed her, yet it wasn't directed at the imminent confrontation on the field. It was Shadick's absence that unsettled her, his silence since their tense encounter after witnessing the embrace between herself and Necron. Efforts had been made to bridge the misunderstanding. Both Amethyst and Starlansha had taken it upon themselves to reach out to him, striving to clarify the innocuous nature of the hug.

Yet, like drops in an endless ocean, their explanations appeared to vanish into the abyss of his silence. Determined to no longer rely on intermediaries, she resolved to seek him out personally. This rift between them couldn't persist; she yearned for him to recognize the depth of his significance to her, to acknowledge that she cherished him above all else. And she refused to allow anything to mar the precious connection they shared.

"Why is it that I always find you lost in thought?" Amethyst asked, walking towards her, "Are you still thinking about Shadick? Or is there something else that is keeping your mind away from the now?"

"A bit of both, to be honest. I think the fact that I can feel the nerves of the warriors isn't helping all that much," she replied.

"There is nothing to worry about as I trust these men, women, and creatures with my life. I believe that the nerves come from them being unsure of when the battle will start. There is an air of uncertainty all over, even between us who do have a vague idea."

"I have also been trying to figure out the best way to get to

Justren and Balditha so that we can make sure that we wouldn't have to worry about them in the future. We both know that it won't be as easy as just approaching them and killing them, as there are always warriors around them."

"Would it not help if you turned into a wolf or an eagle? The same way you did when you killed Diliante?"

"Not a bad idea, but I have to believe that they would expect something like that."

"There is no doubt in my mind that you will figure out how to do it, and not just because Luanda saw it in her vision. But because I have faith in you."

"I wish that I were as sure of that as you are."

"Every single time that I find the two of you together, it looks as though you are conspiring," Sachiel said with a grin. "Would you like to tell me something before I find out a deep, dark secret?"

"We were only discussing strategy, my love. There really is nothing for you to worry about," Amethyst said, smiling up at him.

"I am the King after all, so these things should be discussed with me present."

"These strategies are for me and not the warriors. A discussion on what the best way would be to get to the bastards responsible for all of this to kill them. I need to make sure that we end this before there are too many lives lost."

"I truly have missed walking up here and seeing you guys

talking to each other," Terri said, running towards them. "It really has been too long since I was able to walk upon a battlefield with you."

"Terri! Where in the world have you been? We haven't seen you around in the longest of times."

"I embarked on a mission entrusted to me by Amethyst and King Sachiel – to search for additional warriors who might help our cause. My journey led me to the fringes of the Centaur encampment and through stretches of the neighboring forests. Regrettably, I must convey that my efforts yielded limited results; there weren't many warriors to be found. However, I did manage to encounter a small group of stray Centaurs who expressed a desire to align with our forces.

"Anticipating your next inquiry, I assure you that I have considered the possibility of their allegiance wavering on the battlefield. Yet, their accounts of certain matters have instilled within me a measure of confidence that they harbor no intentions of betrayal," she relayed, offering a detailed account of her mission and the findings she had brought back.

"It is actually Queen Amethyst now. They got married while you were away."

"What kind of things did they tell you exactly?" Amethyst asked, stepping forward.

"Some things are better not discussed in front of certain

people," Terri replied, looking around, "but as she is not with us at the moment, Roslata has been with the Centaurs the entire time, and it is rumored that she is with child. A child who belongs to Justren."

"What?! How would that even be possible?" Sachiel asked wide-eyed. "Was she forced to sleep with him?"

"From what they were telling me, she arrived at their camp not long after leaving your side. And that she was welcomed as though she were a long-lost family member. The very same night, many of the Centaurs heard sounds emanating from his tent that they could only describe as pleasure."

"So that is why she was so upset when Starlansha refused to join her. It had been her plan all along to have them join the Centaurs," she said, shocked. "Even when she knew that her sister would never join her, as she would consider it abandonment. It is something that she would never do and would fight tooth and nail to make sure it didn't happen."

"I now understand why you preferred to not have her around when you told us this information. She would not have taken it well and more than likely argued against it," Amethyst said with a small nod. "That it was just the Centaurs' plan so that they can make us not fight."

"It is very valiant of you to try and gather more troops for our cause, and I thank you for that. And I am truly sorry that you had to be the bearer of bad news," Sachiel said, shaking his head. "Once the war is over, you will receive the highest ranking in my royal guard. You truly have my highest praise and thanks."

"My only request is that when we do win this war, is that I will be able to take those who were forced to take part in the war to a place where they won't be judged for their past action. There is no doubt of course that they will fall under your ruling, but there is no doubt in my mind that they would prefer to be alone with each other," Terrie asked, inclining his head.

"I assure you that you are free to take whomever you wish to take. I will make sure that all the humans and magical creatures alike know that you are their King."

"There really is no need for you to do that, your majesty."

"It has been something that we have been discussing for a while now, Terri. We have come to an agreement that you truly deserve to rule a place of your own. And it would be your choice whether it be just the Centaurs or other creatures," Amethyst said smiling.

"That is too kind, Amethyst."

A delicate flush crept across the Centaur's cheeks, her smile tinged with a subtle warmth. It brought her genuine joy to witness the man finding solace, an emotion that had been elusive due to the agony of witnessing his own kin perpetrate atrocities against those he held dear.

The weight of his helplessness had burdened him, a sentiment she ardently hoped they could alleviate by preventing further escalation of the already dire situation. Amidst the turmoil, the undeniable truth of Roslata's demise loomed, and Starlansha's struggle to come to terms with this reality was palpable, perhaps even manifesting in a subconscious denial.

Chapter 22

Final Battle

It was early morning, and she was one of the few people awake at such an early hour; it was nothing unusual for her though, as she struggled to sleep for longer than two or three hours. It didn't help that Shadick was still mad at her, causing her to sleep even less; she would however never admit this to anyone. He seemed to be the only person who had the ability to calm her soul and mind, allowing her to get the sleep her body craved. She had no way to be sure about a feeling, but there was just something in the air that made her believe something would be happening within the next couple of hours.

When she looked to the other side of the battlefield, she was able to see the shapes of Centaurs as well as some of the Minotaurs. She felt frustrated though that she could see shadows of creatures she could not discern. The Harpea that still remained and had decided to stay in Balditha's army was hidden just behind the hill. The air changed slightly as some of the guards joined her in her vigil, their excitement rising slowly as they watched the Centaurs slowly making an appearance.

"General…" she whispered to the one warrior stepping towards her, "I do believe it would be a good time to wake everyone up, although ensure to not alarm anyone, as it would not be a good way to start the battle."

"Very well, your Grace," he replied, saluting her.

As she watched the opposing side, the shadows grew larger, covering a large part of the landscape as she heard the whispering to wake up the other warriors. It was with trepidation that the day had finally arrived, and she was staring at what she had been expecting for years. She took a deep breath, closing her eyes, trying her utmost to calm her soul, as there was no time for her to start doubting herself.

If there had been any doubt in her mind that she would be the one to take out not just Balditha but Justren as well. She would have argued against it a couple of months ago, but she had known from the start that it was meant to be. The last couple of weeks however it didn't scare her anymore; all that remained was for her to figure out how she would be getting to them.

"Why in the world is everyone being woken up so early?" Starlansha asked sleepily as she walked towards her. "Before I could even make out what the guards were saying, they ran towards one of the other tents."

"The Centaurs have decided that it would be a good day to make their presence known," she replied, nodding towards the shadows. "So I can assure you there will be chaos all too soon."

"Right; it should have been obvious that would be one of the only reasons they would start waking everyone up. It should have crossed my mind earlier if my brain wasn't addled by sleep."

"Why does it sound as though you had done something wrong or stupid? Maybe I should have told the General to ensure everyone knew why the wake-up call was happening. I was afraid however that some of the people might start panicking."

"No, the way you handled it was absolutely perfect. The warriors know that they need to be ready for battle, but in this way, they will not panic and cause a riot," Amethyst said, joining them, still tightening some kind of armor. "If it had been me in your shoes, I would have done exactly the same thing. So please stop worrying about doing the wrong thing."

"I was hoping that the battle wouldn't be happening this soon, even though we knew what was coming," Sachiel said, shaking his head, glancing at Amethyst. "It has been feeling as though none of us has been able to get proper rest the last couple of years, and it shows on everyone's faces. Although we shouldn't forget all of the good things that have happened over the last couple of years."

"Exactly, this mess has brought us back together. The fact that we weren't together until the last year shouldn't have happened. I shouldn't have allowed it to happen in the first place."

"You are not being judged for the decisions you made. The reasons behind those decisions aren't something that should be

286

questioned."

"Have I not told you before, Am? If anyone were to question the decisions you made, let me know, and I will make sure that they understand the facts," she said seriously, not taking her eyes off the battlefield. "I will allow no one to doubt a pure person like yourself."

"Did I miss anything?" Shadick asked as he joined them.

"No, you haven't; they are all still gathering on the other side of the field. From what we can see so far, there are Giants, Minotaurs, some Harpea, and naturally the Centaurs. There are however some new kinds of creatures we aren't able to make out, which is rather worrying," Sachiel informed him. "But there is no doubt in our mind that today is the day the final battle will happen."

"And there was some kind of doubt about when the battle would happen?"

"News reached me that some of the warriors started making bets on when the battle would actually take place and whether it would actually happen. I understand why they would start thinking that way, so it doesn't surprise me that the bets started. A week and a half has passed since we moved them here, and there has been no sign of the Centaurs. Now there can be no doubt in anyone's mind that our estimations were correct, and I can with confidence go and claim my winnings once the battle has been won."

"I don't understand why there was any doubt as to why we've been here for so long. We made the decision not just because of the vision but to make sure that we would be ready when it does happen. Since Luanda joined the village, her visions have been nothing but accurate, which has helped all of us so much."

"Just remember that some people have still been hesitant to accept the visions as real, some have even been arguing that we have been using them as an excuse because we didn't have absolute proof that this would actually happen. Even though we have given them proof of the visions actually being true, they still doubt however as it is not something they have really dealt with before."

"They have been told for many years that the magical community doesn't even exist, so there is no need for us to blame them for not believing the visions are correct. When the children noticed something, they were told it was just their attempts at gaining attention," she said, taking a deep breath. "When we approached them at first, they were thrown into the deep end, and they had to adapt to everything that went against what they had been taught. I can say with confidence though that a lot of the humans still wish they could be oblivious of the magical creatures living around them, as they feel war has been the only thing that's happened since the first day."

"There is movement from the Centaurs!" one of the guards

shouted in their direction.

"So that would be Balditha and Justren preparing to give us this speech on how we have the opportunity to avoid the battle, how they will allow us to continue living. There is no doubt in my mind however it would come with the clause that I would have to be handed over to them so I can be taken care of. They won't stop there however and demand the heads of those closest to me as well," she said, rolling her eyes.

"We have chosen a gorgeous day for all of you to die, don't you think? I have to admit though that it is rather saddening that you wish to spoil it by insisting on fighting what is clearly a losing battle," Balditha shouts across the field. "There is no doubt in my mind that you all will put up a valiant battle, but in the end, it will get you nowhere, except your family members mourning the death of their loved ones that were lost here.

"I will however give you an opportunity to withdraw, and you could rest assured I will not come after those you care about. There is however one thing I need for this to happen. Alexandria needs to drop her weapons and give herself up for all of those around her. If she insists on putting her own well-being ahead of those around her, then she will be the first to die today just to prove we are more caring than she keeps claiming to be."

"After all of this time, one would think he would be able to come up with something more original than just me having to give myself up and dying without putting up a fight."

"He is honestly too narrow-minded for that to happen," Starlansha said, shaking her head. "The fact that Justren is right there cheering him on means he will never realize how terrible he sounds when he repeats the same things over and over again. It wouldn't surprise me if he wrote these terrible speeches for his father."

"So I ask you for the final time, what is your decision on my very generous proposal?!" he shouted at them again.

"We know all too well that even if Alex were to walk across this battlefield empty-handed to hand her life over to you, you wouldn't be happy until those who have gone up against you have been killed as well. That would include everyone standing on the battlefield right now. So, as per your last attempts, no," Amethyst replied, rolling her eyes. "I think it would be a good idea to just stop with the yammering and get the battle underway."

"It brings happiness to my heart to see Starlansha is still amongst you. I have a question for you, Starlansha. Did the thought ever cross your mind what happened to your sister when she stormed away from your little group of misfits?" Justren asked with an evil grin. "I can put your mind at rest. She was with me up until recently; she unfortunately lost her life while giving birth to our son. It has been a rather difficult time the last couple of months with her not around. I wish that she had not died."

As she watched Starlansha's face contort in complete and utter loss, she knew that Luanda had been right once again; there was however no way they could have prepared for anything like this happening. Nor could they have predicted how the loss would turn to anger. She had no time to call a warning or even attempt to stop her, as Starlansha rushed forward towards the Centaurs who had been waiting for exactly that to happen. The warriors behind them didn't hesitate in rushing after her and meeting their enemy in a clash of swords, arrows raining down on the charging Centaurs and Giants.

The Faeries flew towards the Minotaurs, throwing them with energy balls, doing their best to distract, allowing those close to kill them. Some were successful in bringing down the beasts; unfortunately they were also some of the unlucky few who lost their lives. Screams of pain and frustration filled the air as some of their attacks failed and others succeeded better than expected. Her eyes flew to where Shadick took on three of the Centaurs at once, making her heart skip a beat.

It was with great difficulty that she pulled her eyes away from him to search out Amethyst and Sachiel, feeling relieved that they were fighting side by side as she knew they would keep each other safe. If it hadn't been for the fact that she needed to concentrate on Balditha and Justren, she would have joined Shadick without any hesitation. The dragons flew over the Centaurs, going for those at the back quickly, causing them fiery deaths. As shocking as it was to watch, at least she knew they had taken care of a good chunk of the Centaurs.

A Centaur was suddenly in her face, making her quickly duck under his sword in time. He made a quick recovery, kicking her in the stomach, almost causing her to fall over. She took a deep breath and, while still on her knees and ignoring the pain, she pulled out her daggers from the scabbards at her side and thrust them through the Centaur's heart.

Twisting out of the way quickly as his body came crashing down, a Minotaur was in front of her, making her swear underneath her breath. He succeeds in his attack as his spear pierced her arm, making her flinch as he tried pulling it out, and meeting with resistance in the form of her skin. Quickly dropping her one dagger, breaking the staff part off close to the tip, before using it to smack the creature across the face hard enough to make it stumble. Taking the opportunity to jump up, letting her other dagger slide across its neck, slicing through cleanly a scream escaped its lips as the life left him.

Bending down and picking up her dagger, glancing around with a frown, it didn't surprise her that there was no sense in how the Centaurs, Giants, and Minotaurs were fighting. Just rushing onto the field, not stopping to question whether they were making the right choice. Her eyes wandered briefly over a couple of bodies of

292

the Centaurs strewn across the field.

She flinched as she noticed just how many bodies there were of not just humans, but the magical creatures surrounding her. There was however no time for her to dwell on the losses at the moment; she would ensure that there would be enough time to mourn for the lost once the battle was done. Glancing up towards where Balditha was just standing there, seemingly with no plan on joining those fighting for him. His sword wasn't drawn as though he was about to jump in to help those surrounding him. Justren was barely visible, doing his best to get into some of the fighting, but it was clear he was holding back as well.

As she watched, she saw him change direction, running straight towards Shadick. In that moment, she knew it was then or never for her to get through to Balditha to take care of him. So it was without a second's thought that she ran through the fighting creatures, towards her target. She automatically attacked any of the Centaurs when they got in her way and did her best to give the magical creatures any kind of help.

Balditha was still oblivious to the fact that she had run towards him, so she slowed down, blending in with those around them to get the upper hand. As she got closer, she could see a maniacal glint in his eyes as he observed the bloodshed that lay before him.

Rushing towards him, he was only a couple of meters ahead of her as he readied herself for the attack, her dagger crossed over her chest. It was at the last moment that he turned towards her, and she slightly missed her target, only able to cut him across his arms, making her swear softly.

Why had she expected anything else? She didn't allow it to stop her attacks though, and she quickly thrust the dagger towards his throat, hearing him swear under his breath. He reached for his weapon and aimed for her, at the last moment changing his mind and allowing the hilt of his sword to fall on the wound on her arm that still held the spear's tip. It caused her to scream softly, doing her best to ignore the pain as she swung her daggers, this time aiming for his legs. Smiling a little in satisfaction that she was able to injure him before he was able to recover completely, and stepping back.

She stepped towards him, ducking underneath his swinging sword, using her movements to carry her to his side. She jumped over his next attack before landing on his back, where, without a single moment's hesitation, she thrust the daggers through the back of his throat and out the other side. His sword dropped to the ground as he tried breathing and failed miserably, uselessly doing his best to grab the daggers from his neck as the life left him.

He dropped to the ground, a slight vibration seeming to run throughout the field, causing everyone to turn in her direction. Two people, however kept fighting, not noticing what had just happened. It was in that moment that the temperature dropped and a fog drifted over the field, her breath coming in short bursts, realizing that this fog was not normal. It was the same fog that surrounded her childhood village, the same fog that kept the ghosts where they were and ensured no one would be able to stop their attacks.

Glancing around in slight panic, she did her best to figure out where the ghosts were going to appear. Her breath caught in her throat as five of the ghosts surrounded Justren and Shadick, seeming to watch the fight in silence. Right before she could move or open her mouth to shout a warning, the ghosts rushed into Shadick's body, seeming to cause him to levitate.

It was in that moment she saw Justren stepping forward, swinging his swords upwards and severing Shadick's head just as a volley of arrows hit him in the chest. A scream escaped her lips as his lifeless body fell to the floor, the ghosts disappearing as quickly as they had appeared.

All of the fighters, whether on their side or not, stopped and turned towards where Justren still stood watching in silence as Shadick's body fell to the ground. Sachiel ran towards Justren, Starlansha close on his heels. In her mind, it felt as though things were happening in slow motion, as though her brain refused to accept what had just happened.

She allowed her body to turn into wind drifting towards Justren, still grinning and oblivious to what was happening around him. Turning to where his father had been standing, a small frown formed when he couldn't spot him, slowly allowing herself to land on the ground not too far behind him, with black eyes.

"I just had the honor of watching the life leave your father's eyes when I drove my daggers through his throat, and I have to admit it was one of the best moments in my life. Just seeing how the life drained from his eyes was satisfactory, and it would only have been better if there had been a way for me to record the moment and experience it over and over again.

"Your father was a fiend, and he cared for no one but himself, and there is no doubt in my mind that he cared much when I killed your mother during the last battle. In that moment, he may have acted as though I had done the worst thing in the world. I think however it had all been an act and he was secretly pleased about what I had done. Did he even mourn? Did he even take some time so that you and he could get over her loss?" she asked with narrowed eyes, her energy drifting off of her in waves as her hair floated around her

"Tell me how it would be fair for you to live when you just killed one of the best men there were in this world. I saw the glee in your face when you ended his life! And why exactly did you do it? Because you were stupid enough to let your father convince you that we are the enemy? Because he believed you were wronged and that the only way out of what you considered hell would be to fight against those who would be willing to listen? He was blood hungry and had decided to hide behind a mask of being wronged. Did you ever think about asking him why he thought it was a good idea for you to sacrifice your kinsmen for what he falsely believed was for the better good?

"Or were you just so desperate for his love and approval that you believed his opinion was the only one that was right? And that if you were to go against what he said would be wrong. Were you just his perfect little soldier? Or at least tried to be, as we both know he hated the fact that you turned out to be a half breed. What a disgrace you were to him, no matter how hard you tried to prove him wrong. Your mother was trying her best to make it better by doting on you, but it was never enough because you only wanted your father's approval. The approval of a monster who would rather kill a person or even a child because he only saw them as evil. When he was the one who was evil to the core.

"Now, before I kill you, where is Roslata's body as well as her son? And I can assure you, I won't be making empty promises like your father did. Whether you give me this information or not, you will die. There is a very small chance that it would make it a little less painful for you to bear."

"My father did care when you killed my mother, but he took the option of trying to ignore what had happened so we could go on with our lives. As for whether I was just a mindless soldier? Yes, I am. And there is no way for me to change it, not that I would. He was my father, whether he showed it or not. There were even a couple of times that he proved just how proud he was of me, so stop making him out to be a complete monster. My father had Roslata buried near our camp over the hill. Our son is also at the camp, being cared for by an elder female Centaur," he told her, spitting on the ground. "You can do your best to try and kill me, but you will not find it as easy as you believe. My father did not raise a coward, and I was taught how to fight since I was a young child. As you have faced me before, you should know that I will not just give you another kill."

"Your death was predicted, so you can rest assured it will happen."

"Let me guess, you were also told that you will be the one to kill me?"

"Even if it hadn't been in the vision, I would have ensured that it would be by my hand that your life is taken away from you. It was you who was trying to fool me into believing in a fake sob story, all while pretending to be someone I could trust as a friend. You even convinced Amethyst you were a good guy. When I told her that you had been playing us all for fools, she didn't want to believe it," she replied spinning her daggers around, getting ready to attack.

He started laughing as though he had completely lost it, making her frown. Ignoring it and stepping closer to her, swinging her right-handed dagger at his chest, following up with the left dagger to his face. The laughter died on his face as she drew blood, before he was even able to make a move to ready his sword, she swung her daggers and sliced his right hand off. Slightly pulling her dagger back up and shoving the one through his eye. Adding the elemental powers in her veins without even thinking about it, causing his head to explode outward in blood and bones.

From what felt very far away, she heard happy shouts and cheers surrounding her. She was still enraptured by the power flowing around her, so it took her a couple of seconds to realize someone was trying to get to her. She quickly spun around towards the attackers, glaring at the person, her eyes still completely black, quickly realizing it was Amethyst, and relaxing slightly and allowing her to approach her.

"Alex? Are you feeling alright?" Amethyst asked, lightly touching her cheek. "Your eyes are darker than the night sky."

"I apologize," she whispered, closing her eyes, shaking her head. "It is something that has been happening ever since I was taken by the Elementals to train under their boss. He said that it was one of the few moments where I lost all sense of what was happening around me, making me concentrate on just one thing. In this case, it was Justren."

"You succeeded! You were able to take out their leaders, as soon as they saw you killing Justren, they all threw down their weapons and fell to their knees. We have finally won the battle!" one of the Generals shouted, running towards them. "Today is the day of celebrations!"

"We have lost many fighters, and we will need to inform their loved ones before we can celebrate. Yes, we have won the battle, and everyone wishes to celebrate, but there is a time and place for everything," Sachiel shouted, stepping closer to them slowly. "Today, you have all lost friends and family. As happy as they would be at the outcome of this battle, they would much rather be here with us."

"I think one of the most important things for us to do right now is to go and find Roslata's son. Justren told me where they were before he died, there is no way that it will stop Starlansha from mourning her sister but I think having her son close by would help a little in the healing," she said turning towards Amethyst again. "We will need to gather all of the bodies together of those that stood by our sides so a list can be made of the families that needs to be informed. Where is Michael? I don't wish to give Luanda the bad news if he had died."

"He is busy doing the rounds and checking up on everyone. I asked him to go around and make sure that if someone is in need of medical attention, they will get it. So you don't have to worry about him, besides Luanda would have known if something were to happen to him and prepared if that had been the case."

300

"Honey, I think it would be for the best to get off the battlefield. That way we can make sure Shadick's..." Amethyst started saying.

"You are right, of course. Luanda would have informed me of it if that had been a possibility. We should make sure the guards know to not hurt any of the Centaurs unless provoked. I do however believe they were just following orders and won't be trying anything. Also, everybody will need a place to sleep for the time being. Until we can figure out a more permanent place for everyone to stay."

"Why isn't she over there with Starlansha? I was sure that she would have been the first one to be there after it all ended. It is Shad..." Terri asked as he walked towards them, but was cut short.

"We also need to make sure that even the Giants get some medical help if it is needed. There is no doubt in my mind that they were injured as well. They may be big, but they also get hurt and need us to show them that we aren't the enemy."

"She is currently cutting off anyone who might start mentioning Shadick's name," Sachiel said. moving towards Terri, "She is in denial and doing her best to not think about it."

"Denial would be me saying it can't be possible for him to be dead. I am just concentrating on other things right now so we can be sure we don't lose anyone else, not to mention it would have been what he was doing," she finally said, taking a deep breath, "because right now, if I stop to think about things, I will not be able to keep it together."

"There is nothing wrong with allowing yourself to have a little breakdown, Alex. You are human after all," Amethyst said, wrapping her arms around her in a hug. "You loved Shadick, and you are allowed to mourn for him, from what I was able to make out from your conversation with Justren. It is one of the things you took him on about, about his father not mourning Diliante."

"Alexandria, please allow me to escort you to your tent so you can get some much-deserved rest," Terri added. "There is nothing wrong with leaving things in capable hands. You know you can't argue that when Sachiel and Amethyst make sure everything gets handled and that things get done as they see fit."

She glanced around at all of the humans and magical creatures standing around, all talking to each other quietly. Not too far from them, she could see Starlansha still bent over what she was sure was Shadick's body. Turning back to Amethyst, Terri and Sachiel, she let out a breath, nodding in silent agreement. There really was no need for her to worry about stuff when she knew Amethyst would make sure it would all be organized.

If she hadn't been in shock, she would have protested when Terri picked her up and started carrying her away. Instead, she leaned her head against his shoulder, staring straight ahead of her. People lowered their heads as they passed, and she knew that it was their silent way of showing support; she couldn't respond however as the world became blurry with the tears running down her cheeks in silence.

Chapter 23

Embers of Mourning

A couple of months had passed, and she could finally see how things were calming down once again. At first, she wasn't sure if it would happen that some of the Centaurs would freely walk among their own warriors, but it made her happy when she saw them stop to have a quick conversation.

"It is true that we were once enemies, but now we have the opportunity to build a future of understanding and cooperation. We have learned from our past mistakes and have chosen a path of peace and unity. The Centaurs will no longer be exiled, and we will welcome them as our neighbors and friends. Together, we will heal the wounds of the past and create a harmonious community where everyone can thrive. I understand that some of you may still have reservations and concerns, and I want to assure you that your feelings are valid. Change is not always easy, but it is necessary for growth and progress. I encourage you to have open and honest conversations with the Centaurs, to listen to their stories, and to share your own.

"Through communication and empathy, we can bridge the gaps that once divided us. Let us not forget that Balditha's actions were those of one individual, and they should not define an entire race. We cannot let hatred and prejudice cloud our judgment. Instead, let us focus on building a better future, where all creatures can live in harmony and peace. As we move forward, I ask for your patience, understanding, and support. Together, we can overcome any challenges that may come our way. Let us be the example of unity and compassion that the world needs. Our strength lies in our diversity, and together, we can achieve great things. I want to thank Terri and the Centaurs for their willingness to embrace change and work towards a better future with us.

"Their courage and openness are commendable, and I believe that their presence among us will enrich our lives in ways we cannot yet imagine. Let us stand together as one community, bound not by fear or hatred, but by love, understanding, and respect. Together, we can create a brighter and more hopeful future for ourselves and the generations to come." The crowd listened attentively to Sachiel's speech, and there was a palpable sense of hope and unity in the air. "The path ahead might still have its challenges, but they were ready to face them together, as one united community. As for the people of Dargona Village, I understand that the memories of the battle might still be fresh in your minds. The wounds of war take time to heal, but I want you to know that you are always welcome here, in our castle and among our people. We hold no grudges, and we understand the hardships you have endured. If you wish to return to your homes in Dargona Village, you have our full support."

Astarte and Chadromida, who were standing among the crowd, exchanged a glance. The loss of Shadick was still a heavy burden on their hearts, and returning to Dargona would undoubtedly bring back painful memories. However, the sense of belonging they had felt among the people of the castle and the support they received from everyone made the decision more difficult. Amid the uncertainty, a voice rose from the crowd. It was Adriata, the young girl who had been trying her best to console and support Luanda after the loss of Shadick.

With tears in her eyes, she stepped forward and said, "Aunty Astarte and Uncle Chadromida, I will miss you if you go, but I want you to be happy. You have been so kind to me, and I don't want you to be sad because of me. If returning to Dargona will make you feel better, I understand."

"Thank you, sweet Adriata. Shadick would be so proud of you," Astarte whispered. "You are a precious soul, and your kindness means more to us than you can imagine."

"Is there something bothering you?" Terri approached Alexandria with a concerned expression, noticing that she seemed lost in her thoughts.

She sighed, her mind filled with the events that had unfolded since the battle's end. "I've just been thinking back to everything that has happened. So much has changed."

"A lot of things have happened that is true, but most of those things have been good. The humans and magical creatures have accepted the Centaurs within their midst without too many issues. Yes, there had been some hesitation at first, but I think they have been seeing me enough for the last couple of years, which has been helping, if even a little bit."

"It most certainly did..." she whispered, her eyes following Astarte and Chadromida as they walked towards the villagers of Dargona, who were preparing to return to their homes. It had been one of the most difficult things for Alexandria to do - approaching Astarte and telling her that her brother had died during the battle. The shock and pain that had flashed in Astarte's eyes had almost overwhelmed her. The shock had quickly turned to hate as Astarte started shouting at her, asking her to leave the house and never darken their doorstep again. Chadromida had been kinder, understanding that it was a part of battle.

He had promised to talk to Astarte and let her know when she felt more reasonable. However, that day had not come, and deep in Alexandria's heart, she knew it never would. She mourned Shadick on a daily basis, wondering whether things would have been different if he hadn't been mad at her. But there was no way for her to know if it would have changed anything. So she had been keeping to herself, trying to allow her heart to heal. She had been putting up a mask so that people wouldn't pity her or make them feel sorry for her, because her heart had not healed even a little.

Taking a deep breath, Alexandria's gaze shifted towards her sister, Luanda, who was busy working on her latest project. It had been a shock for her to realize that she was pregnant right before the battle had started, especially as she knew when she was expecting Demiane. Michael of course had already been on the battlefield, but there had been no doubt in her mind that he would be in any danger. She had been doing her best to make her feel better, but as much as she tried, there was no way for her to bring Shadick back.

When Amethyst had asked whether she knew what the sex of the baby was, she had insisted it would be a boy, and they had already chosen a name. No matter how much the Faerie Queen had tried to coax it out of them, she had not been successful in getting them to reveal the name. Even though she hadn't been able to show it much, she was happy for them and excited to see what their future held.

She observed from a distance as Amethyst, the kind-hearted Faerie Queen, strolled through the village hand-in-hand with Adriata, a young and compassionate fairy. Amethyst's smile, which had been rare in the aftermath of the battle, seemed to shine a bit brighter in Adriata's presence. Adriata had taken it upon herself to be Alexandria's source of comfort and support. In her gentle way, she did everything she could to lift her spirits. Picking wildflowers from the meadows and presenting them to her, creating colorful drawings to bring cheer, and leaving these thoughtful gifts on her bed were just some of the little gestures Adriata performed selflessly. But it was the hugs that made the most significant impact.

Adriata seemed to sense when she needed a moment of warmth and reassurance. Whenever she spotted a glimmer of sadness in Alexandria's eyes, she would embrace her tightly, enveloping her in a comforting embrace that conveyed the unspoken message: "You are not alone." One night, she had heard muffled sobs coming from Adriata's room. Worried, she rushed to check on the young fairy.

To her surprise, Adriata's tears were not for herself but for her. In her innocent honesty, Adriata confessed her longing to bring back Shadick, Alexandria's beloved partner, so she could see her radiant smile once more. The depth of Adriata's empathy touched her heart, and it reminded her that even in the midst of her own grief, others cared deeply for her. Sachiel, the wise and caring leader, had recognized the pain she was going through. He ensured that the villagers respected her need for space and solitude. His considerate actions allowed Amethyst to grieve and heal at her own pace, knowing she had the support of the entire community.

She turned back towards the Castle and saw Starlansha walking around with Prince Jacques, who had shown up shortly after the battle started and pronounced his undying love to her. Then made sure that she knew he had gone to her grandparents and asked if they would please allow them to get married whenever she felt ready for it.

He had been so happy as they had just won their own battle that he had laughingly agreed before handing him her mother's ring. He had been taken aback when Iva had brought out William. At first, he had been outraged that she had been with another man. But when she explained that he was her sister's and she had taken responsibility for his upbringing, he had grown with pride; they had become a family that day with an adopted son.

Starlansha had been touched by the prince's willingness to give her the time she needed to heal and grow stronger after the battle. When Starlansha introduced William, Prince Jacques couldn't help but feel surprised. He had no idea that Starlansha had a son, and the revelation caught him off guard. For a moment, he was unsure how to react, as he hadn't expected this new piece of information. As the initial shock subsided, Prince Jacques composed himself and listened attentively to Starlansha's explanation. She revealed that William was her twin sister's son and that she had taken on the responsibility of caring for him. Her dedication to her nephew and the love she had for him were evident in her words and actions.

The village flourished under Amethyst and Sachiel's leadership.

The Centaurs integrated seamlessly, and the humans and magical creatures embraced their new neighbors with open hearts. The wounds of the past were slowly but surely healing. One evening, the village celebrated its newfound unity with a grand festival. The village square was adorned with colorful decorations, and the air was filled with laughter and music. Amethyst and Alexandria stood side by side, their hands linked in a display of sisterly solidarity.

As they looked out at the joyful crowd, Alexandria whispered, "Thank you for being there for me, Amethyst. I don't know what I would have done without you."

Amethyst squeezed her sister's hand. "And thank you for reminding me of the importance of family. Together, we've shown our people the power of unity and love."

* * * THE END * *

Character List

The Protagonist

Alexandria — A powerful Witch and the central figure of the story. Brave, compassionate, and burdened by destiny, she stands at the crossroads of magic, loyalty, and war.

The Fey Court

Amethyst — Fairy Queen and Alexandria's closest friend. Wise and regal, she rules with grace and resolve.

Sachiel — Human King and husband of Amethyst, bound to the Fey Court through love and alliance.

Adriata — Daughter of Amethyst and Sachiel; a symbol of unity between worlds.

Valencia — Mother of Amethyst; the village of Valencia is named in her honor.

The Wolfane

Shadick — A Wolfane warrior and Alexandria's love interest. Fiercely loyal and guided by honor.

Managwa — Shadick's loyal wolf companion.

Freya — Alexandria's devoted wolf, her protector and shadow in battle.

Family of Blood and Magic

Thalia — Alexandria's mother; a formidable Witch with deep ties to ancient magic.

Damon — Alexandria's father; a skilled Warlock whose past influences the present.

Luanda — Half-sister of Alexandria.

Michael — One of the Head Guards; a trusted friend of Alexandria and husband of Luanda.

The Mermalani

Starlansha — One of the Mermalani twins; a loyal friend to Alexandria.

Roslata — The second Mermalani twin; she flees to the Centaurs, setting darker events in motion.

Elementals

Claudia — Fire Elemental, fierce and unyielding.

Necrontyr — Nature Elemental, ancient and patient.

Jace — Spirit Elemental, bound between worlds.

Maya — Wind Elemental, swift and untamed.

Creneis — Water Elemental, calm yet devastating.

Dragons and Kin

Chadromida — Dragon Master; Shadick's closest friend and husband of Astarte.

Astarte — Shadick's sister; strong-willed and fiercely protective of her family.

Kaedyn — Daughter of Chadromida and Astarte.

The Centaur Conflict

Balditha — Leader of the Centaur uprising.

Diliante — Wife of Balditha.

Justren — Son of Balditha; a half-breed caught between two worlds.

Terri — A Centaur who defies her kin to fight alongside Alexandria.

Terrae

The Master — Supreme leader of the Terrae; a shadowed force shaping the greater conflict.

The Guard

Captain Davies — Head of the Guard; steadfast and loyal to the realm